Forgotten Memories

Forgotten Memories

PENNY ZELLER

Maplebrook

Forgotten Memories

Copyright ©2022 by Penny Zeller

www.pennyzeller.com

www.pennyzeller.wordpress.com

All rights reserved.

Published by Maplebrook Publishing

No part of this publication may be reproduced, distributed, or transmitted in any form or by any means, including photocopying, recording, or other electronic or mechanical methods, or by any information storage and retrieval system without the prior written permission of the publisher, except in the case of very brief quotations embodied in critical reviews and certain other noncommercial uses permitted by copyright law.

Cover design by Savannah Jezowski

Editing by Mountain Peak Edits & Design

Proofreading by SnowRidge Press

This novel is a work of fiction. Unless otherwise indicated, all the names, characters, businesses, places, events, and incidents in this book are either a figment of the author's imagination or used in a fictitious manner. Any resemblance to actual persons, living or dead, incidents, locales, settings, organizations, businesses, or actual events is purely coincidental. Any brand names or trademarks mentioned throughout are owned by the respective companies.

All scripture quotations are taken from the King James Version of the Bible.

Print ISBN: 978-0-9760836-8-9

ALSO BY PENNY ZELLER

Maplebrook Publishing

Standalone Books
Love in the Headlines
Freedom's Flight
Levi's Vow
Heart of Courage

Wyoming Sunrise Series
Love's New Beginnings
Forgotten Memories
Dreams of the Heart
When Love Comes
Love's Promise

Horizon Series
Over the Horizon
Dreams on the Horizon
Beyond the Horizon

Hollow Creek Series
Love in Disguise
Love in Store

Love Letters from Ellis Creek Series
Love from Afar
Love Unforeseen
Love Most Certain

Love in Chokecherry Heights Series
Henry and Evaline (Prequel)
Love Under Construction

Whitaker House Publishing

Montana Skies Series
McKenzie
Kaydie
Hailee

Barbour Publishing
Love from Afar
(The Secret Admirer Romance
Collection)

Freedom's Flight
(The Underground Railroad Brides
Collection)

Beacon Hill Press (Nonfiction)
77 Ways Your Family Can Make a
Difference

Dedicated to those who have found forever homes through adoption.

Therefore if any man be in Christ, he is a new creature: old things are passed away; behold, all things are become new.
2 Corinthians 5:17

Chapter One

Wyoming Territory, 1877

A FLEETING MOVEMENT CAUGHT twelve-year-old Annie Ledbetter's attention. She squinted at the grove of trees on a distant hill and willed her eyes to focus. A quick flash of something—or someone—appeared. Annie tipped her head to the left and stood on tiptoe, anticipating a better view.

The vacant prairie previously held nothing but miles and miles of grasslands, sagebrush, and the occasional rolling hill.

Until now.

Annie's feet stalled in the soft dirt as if rooted. Could it be? A man, or maybe more than one man, watched and scrutinized Annie and the rest of the travelers.

But as quickly as the figure appeared, he vanished.

A shiver of fear traveled up her spine.

Annie's heart skipped a beat and her arms tingled with numbness. What had she just seen? She rubbed her eyes and took a second glance, but now saw nothing. Stumbling, she began to walk again.

Should she mention what she had seen to Pa? Surely Pa, with his perceptive eyesight, had noticed the elusive movement. In the wagon, he and Ma carried on what appeared to be an important conversation, although Annie couldn't hear the words over the creaking of the wagon wheels and the commotion from the other families in their wagon train. Ma nodded at whatever Pa said, her hands propped comfortably on her large belly. The baby would be here soon.

Hopefully, they made it to Nelsonville before that happened.

Annie stared in the direction of the grove of trees. Had she imagined what she'd seen? After all, Ma had commented on more than one occasion that Annie had an overabundance of imagination. If so, best not to tell Pa. He and her brother, Zeb, would give her a good ribbing about how the lonely boredom on the journey from their home in Hollins, Nebraska, to the Wyoming Territory, caused her to conjure up things that weren't really there. From the beginning of their trip several days ago, it had been an uneventful adventure with no Indian attacks, no severe illness among the travelers, and no unexpected deaths. Why should that change?

Annie rubbed her stomach then and groaned, attempting to appease the intermittent discomfort. Was it nervousness from what she thought she saw or were the berries she'd eaten at lunch causing a disturbance?

"Hiya, Annie." Zeb ran up alongside her and matched his steps with hers.

Annie diverted her attention from her nausea and turned to face her fourteen-year-old brother. She weighed her options. *Should I tell him about what I saw? Surely there would be no end to the teasing, but maybe he saw it too.*

"I think I saw someone hidden behind those trees."

Zeb shielded his eyes from the sun and focused where she pointed. "I don't see anyone."

"It must have been my imagination." Annie sighed and brushed aside a stray hair that had fallen from one of her braids. Zeb's confirmation somehow soothed her, yet her stomach was still in upheaval. "I wonder if we'll stop soon for supper."

To rest for a while sounded appealing.

"Our noonday meal wasn't that long ago. Are you all right?"

"I think the wild berries are causing a fuss in my stomach."

"Perhaps you can ride in the wagon for a spell."

Without awaiting her response, Zeb garnered Pa's attention, and moments later, Annie climbed into the back of the wagon, anxious to lie down in the hopes of settling her stomach.

The canvas provided a respite from the sun, even if the space was hot, crowded, and stuffy. The wagon housed all they owned and didn't leave much room for a growing twelve-year-old girl. Listless, Annie reached for her diary, the simple, well-worn book that had long ago become her companion. Perhaps penning an entry would relieve her nerves. She opened it and began to write for the first time since leaving her home.

July 14, 1877
Dear Diary,
Pa says we will soon be reaching Nelsonville in the Wyoming Territory. I, for one, am thankful we are almost to our new home.
Having lost nearly everything and having to start over has been difficult for Ma and Pa, and I revisit often the memories of our old soddie and the mismatched round table and four chairs Grandpa

Ledbetter gave Ma and Pa on their wedding day. *I miss supper with stew, cornmeal muffins, and apple pie for dessert. Much more decadent than the plain beans we eat day after day on our journey.*

Only one other family in our wagon train will settle in Nelsonville. Everyone else will continue to other destinations.

I had a nervous fright today when I thought I saw something in the distance, perhaps a man. I pray it was only my imagination.

⋯❀⋯

Caleb Ryerson stood beside his horse and watched as his older brother, Cain, peered through a brass monocular spyglass. Another plot to commit a crime. Would Cain and his friend, Roy, ever tire of taking things that didn't belong to them? Would they ever tire of ruining the lives of others?

Cain snickered. "You won't believe this, but that ain't no stagecoach that's comin'. It's a band of wagons."

He was crouched out of sight behind a grove of trees overlooking the valley where the travelers journeyed.

"What? I thought we was supposed to be watching for a stagecoach. Give me that." Roy Fuller grabbed the spyglass from Cain and peered through it. "Well, I'll be. Little wagon train, likely four or five wagons."

Roy spit to the side, barely missing Cain's foot.

"Don't matter none, though. We can rob them just the same as we rob a stagecoach. And anyways, we might even get more loot out of the deal." Roy lifted the spyglass and gazed through it again. "Definitely ain't no big wagon train."

"I think we should stick to stagecoaches," Caleb interjected.

"Keep your opinions to yourself, Little Brother, 'cause no one even asked you," snapped Cain. "I'm tired of you trying to make 'polite' decisions. This ain't no time for politeness. As I've told you a dozen times, if you wanna eat, you'll do as I say. It's as simple as that."

Caleb sighed and kicked the soft dirt with the toe of his worn boot. He, Cain, and Roy had taken to robbing stagecoaches in a variety of Wyoming and Dakota Territory towns. Oftentimes, the loot was bountiful and the thievery simple. Twice there had been casualties. He cringed at the thought of his brother's and Roy's disregard for life and willed the memories to vanish from his mind. Those casualties had been someone's pa, brother, or son. He had never participated in taking the life of another and never would. His conscience wouldn't let him. If he someday wanted to leave the lifestyle he'd been born into, Caleb knew he would have to abstain from as much crime as possible, even if it meant suffering Cain's wrath.

"It pays better than trying to earn a living the honest way," Cain told Caleb on more than one occasion. "We're so good ain't no one ever gonna catch us. You'd think they'd have better lawmen in this part of the country."

Maybe the lawmen were smart and luck played a major role in their failure to be apprehended. What would happen someday when there was no more luck? Prison time? Hangings? Death from a gunfight like what happened to Pa? Caleb shivered. Would he ever escape the life he lived?

The coarse conversation between Cain and Roy drew Caleb back to the present. He attempted to ignore their discussions until Cain directed a question at him. "What do you say, Caleb?"

Caleb cleared his throat. "I'm just saying these are probably families without much. Let's wait for the stagecoach."

Hearing himself attempt to dissuade Cain and Roy made his insides churn. Yes, while he was trying to talk them out of robbing a wagon train, he was consenting to rob yet another stagecoach. No matter who they robbed, stealing was stealing and Caleb knew, although no one had ever taught him so, that stealing was wrong.

"I don't care what you think or what you say," Cain sneered. "Look at your hand. Do you want to work for someone who does that to you again?"

Caleb rubbed a finger over the wide three-inch-long diagonal burn scar on his hand. No, he never wanted to work for someone like the mean Mr. Yager again. A man whose punishment included a hot piece of steel seared into Caleb's flesh as a permanent reminder of his wrongdoing.

Still, the thought of stealing from families unsettled him. There had to be a better way to make a living.

"Now, here's the plan. Caleb, you're gonna be the one to find the loot inside the wagons. You'll raid them and take anything you see worthy of selling. And I mean *anything*. Sometimes these folks have coins and jewelry, so be lookin' for that." Cain handed him a burlap sack. "Roy and me, we're gonna order everyone off the wagons before the search and we'll be sure no one fights back. There's likely to be at least one man in each wagon, so we don't want to be overpowered. 'Course, if anyone decides to give us any guff or attempts to reach for a gun, we'll shoot them."

Roy chuckled. "I like this plan. I always get the fun parts." He pulled his Colt .45 Peacemaker from its holster and ran his left forefinger over the barrel. "This gun has served me well."

Caleb had never shot anyone and never would unless it was in self-defense. He just wasn't like Cain and Roy. They'd killed before and hadn't thought much of it. They'd once been apprentices in a life of crime. Now they were professionals, shooting anyone who dared cross their path. Caleb recalled a time only a few months ago when Cain had threatened to take Caleb's life for disagreeing with something he and Roy said. It was that memory that reminded him not to provoke the two any further.

"Did you hear what I said, Little Brother?" Cain snapped, elbowing Caleb hard enough to nearly knock him off his feet.

"Yes." He struggled to maintain an upright position as pain shot through his side.

"Ain't no way and no how Caleb's ever gonna shoot nobody," sneered Roy. "You ain't never shot no one, have you, you stupid fool? Think you're better than me and Cain anyways, just 'cause you ain't never shot no one. Maybe we should just leave the coward here while we take care of business."

"It would be the easier way," Cain agreed. "But, if he wants to eat supper tonight, he's gonna have to help. I know I, for one, am not going to continue to support someone who doesn't work for their meals. There ain't no free supper to be had here."

Roy nodded. "So is you in or ain't you?" he asked Caleb.

"I'm in."

Caleb didn't want to let the thought of hunger cross his mind. He'd been hungry too many times in his life. In response to the thought of food and lack thereof, his stomach rumbled. If only he could make a decent living—maybe own a ranch or apprentice for a local merchant. Instead, his destiny had been planned for him—a destiny that included stealing what didn't belong to him. His father had been an outlaw. Now he and Cain followed in Alvin Ryerson's footsteps. Caleb couldn't deny the trapped feeling smothering him when he thought of the lack of choices he had for his future.

What about the innocent people whose lives would soon change at the hands of Cain and Roy? Had it been Caleb's choice, he would have asked the people in the wagon train if they would be willing to share their supper with him in exchange for work. Cain, of course, had different plans. He believed he was owed everything. Entitled. How could two brothers born of the same parents be so different? He reasoned with himself that Cain was a lot like what Caleb remembered of their father. He recalled the times their pa had taken them on what Alvin termed "jobs". Cain had gleaned what he could from watching Alvin Ryerson in action. Caleb had closed his eyes and begged to be taken home. Such a response received nothing less than a tongue lashing followed by a whipping from Pa. He still had the scars to prove it.

"They better have some loot, that's all I gotta say," Roy grumbled with a scowl. "I don't believe in wastin' no time."

"They probably don't have much," Caleb muttered.

"You don't know that, you stupid idiot." Cain again jabbed his elbow into his brother's ribs. "If they're moving, it's likely they have everything they own. Wouldn't you take some money with you if you were moving? 'Course, maybe not, since you ain't that smart."

"Yes, I would take money with me," Caleb answered. He took his hat off and wiped his brow with his forearm. How had he and Cain come to this? His brother was only seventeen and already a hardened criminal. Their father had been dead for six years and for those six years, they'd fought to survive. Caleb shuddered at how things transpired since they'd become orphans.

He never thought he'd be an outlaw at the age of fourteen.

Roy let loose a string of swear words. "Is you comin' or is you just gonna stand there and look dumb?"

Caleb wished he could be anywhere but here at this moment. As he always did when they planned a heist, he covered his face with the handkerchief so only his eyes were visible. He pulled his dingy cowboy hat low over his forehead as he'd been instructed and followed his brother and Roy toward the unsuspecting travelers.

Annie wasn't sure how long she'd been asleep in the back of the wagon, nestled against the rough edges of the trunks, when a loud noise startled her. She sat up and shook away the feeling of pins and needles in her right leg from holding it in one position too long.

She no longer heard her father's low rumble of laughter or her mother's sweet singing of their favorite hymns as they rode across the prairie. Those noises had been replaced by raucous, unknown male voices, a woman shrieking, and a young child crying.

Was she still asleep and having a dream?

Was her creative mind once again getting the best of her?

Annie fluttered her eyes, attempting to rid herself of the drowsiness that remained from her nap. Somewhere nearby a horse neighed.

More yelling.

More commotion.

"Ma?"

No answer.

Annie inched to where she could see out of the back of the wagon. It was then she saw something that horrified her—nothing made of imagination, but something of pure reality.

If only she had told Pa.

※

Cain fired a shot in the air as they neared the wagons.

"Get out of your wagons and get over there by that tree!" he bellowed, pointing to the lone tree thirty feet away. "Try anything and you'll be shot. Believe me when I say that, because I've done it before, and I will do it again."

With one hand Cain held his gun, never taking his eyes from his victims while removing his hat with his other hand and wiping the sweat from his brow.

"Leave all your weapons by the wagons. Everyone over there *now*."

Hushed murmurs mingled with a child's whimpering in the stifling heat.

Caleb loathed how his brother's voice penetrated the air with its brash, hateful, and disrespectful tone. Cain loved to be in control of others, especially in his mean-spirited way. How long had he exercised his authority over Caleb?

They dismounted. Caleb attempted to ignore the roiling in the pit of his stomach.

Commotion ensued as the travelers gathered by the tree in unorganized panic. Caleb shook his head. *They're families, likely good people.*

"Please, don't do this," pleaded one of the men.

"Quiet, old man." Roy repeatedly struck the man with the butt of his revolver. "Speak again and I'll shoot you."

The man collapsed to the ground.

"Whatcha waitin' for?" Cain sneered. "Don't you have a job to do?"

Caleb sprinted toward the first wagon. His hands shook as he prepared to enter. He detested this part, but the alternative was worse.

As Caleb lifted his leg to step into the back of the wagon, he saw someone and his heart nearly stopped. It wasn't so much that he feared for his life at the hands of the stranger before him, but he *did* fear for her life. Cain told *everyone* to remove themselves from the wagons and here was someone who blatantly disobeyed his orders. Cain held no prejudice for taking out his wrath on whoever decided to ignore his commands. Whether it be man, woman, or child, the punishment was the same.

Caleb groaned. A girl, eleven or twelve with two long blonde braids, sat cross-legged staring at him. She blinked rapidly and her breath came in gasps. Despite the oppressive heat, the girl's face shone an ashen white and her lips trembled. He had caught her by as much surprise as she had him.

"Shhh." Caleb held a finger to his lips. If Cain and Roy knew she was in the wagon, they'd take necessary action.

"Just be real quiet and don't say a word. Everything will be all right."

Caleb's attempts to pacify her were likely for naught. From the way she shook, his words did little to appease her fright.

⁂

Annie scrutinized the gun tucked in a holster on his waist as he stood in front of her. *Could this be the man I saw earlier? Why, oh, why hadn't I told Pa?* She fought to keep the meal from many hours ago from resurfacing as fear enhanced the rising nausea in her unsettled stomach.

Who was this man and what did he want? She'd heard raucous voices ordering everyone to stand by a tree, but at the insistence of this unknown voice, Annie froze. Too late to climb from the wagon, she found herself trapped and face-to-face with one of the outlaws.

Lord, please help me.

She struggled to breathe as the suffocation of nervousness rippled through her.

Annie crouched among the contents of the wagon and attempted to back further away from the man, but there was no place for her to go in the cramped quarters. *The Lord is my Shepherd, I shall not want.*

The man squeezed through the close confines of the wagon and pilfered through the Ledbetter belongings with expertise. Although she couldn't see his mouth or nose because of the red bandana, she could make out his blue eyes, nearly hidden by a dirty black hat. Scrawny, thin arms attached to narrow shoulders swiped random items from their places. What possessed someone to take what didn't belong to him? Her heart raced, causing unbearable thrumming in her ears.

She fought to cling to the Scripture verses hidden in her heart since early childhood: *The God of my rock; in him will I trust: he is my shield, and the horn of my salvation, my high tower, and my refuge, my saviour.*

Annie closed her eyes and clasped her clammy hands together. She continued to pray, her mouth moving silently as she sent her request heavenward. When she opened her eyes, the young man was watching her, his gaze steady.

Annie pondered how the man's eyes were kind and not hardened like how she imagined an outlaw's would be, not that she had ever seen an outlaw before. Yet, the man—rather a boy—held no shame in stealing what belonged to others. She couldn't tell his age, but surmised he wasn't much older than she, probably about the same age as Zeb. He was dressed in clothes in need of a good washing. She did a double-take when she saw his right hand. A lengthy scar covered nearly his entire hand and was raised and red. When had he received it? Was a knife fight on the streets of an unkempt Wild West town to blame? Had this man won the knife fight? She trembled at the thought of the demise of his opponent.

She glanced again at his revolver. Would a gunfight take place here on the open prairie with no one to save them? *God is our refuge and strength, a very present help in trouble.*

Entranced by the prominent scar, Annie couldn't take her eyes off of his disfigurement, the sight now fully embedded in her memory.

She was a prisoner in the wagon. Thoughts of what she should do cluttered her mind. Annie released a long-held breath. "Please—please don't hurt me," she stammered.

"Try to be quiet and nothing will happen to you."

His whispered response took her aback. She would heed his advice.

※

"You finding anything, Little Brother?" yelled Cain.

"Almost finished," Caleb kept his attention on the girl. The last thing he needed was for her to wallop him on the head once his back was turned. That wouldn't sit well with Cain and the ruckus could cause his brother to lose control. And Cain hated losing control.

Continuing to pilfer through the belongings in the wagon, he threw some things aside and placed other items into his burlap sack. It was then that Caleb found a tin box and opened it to find a meager stash of money and coins.

"Please don't take that," the girl whispered. "It's all we have."

He hated having to steal to make his living, especially from good folks, and chided himself for casually going through her family's belongings as if they were his to do with whatever he wished.

"Take anything else, but not that. We have so little left..." her voice trailed and her wary eyes searched his face for what his answer might be.

Caleb sighed. Although the temptation was great because of his need to obey Cain, he knew the decision he must make.

Without removing anything from the box, he opened the top of a sack of cornmeal and tucked it inside.

Caleb was ready to climb from the wagon when the girl whispered again, visibly shaking as she spoke.

"Please, sir, please don't let them hurt us. My ma is going to have a baby soon. Have mercy on us."

Bile rose in Caleb's throat. His own ma died giving birth to him. What if her life had been spared?

His eyes locked with hers. Had he been a normal fourteen-year-old, he would have probably sat next to her in school. She didn't appear much younger than he. Had he been a normal fourteen-year-old, he wouldn't be robbing wagons and stagecoaches. He'd be helping on the family ranch, if his family had a ranch. If he were a regular fourteen-year-old, he wouldn't be rummaging through the belongings of others and deciding what was worth taking. The realization hit him hard that in order to survive, he must do what his brother commanded.

"I wish I could promise you no one will get hurt," he said quietly, "but I can't."

With that, Caleb left and continued to the second wagon.

―――✦―――

Annie cautiously scrutinized the situation from a thin tear in the canvas. She saw the wagon party gathered near a tree, many of the women crying. The children clung to their mothers and the menfolk's expressions told of helplessness and despair. Two men held them hostage. But why? Annie's family and friends had done nothing to them. Nothing at all.

Yet their lives were in danger at the hands of strangers, just miles from the wagon party's first destination.

Annie saw the younger man rush from wagon to wagon, likely rifling through the contents in search of anything of value.

Her gaze fell upon her family. Ma leaned against Pa. Zeb stood completely still. Pa's eyes narrowed and he rolled up the sleeves of his shirt. He would do anything to protect his family.

Please, Pa, don't do anything foolish.

❦

"Did you find anything?" Cain asked Caleb.

Caleb held up his sack. "Yes."

"That ain't nothin', coward," Roy said, punching Caleb hard in the arm. "Why is he such a good-for-nothin' ninny? You shoulda done the searchin', Cain. You'd have gotten us some real loot."

"I said *don't use my name*," Cain sneered through clenched teeth. "I'll go look again and see if he got everything."

He shoved Caleb aside and stomped toward the first wagon.

"I can check again." Even in his own ears, his voice exuded desperation.

Cain paused. "You really are worthless," he hissed. "Nah, this time I'll check."

What of the girl? Caleb held his breath. Indecision rose within him, but to defy Cain would be a death sentence.

His brother reached the wagon within seconds.

"What are you doing in here?" Cain's harsh words competed against the whimpering of a child.

"I was sick."

Her voice was so timid. So frightened.

"Please don't hurt her," a pregnant woman begged.

"Shut up. And you, get near that tree." Cain yanked her arm and shoved the girl as she exited the wagon. She stumbled, fell to the ground, and stood again before running toward the rest of the travelers.

Caleb fought to remain planted where he was. He stood no chance against Cain and Roy.

A man standing with the pregnant woman started toward Cain, but was restrained by another man who shook his head.

Voices murmured.

Roy fired a shot into the air. "Shut up or I'll start shootin'!"

"You're right for once, Little Brother," Cain announced upon returning from the first wagon. "I didn't find nothing else."

Caleb exhaled, thankful Cain hadn't found the box with the family's money.

Cain shoved Caleb toward the remainder of the wagons. "You go and search the wagons again, coward. It shouldn't be my job."

While Caleb was in the third wagon, he heard a gunshot. He peered out the back just in time to see a man collapse.

A woman screamed and fell to the ground next to him.

"That's what he gets for bein' so dumb." Roy scowled. "If anyone else would like to try somethin', go ahead, but don't say I didn't warn you."

"I think we got everything," Cain said. "Let's get out of here."

Powerlessness and frustration consumed Caleb, and he clenched his fists at his sides. Would the man survive? When would the senselessness that had become part of his life end?

Had he known how to pray, he would have done so.

Caleb climbed from the wagon and scanned the group of people. The girl from the wagon cowered next to whom Caleb presumed was her pa. Caleb released the breath he'd been holding, grateful it wasn't her pa who had succumbed to Roy's wrath.

But her pa could be next.

His eyes briefly connected with hers. She blinked and avoided his gaze. He had hoped no one would get hurt, but as he told her in the wagon, he couldn't make that promise.

Next to the girl's pa, Caleb noticed a woman very much with child. He assumed it to be the girl's mother.

"Walter," the woman said. "I think the baby is coming."

The girl's pa gently assisted his wife to the ground. Would her baby be all right? Would the woman be all right? Had his own ma suffered before she passed?

Caleb wished he could help, but knew he could not.

"My husband, he needs a doctor." The pleading voice of the woman whose husband had been shot tore at Caleb's heart.

The man didn't appear long for this life. Several people crowded around him offering assistance and comforting the woman.

Caleb hated seeing death, and he'd seen far too much.

Roy held his gun on the wagon party and backed away slowly. "Don't care none what your husband needs. Now don't nobody move or I'll shoot again. You done saw what I did to that other fella."

Cain sauntered up next to Roy. "Quit your yappin' and let's get out of here."

Roy backed slowly toward the horses while shooting wildly into the air.

As if they had never been there, they vanished, leaving several families in turmoil and grief.

As the three outlaws neared the town of Willow Falls, Caleb knew what he must do. "I'll meet you near the rocks," he mumbled.

Earlier that day, they had discovered huge, magnificent rock formations that afforded them shelter as well as a hiding place until they left tomorrow morning.

Cain glared at him. "We don't have much time, so whatever is so important, get it done."

"I will."

"The sooner we get to the rocks, the better," said Cain. "Besides, I'm lookin' forward to seeing what it is we collected from the raid."

Roy slugged Caleb. "Don't do nothin' stupid, coward."

"I won't."

"Give us the sack, just in case you get your stupid self caught or somethin'." Roy snatched the bag from him.

"Come on, we don't have time to wait for him." Cain beckoned his horse toward the outskirts of town.

Caleb stood for a moment, his heart pounding and his knees shaking, as he wrestled with the aftermath. Minutes ticked by.

Finally, he pulled his bandana from his face and took a deep breath. In the distance, Cain and Roy rode hastily in the opposite direction, leaving a puff of dust behind them.

Caleb was thankful neither of them asked about the "business" he had in Willow Falls. It hadn't surprised him, however, because to Cain he was a burden, and Roy just plain hated him.

He would never turn in Cain and Roy for fear of what might happen to him if he did so. But there was something Caleb knew he must do, even if it meant risking his freedom and possibly his life.

Chapter Two

Wyoming Territory, August 15, 1884

Annie Ledbetter and Hetty Milstrap sat on the porch of Hetty's parents' house attempting to tend to their sewing between bouts of lively conversation.

"I must say I'm thrilled you're courting my brother, Hetty. You and I shall be sisters someday for sure."

"We haven't talked about marriage yet, but I admit the thought has crossed my mind. Of course, I *only* speak of such matters with my best friend. What would the etiquette books say about me mentioning marriage before being proposed to?" Hetty held a hand to her chest. "I'm sure I'm breaching the rules."

Annie giggled and glanced at her sewing in her lap. "Do you realize we have been sitting here for the past two hours and have only succeeded in sewing a single line of stitches? What dawdlers we are."

"Dawdlers we may be, but isn't it much more enjoyable to share in delightful conversation with one's best friend?" Hetty paused, a wistful glint in her eye. "I remember the day we met."

"As do I. Zeb and I arrived at school that day and knew no one. I missed my friends in Nebraska something dreadful. But then you shared your noonday meal with me and introduced me to the delightful tradition of eating dessert first."

"You were the first person who agreed with me about my noonday meal tradition. I knew then that we would be the best of friends."

"I will *always* honor that tradition."

"And pass it on to our children," declared Hetty.

Annie smirked. "Seems you have your future with Zeb on your mind today."

"Perhaps." Hetty's face reddened. "But just you wait, Annie Ledbetter. Someday you'll fall in love."

"Not with anyone in Nelsonville. Have you seen the prospects? It would be quite easy to become a spinster in this town…not that I'm worried at present. There'll be plenty of time for courtship."

An image of the unpleasant Hank Struna flashed through her mind. He'd asked Annie to court him no less than four times, and likely would still be pestering her if Zeb hadn't warned him away.

"Far be it from you to concern yourself with being a spinster at the tender age of nineteen. And who knows who you might meet if you procure the teaching position in Willow Falls." Hetty bit her lip. "Will it bother you dreadfully to be so close to where your wagon train was robbed?"

"No. While I think about that day from time to time, I no longer have the frequent nightmares I once did." Annie shivered. "I'm thankful we survived the ordeal and arrived in Nelsonville safely. I'm especially grateful God performed a miracle by allowing a doctor to arrive to care for Ma and the baby at just the right time. He saved Mr. DeGroot's life as well, and tended to the man who was beaten."

Hetty's mother paused on the stairs of the porch, a basket on her arm. "Annie, Mr. Ackerman told me to tell you he has a letter for you."

"Thank you, Mrs. Milstrap. I'll go right over and retrieve it." Annie rose. "Care to come along, Hetty?"

"I do need a respite from sewing."

Annie always thought it was convenient for Hetty to live in town rather than a mile away, especially in the winter. It was the only logical choice since Hetty's parents owned the mercantile.

Moments later, she and Hetty entered the post office.

"Mr. Ackerman?"

"Ah, yes, Miss Ledbetter. I do have a letter for you. Hello, Miss Milstrap." The postmaster reached behind his desk and placed a letter on the counter. "It didn't come very far, only from Willow Falls. Still, it appears to be of utmost importance."

Butterflies fluttered in Annie's belly. Could this be the letter she'd been anticipating?

Mr. Ackerman watched her, likely awaiting the chance to be privy to the letter's contents. His eyes magnified beneath his spectacles and his arms folded across his chest. He tilted his balding head toward Annie, hinting for her to share a morsel of information regarding the details of whatever may be inside the envelope.

"Thank you, Mr. Ackerman." Annie removed the letter from the counter and proceeded to leave.

"But, Miss Ledbetter, aren't you going to open it? Surely Miss Milstrap and I would appreciate a read-aloud of whatever it contains."

Annie gave Hetty a knowing glance. "I think I'll wait to open it."

"It must be of high importance to have been mailed from Willow Falls when it could have been delivered by word of mouth."

Annie attempted to stifle a laugh at Mr. Ackerman's persistence. "I have no doubt it is of high importance. Why else would one waste money on a stamp when delivering it to such a close location?"

"Indeed." Mr. Ackerman shifted the weight of his stout body to the other foot and adjusted his thick, round glasses.

"I should be on my way now so that I may open it posthaste." Annie started toward the door. "Good day, Mr. Ackerman."

"Are you sure you don't want to open it here?"

"I'm quite sure, but thank you just the same."

With a smile and a wave, Annie and Hetty left the post office and returned to Hetty's house.

They again took their places in the chairs on the porch.

"That Mr. Ackerman is so nosy," Hetty said. "Ma said she went to retrieve a parcel yesterday and Mr. Ackerman nearly held her hostage at the post office in an attempt to see what was inside."

"That sounds like Mr. Ackerman. I think he's lonely since he has no wife or family so he finds his excitement in being meddlesome."

Hetty placed a hand on Annie's arm. "Do you think it's a letter about the teaching position?"

"I hope so...and I hope it's good news."

Annie offered a brief prayer heavenward before carefully opening the envelope. She then removed the letter and read the words aloud.

Dear Miss Ledbetter,

It is my honor to inform you that you have been accepted for the teaching position at Willow Falls School. The board was greatly impressed with your grades and achievements while a student as well as your passion for teaching. What you shared about your desire to teach was well received.

As discussed at your interview last month, room and board will be provided, along with a small monthly stipend.

School is scheduled to begin on the first Monday in September.

On behalf of the school board, the parents, and the students of Willow Falls, we welcome you to our town.

Sincerely,
Reverend Solomon Eliason
School Board Chairman

Annie re-read the letter, not once, but twice. "I'm going to be a teacher! I never imagined I would have been the one they would have chosen. Surely at least one of the other applicants was more experienced and educated."

"Experience and education weren't the only things the school board was looking for. He mentioned your passion for teaching."

"Oh, Hetty, I shall miss you so!"

"I hope you'll be returning home frequently. After all, Willow Falls isn't that far."

"Oh, I will. I'll miss you and my parents and Sadie, and I'll even miss Zeb, just a little bit." She held up her finger and thumb to indicate how much she would miss her brother.

"This is going to be a big change for you, Annie."

"It's been my dream to teach since I can remember, a dream that's now coming true." Annie placed her fabric, needle, and thread in her sewing basket. "I can't wait to tell Ma. Maybe I should stop by the post office and tell Mr. Ackerman first. After all, he had a hunch there was some mighty important information inside this envelope."

Annie deepened her voice and adjusted her imaginary spectacles on the tip of her nose: "Miss Ledbetter, aren't you going to open the envelope here? Surely Miss Milstrap and I would appreciate a read-aloud of whatever it contains."

"Annie, you silly girl," giggled Hetty. "Hurry home and tell your ma. I'll see you Sunday."

"Where has the time gone?" Ma's voice was thick with emotion and her eyes glistened. "Look at you, so grown up. When did this happen?"

"I'm still your little girl, Ma. Only older and taller." Elation mingling with trepidation consumed her thoughts. "I'm unsure how grown up I'll feel on my first day of teaching school. I've wanted to teach for so long and now that the day is nearly here, my nerves are in a bit of a shambles."

Pa, Sadie, and Zeb were outside, and Annie treasured this time with Ma.

"I know you'll do a splendid job. Now, close your eyes. I have something special for you for your first day of teaching."

Annie closed her eyes and held out a hand. She felt Ma place something thin and cool in her outstretched palm.

"You may open your eyes."

Annie opened her eyes to see Ma's elegant black glass beaded earrings. "Oh, Ma, I couldn't. This is your most prized possession besides your Bible."

Ma's only other special possession besides her Bible.

"Yes you can, and you shall. It's an important event and I want my favorite eldest daughter to have these."

"I don't know what to say."

Annie fingered the ornate pendant-style earrings. The jewelry had been Ma's gift from her own mother on her eighteenth birthday. Her family, as immigrants, had been poor, but Grandmama saved what meager funds she had to make a one-time treasured purchase for her daughter.

"I wanted to wait for a special occasion. Yes, your eighteenth birthday was special, but I found this to be more appropriate. I'm glad I waited."

"Ma, they are beautiful. I promise I'll take good care of them."

"Of course you will, of that I have no doubt. I'll help you put them in."

Annie stilled while Ma clipped on the earrings.

"You look lovely." Ma took Annie's face in her hands. "I shall miss you. But remember, we are not far from Willow Falls. Please come home as often as you can."

Annie kissed her mother's soft cheek and nestled against her shoulder. "I will miss you all so much."

"Are you ready, Annie?" Walter Ledbetter opened the door to the house and stepped inside. "I have the team hitched up and ready to go. I reckon we mustn't dawdle if we want to make it to Willow Falls before nightfall."

"I'm gonna miss you, Annie." Seven-year-old Sadie slipped in the door under Pa's arm.

"I'm going to miss you too, Sadie Girl." Annie gave her sister a hug. "You behave for Ma and Pa while I'm away."

"Can I sleep in your bed?"

"Sadie..." Pa scolded.

"It's all right, Pa. She can sleep in my bed, but only while I'm away. When I return for visits, it's back to your bed you go. Promise?"

"I promise." Sadie beamed with a mouthful of missing teeth.

"Do you reckon we'll be leaving in this century, Annie?" Pa teased, his mouth forming a wry smirk beneath his brown-gray beard.

Zeb walked in then, hands in his trouser pockets. He placed an arm around Annie's shoulders. "Don't forget us back here in Nelsonville."

"Not a chance, Zeb. Not a chance."

There was something comforting about Pa's presence—always had been. What he lacked in stature, he made up for in personality, opinion, protectiveness, and concern for his family.

"I find it hard to believe my little girl is all grown up and moving to a new town to teach school. Just yesterday you were Sadie's age."

Annie's eyes stung and she allowed a wistful smile. "Time does go fast. Do you think I'll be a suitable teacher?"

"I think you'll be the best. You spoke of being a teacher from the time you could talk. I have no doubt in my mind the Lord will use you mightily to instruct the students of Willow Falls."

"I sure will miss everyone."

"And we will miss you. Just remember that while disconcerting, change can enable us to grow. Remember how you didn't want to move to Nelsonville? Now look at what a good experience it's been for us."

Annie nodded. Yes, it had been a fine experience, except for the haunting memories the robbery still caused on occasion. She attempted over the years to forget, and most days that wasn't a problem. While the men's faces had long lost their clarity and she doubted she could pick them out from a crowd if she were to ever cross their paths again, their actions would forever remain ingrained in her mind.

"Don't worry, Annie. The Lord will go before you. He'll take care of you and He'll take care of us."

The truth of Pa's words comforted her. Annie did know the Lord would go before her and she praised Him for His faithfulness.

"Since the distance between Nelsonville and Willow Falls is too far to ride each day, especially in winter, room and board will be provided in our home." Reverend Solomon Eliason led Annie and Pa through his house and stopped at a bedroom. "This is where you'll stay, Annie."

She placed her carpetbag filled with clothing and personal items on a quilt-covered bed. A bureau with a lantern and washbasin atop stood to one side with a wood-framed mirror hanging above it. A window with a cheerful plaid curtain afforded a view of green fields dotted with cattle.

"This was once our oldest son, Caleb's, room. He has his own place now, just down the road." Reverend Solomon paused. "I'd like to introduce you both to our family."

Annie and Pa followed Reverend Solomon out of the house and near the garden in the back. "This is my wife, Lydie, our thirteen-year-old son, John Mark, and our eleven-year-old daughter, Charlotte. Everyone, this is Annie Ledbetter, the new teacher for our school, and her father, Walter Ledbetter."

Lydie stepped forward and grasped Annie's hands in her own. "We are so thrilled you are taking the teaching position. I think you'll find it worthwhile and somewhat adventurous." She winked at John Mark.

The potential troublemaker scowled. "Ma, that incident with the mouse was not my idea."

"Still, if we ever catch you concocting such an idea, there'll be a punishment," Reverend Solomon warned.

"Yes, sir," John Mark muttered. "Why is it parents never forget anything?"

"You'll like teaching at Willow Falls. We even have a new schoolhouse," Charlotte twirled one of her blonde braids. "I'm quite smart at parsing sentences, and I love to read."

Her impish grin and pert nose insinuated she might also be a bit mischievous.

"The last schoolhouse could only accommodate twelve students, so when we had seven new students arrive at the end of last year, we were cramped. Although it's still one room, the new school will be much more spacious," said Reverend Solomon. "And an added benefit was that we were able to sell the old schoolhouse at a very reasonable price to the town's seamstress."

"Sounds like Willow Falls is growing," said Pa. "Nelsonville has retained a similar population for quite some time."

"Willow Falls is a fine town in which to live if I do say so myself. Once we are finished here, I'll take you into town and show you the school."

"What happened to the previous teacher?" Pa asked.

"She accepted another teaching position in a town about fifty miles from here. Miss Barry will surely be missed. She had a special way with children."

Annie's mouth went dry. Not only was she new and unknown, but her predecessor had, apparently, been beloved.

Exhaling, she offered a silent prayer for fortitude.

"Caleb is building several new desks and installing the wood stove. In the winter, he will ensure you have plenty of wood for the stove and anything else you may need." Reverend Solomon stopped in front of the school. "I think you'll enjoy this teaching position and living in Willow Falls, Miss

Ledbetter. Most of the folks here, while not perfect, are a wonderful group of God-fearing people."

The white, one-roomed schoolhouse with the tall belfry reminded Annie of the school she'd attended as a child, only newer and much smaller. The building boasted one door and windows on each side. As she entered, she saw the rows of desks and the chalkboard at the front of the room. Her desk was placed not far from the chalkboard, and an American flag hung in the corner, along with pictures of George Washington and Abraham Lincoln. Slates waited on the desks, ready for eager learners.

Uncertainty rippled through her. The prospect of being responsible for instilling education in children, some of whom might not care to learn, again dawned on her.

She swallowed hard.

Was it too late to change her mind?

Chapter Three

Annie stood at the front of the room and admired the classroom. *Her classroom.* A sense of pride washed over her. She mentally rehearsed in her mind last night, when she ought to have been sleeping, what she would say to the students and how she would react to various scenarios.

Once the final pupil settled at his desk, Annie wrote her name on the chalkboard in broad strokes.

"Welcome, class. My name is Miss Ledbetter. I am your new teacher. The same rules that have applied with your past teachers will apply with me, including proper behavior. We will now introduce ourselves."

She was thankful she already knew two of the students: John Mark and Charlotte Eliason. They had promised to assist her in her transition as the new teacher.

Just as the last pupil stood and introduced herself, a man strode through the door.

"May I help you?"

"Uh, yah, is you the new teacher?"

Dirt smudges lined the man's cheeks and he wore faded threadbare overalls that fell at mid-calf, a straw hat that unraveled on the sides, and oversized gloves.

Gloves on a late summer day?

"Yes, I am. How may I help you?"

Poor, poor man. Perhaps he is the pa of one of the students.

"I is a new student."

The man wedged his tall self into a limited space behind one of the desks at the back of the room. His left leg stuck out into the aisle as he clasped his hands behind his head and leaned against the back wall.

"A new student?" Annie gasped. "I don't believe I was informed you would be here."

Wouldn't Reverend Solomon have told her that a new student would be arriving, and a much older one at that?

Unless, perhaps, the Reverend didn't know.

❦

"Didn't know you needed no informin'."

Caleb Eliason pushed up the sleeves of the white soiled shirt with about six holes in it and threaded his thumbs beneath the clasps of his overalls. Were it not for the offensive odor lingering from the borrowed clothes, he might have considered wearing these comfortable, well-worn trousers more often. Many of the young boys in Willow Falls wore overalls but Caleb only knew one man who did, and that was elderly Mr. Paasch who had reluctantly loaned Caleb his favorite set of clothing.

The gloves were part of his costume since the weather was still far too warm to wear gloves unless work demanded it. How would Miss Ledbetter react when he attempted to hold a pencil? Maintaining a nonchalant disposition throughout this ruse would be a challenge.

It was the first time he'd laid eyes on the new teacher, although he'd known she was supposed to arrive soon. She was a pretty woman with blonde hair, expressive green eyes, and a tiny dimple in her left cheek. Something about her was familiar.

Caleb suddenly wished he was meeting her under different circumstances.

It was a tradition in Willow Creek that on a new teacher's first day a few harmless jokes would be played as an initiation of sorts. The tradition started when the town was founded fourteen years ago. Caleb, as the nominated adult in charge, had taken each pupil aside on their way to school. After giving their word they would remain respectful and only carry out the prank on that first day and not the rest of the school year, they had bounded toward the schoolhouse.

A whiff of the pungent odor again filled his nostrils. There had been no need to muck out the stalls this morning on his way to work, as Mr. Paasch's borrowed clothes boasted enough of a stink. He fanned himself. It wouldn't be long before the foul odor emanating from him served its purpose.

If he ever pulled this prank off, it would be a miracle. A bigger miracle if none of the pupils squealed on him. Caleb always tried his best to be honest and upfront, so pretending to be an old student named Franklin Benjamin presented a challenge. Would he be able to achieve his goal?

Annie stared, flabbergasted at what she saw. The man was over six feet tall and appeared to be in his early twenties. And oh, my. What was that stench?

She searched her memory—had she seen him somewhere before?

"I'm Miss Ledbetter, the new teacher. What is your name?"

She so hoped he was a well-behaved student. Would he take kindly to being reprimanded by a teacher shorter and younger than him?

"Name's Franklin Benjamin." He chewed on a piece of wheat with his mouth wide open, making obnoxious smacking sounds.

His manners were atrocious, yet Annie pitied the student who was so obviously out of place. He was much older than the rest and she wondered what had brought him to Willow Falls. Her mind threatened to fabricate a creative story.

With soiled and disheveled clothes, his person in need of a bath, his education sorely lacking, and in desperate need of a tutor, how could she not feel compassion for him?

"Franklin Benjamin? Your name reminds me of the great inventor and signer of our Declaration of Independence, Benjamin Franklin. Only the names are reversed."

"Yah. My Ma and Pa done name me Franklin Benjamin. Ain't sure why though."

Annie cringed at the word "ain't". She remembered her own teachers correcting students when they used that word, but she decided, out of consideration for Franklin and not wanting to embarrass him on his first day, she would forego the correction this one time.

"You don't have to worry none about me givin' you any trouble, Miss Teacher." Franklin reached up and attempted to remove something in his teeth. "When I grow up, I'd sure like to be a teacher myself."

At this, howling laughter echoed through the schoolhouse.

"Children, children, please." Annie attempted to ignore the fact that Franklin was already grown up. "I believe it's important that we all have dreams. I've wanted to be a teacher for many years now. If Franklin would like to be a teacher, I see no reason why his dream can't come to fruition if he strives hard enough."

She paused. "How old are you, Franklin?"

"Gonna be twenty-five tomorrow."

A twenty-five-year-old student? How dreadfully sad. She assigned tasks and watched in disbelief as Franklin attempted to write on his slate with a gloved hand. He fumbled, causing the pencil to clink against the desk. He retrieved the pencil, fumbled again, and finally, after several tries, commenced to writing.

An hour later, Franklin announced he should leave.

How could Annie assist this poor man in his education if he only attended a partial day of school? "But school just started. It isn't even lunchtime yet."

"That's okay, Miss Teacher. Tomorrow I'll go to school in Nelsonville, so I best be on my way before nightfall. Ma says it's only fair that I spend the same amount of time in both schools. Ma don't believe none in favoritisms."

His rationale lacked merit, but Annie didn't mention that fact. What had she gotten herself into by agreeing to a teaching position in Willow Falls?

Chapter Four

Annie was walking up the aisle after having just finished assisting one of her younger pupils when John Mark raised his hand.

"Miss Ledbetter?"

"Yes, John Mark?"

What Annie surmised would be a brief inquiry turned into a lengthy discussion. John Mark didn't think it fair that he should have to do any writing assignments or parsing sentences and proceeded to explain all of his forty-two reasons.

"John Mark, sometimes we don't cotton to a task given us, but we still must endeavor to do it."

She was about to dismiss the conversation when John Mark again garnered her attention.

"But, Miss Ledbetter, can you tell me the history of parsing sentences? Who invented it and when? And most importantly, why?"

Annie fully believed in giving her full attention to her students to ensure they had a quality education, even if they could be exasperating at times. Perhaps John Mark was genuinely interested. She took a deep breath and commenced explaining.

But when he began staring into the distance only a minute into her answer, she feared she'd lost his attention. It was just as she was about to try a new method of explanation when a distinct sound came from the back of the schoolhouse.

She spun to see Franklin leading a calf into the school.

"Oh, goodness, Franklin! Cows are not welcome in the classroom."

The Red Angus calf mooed its way through the door and toward the front.

"Yes, ma'am, I know, but this here is Louie. She's a pet and as harmless as they come."

Franklin patted the bovine on the flank. He beamed, a contagious smile lighting his face.

A female animal given a male name? And just how did she manage to fit through the door?

"Hello, Louie," several students chorused.

"You do realize you're going to have to remove her from the school—I can't teach the class with her in here."

"Yep, I know. I was takin' Louie for a walk and done wanted to share her with the class. Seems she wants to learn too."

Laughter reverberated throughout the schoolhouse.

"Children, please. Franklin, Louie is causing a disruption, and I'm going to have to ask you to please remove her."

"Sure thang, Miss Teacher. After all, I don't want to make you upset none. Come on, Louie."

"I thought you were supposed to travel to Nelsonville this afternoon in anticipation of your school day there tomorrow."

"Nah, I done change my mind. Ma don't show no favoritisms, but I does. I like it here in Willow Falls much better. Think I'll just stay at this school from here on out."

Franklin Benjamin would be her permanent student? What would happen next? Would she arrive at school tomorrow to find a chicken coop built near her desk? *Father, please give me strength.*

***

The walk after school to the Eliason home gave Annie some much-needed time to think. The destitute and peculiar Franklin Benjamin dominated her thoughts. She allowed her "overabundance of imagination", as Ma called it, to run wild. Perhaps Franklin had moved here from a far-off state. Maybe he and his Ma and Pa had to walk the entire way, with only one set of clothes and their pet calf, Louie. Annie imagined Louie on a rope, meandering behind the family as they journeyed over rough terrain and barren prairies.

Poor Franklin hadn't had a chance to attend proper schooling because his pa needed him to help with the farm. As such, his speaking skills and reading abilities had suffered. Franklin's parents failed to teach him proper manners and forgot to tell him that wearing gloves in the summer was unnecessary unless he was doing chores.

Before supper that night, Annie slipped into her room to write in her diary. The words flowed freely from her pen.

September 2, 1884
Dear Diary,

I am shocked to report I endured some amusing occurrences at the school during my first day. Not only did I have a peculiar new pupil who is too old to be a student, but he also brought his pet calf, Louie, into the schoolhouse. I am not sure what to think about the animal, nor about her owner, a young man named Franklin Benjamin. Mr. Benjamin is no ordinary student. On the contrary, he is a twenty-five-year-old man who lacks both adequate hygiene and a proper grasp of the English language.

What will tomorrow bring?

On a more positive note, the Eliason family is nice, although I have yet to make the acquaintance of their oldest son, Caleb, who will be building additional desks and tending to the school's stove when winter comes. Reverend Solomon and his wife, Lydie, are kind. I shall enjoy staying with them.

There is a face I do recognize in Willow Falls: that of Doc Garrett. He is the one who arrived that day to save Ma, Sadie, and Mr. DeGroot.

⁂

Caleb placed Louie in the corral. It had been no minor miracle to have wedged her through the front door of the school. She was a smaller calf than most, so that helped, but her stubborn nature hadn't been conducive to a successful prank.

Finally, Louie cooperated, but Caleb had nearly lost his composure after seeing the expression on Miss Ledbetter's face. Her widened eyes, rapid blinking, and mouth falling open when she first saw him nearly caused Caleb to reveal the truth. To avoid chuckling had been difficult.

And Louie as a female name? He recalled how, when Charlotte was younger, she had named every chicken in the coop "Louie", hence the idea for the bum calf.

Even more amusing was Miss Ledbetter's attempt to hide her grimace when he'd said he preferred to stay in Willow Falls, rather than Nelsonville, for his schooling.

For certain, Miss Ledbetter's first day had been far more memorable than even Miss Barry's first day several years ago when Caleb himself was a student at the school.

Miss Ledbetter was pretty and he wished they could have met for the first time under different circumstances. But he would be *meeting* her tonight as Caleb at his parents' home. Thankfully, Ma would be revealing the truth to her about Franklin and Louie before he arrived for supper.

Caleb tended to his chores, then headed back into town. One of the townsfolk needed assistance with a rambunctious horse, and Caleb never refused the opportunity to assist someone in need.

Chapter Five

That evening, Annie, Lydie, and Charlotte prepared supper.

"There's something I've been meaning to tell you about school, Annie," said Lydie, who had just arrived home from a trip to the mercantile.

"Oh?" Annie carried the plates to the table.

But Reverend Solomon and John Mark's arrival interrupted Lydie, and the hustle and bustle of putting supper on the table took precedence.

"It sure smells good in here." John Mark took a step toward the table and reached his finger into the bowl of mashed potatoes.

Lydie swatted his hand. "John Mark Solomon Eliason, that is for supper. And besides, you have yet to wash up."

"Sorry, Ma. The taters look so tasty."

"The potatoes look tasty because *I* prepared them." Charlotte sashayed around the supper table, setting silverware at each place setting.

"Nevermind. I suddenly don't feel like any potatoes." John Mark shivered. "The thought of Charlotte preparing them has squelched my appetite."

Reverend Solomon chuckled. "Never did I imagine my son using a word like 'squelched.' I'm glad to see that attending our fine Willow Falls school is enhancing your vocabulary."

"That's funny, Pa, because I don't think John Mark really learns anything at school," said Charlotte.

John Mark directed a crusty look toward his sister. "And what of your arithmetic scores, dear Charlotte?"

"Now, now, that's enough, children," warned Reverend Solomon. "There'll be no bickering at the supper table."

"Speaking of the supper table, if everyone would like to take a seat, I think we're ready to eat," said Lydie.

Reverend Solomon led the prayer to bless the meal, and during supper, Lydie asked about Annie's first day. It surprised her how comfortable she felt sharing with her host family.

"Reverend Solomon, would please pray for this new student at school?" Annie told the family about the arrival of Franklin Benjamin and his pet calf, Louie. "For a man of that age to still need schooling...it must be so embarrassing. And he appears destitute and poverty-stricken with his torn and soiled clothing."

Reverend Solomon scooped some mashed potatoes. "I have a feeling that the Lord will take care of Franklin. I don't think you need to worry about him."

Lydie tossed her husband a stern look. Perhaps she understood Annie's discomfort since she mentioned she had been a teacher before her marriage to the Reverend. "That reminds me, Annie, there's something I need to tell you about Franklin."

"Still, we'll pray for him." Charlotte smiled.

"He needs all the prayers he can get, and more," muttered John Mark.

"John Mark…" Reverend Solomon warned.

"Yes, you see, Franklin…" Lydie began but was unable to finish as just at that moment, the door opened and Franklin Benjamin removed his hat, hung it on the hook near the door, and sat down at the table across from Annie.

<hr />

"I'm so glad you're here. We were just about to start eating." Ma rose to retrieve a plate.

"Sorry I'm late. I had an accident involving a horse at Mr. Dixon's today." He held up a bandaged hand. "Painful experience, but Doc reckons I'll make a full recovery."

"Oh, that's awful. And you look so pale."

Ma, as usual, fussed over him. Not that he was complaining; he appreciated her concern.

Pa leaned toward him. "I'd like to take a look at that after supper."

As Caleb glanced up, he noticed for the first time that Miss Ledbetter was sitting across from him. She stared at him, confusion and bewilderment clouding her pretty features. Her brows knit together and she tilted her head to one side, sitting still as if frozen in place.

Had Ma not yet told her about the prank tradition? If not, what must she think?

The discussion continued about Caleb's hand before the passing of the food around the table commenced. Conversation ceased temporarily while everyone ate. A multitude of thoughts crowded Caleb's mind. When would be the right moment to tell Miss Ledbetter he wasn't really Franklin Benjamin, but Caleb Eliason?

He fumbled with his fork while using his left hand. It would take some adjustment to become at least somewhat proficient in doing things while his injury healed. The incident today brought back a slew of memories about a previous wound on the same hand.

The scar was an ever-present reminder of the burn he'd suffered, along with hateful and cutting comments from the cruel lips of the malicious Mr. Yager since Caleb had failed to do anything right in the man's eyes.

Seven years ago, the Lord saw fit to give Caleb a new family, one that cared for him.

And a new start.

It was obvious the man was in pain from his injury. Annie recalled when a horse kicked Pa years ago. Horses were powerful creatures. It was only by God's grace the injury hadn't been worse.

Her thoughts turned to confusion. The Eliason Family had invited Franklin Benjamin to supper? Or at least, he *looked* like Franklin. Except his appearance was now that of a working man, but clean and tidy nonetheless. But what of his familiarity with the Eliason family? She supposed it was the Reverend's duty to do what he could to provide for his congregants.

But how had Franklin's vocabulary improved so significantly in a matter of hours?

Annie realized she'd been staring at Franklin, her spoon in midair between the mashed potato bowl and her own plate. She hastily lowered it, her mind still a maze of confusion.

"I was hoping to have spoken to you about, um, Franklin, before now." Lydie's statement caused Charlotte and John Mark to pass a knowing glance between them.

Reverend Solomon began to chuckle. "This must be mighty baffling for you, Annie."

"I must admit, I am somewhat befuddled. I never imagined the Lord to answer this particular prayer for Franklin so expeditiously. How ironic I just requested prayer for him and now here he is! It's admirable you invited him to supper and are offering to care for his injured hand." She adjusted her napkin on her lap. "Does he eat here often?"

John Mark snorted. "Only when Ma makes his favorite meal."

"His favorite meal?" asked Annie.

"We should probably explain," said Lydie. "Caleb, would you care to?"

Annie searched the table for who Caleb might be. She stared from one person to the next—from the Reverend, to Lydie, to John Mark, to Charlotte, and finally to Franklin.

"Well, my name really isn't Franklin."

Annie gaped at the man across the table from her. His blue eyes held a mischievous twinkle.

"My real name is Caleb Eliason."

"I beg your pardon?"

Lydie tossed her a sympathetic glance. "I do apologize. I was going to tell you before supper about Caleb. You see, each time there is a new teacher in Willow Falls, it's the town tradition to play a harmless prank or two on the first day of class. Although he begged not to be chosen, Caleb was nominated by the students to be the adult in charge of the pranks this year. By nominating an adult to oversee the plan, we are assured it won't get out of hand, that the pranks remain innocuous, and the students respectful."

"All of the students knew?"

"Yes," answered Lydie.

"Each and every one?" Annie peered from John Mark to Charlotte, who both nodded.

"Oh, dear," her voice squeaked, not at all sounding like her own. "Franklin, or Caleb, is not really a new student in my class?"

"No, I'm not really a new student," Caleb said. "That was part of the prank."

"And these pranks only last the first day?"

John Mark shook his head. "Unless one of the students…"

"And that student best not be you," Reverend Solomon reprimanded.

"No, sir. It won't be. I was just saying that it happens to be the case sometimes with other students, but not me, of course."

Annie wasn't sure how she felt about the prank. On one hand, it was humorous. But on the other, quite an embarrassment.

"I should hope you weren't a new student…especially since, how old did you say you were? Twenty-five?" She suddenly felt gullible.

"I'm not really twenty-five. I'm actually only twenty-one, but…"

"Well, gracious! It is a relief you are not actually a student at the school."

Charlotte giggled. "And you don't have to worry about Louie ever again, either."

Oh, yes, Louie.

Caleb caught her eye and held her gaze. "Believe me, Miss Ledbetter, I didn't want to partake in the prank tradition. Charlotte and John Mark, along with their friends, coerced me into being the adult in charge this year. Each year, the students can pick and vote on which adult they want to lead the prank. Unfortunately, they chose me."

Confusion overwhelmed her and Annie sought to set the perplexing episode straight in her mind. She had been naïve in thinking Caleb Eliason was a twenty-five-year-old man named Franklin Benjamin, and a new student to boot. And the horrible English usage—it had all been a ploy to initiate her into the town of Willow Falls and into her teaching position. Everyone knew—every one of her pupils, every one of the Eliasons, likely everyone in Willow Falls.

"So is Louie your real pet calf?"

At this, the entire family laughed.

"She is," said Caleb. "That part is true."

"Well, of all things..." Annie pressed her hands in her lap.

She had the mind to take out her wrath on Franklin...or, rather, Caleb.

"Annie, if it makes you feel any better, I was a new teacher in Willow Falls many years ago. The students played a prank on me too. I believe I was the first teacher to succumb to these shenanigans, and when I discovered the truth, I was so upset I ran to tell the young new reverend in town what had happened. Well, I didn't know the new reverend very well because he had just arrived a week prior, but he knew all about the prank too," said Lydie.

Reverend Solomon's eyes crinkled at the corners. "Oh, yes, I knew all about it. And this lovely young teacher, frustration on her face, visited me in the middle of writing the second sermon I'd ever preached. On telling the truth, no less."

"There was one favorable result, however. I fell in love with the new reverend," Lydie fluttered her lashes at Reverend Solomon.

"And I fell in love with her as well."

Charlotte wrinkled her nose. "Ma, Pa, can we please eat supper now and not talk about sappy topics?"

"Just wait, Charlotte. Someday you'll fall in love. Maybe with Tobias."

Charlotte nearly leaped from her seat. "You take that back, John Mark Solomon Eliason! Tobias is repulsive and abhorrent. Ma, make him stop."

"Now, now, John Mark. Apologize to your sister."

A few seconds ticked by before a begrudging, "Sorry, Charlotte."

Annie noticed his apology didn't seem all that sincere, but she had so much on her mind about processing the entire Franklin and Louie episode that she didn't give it a second thought.

"Since I'm apologizing, I might as well say I'm sorry you had to be the one we played the pranks on, Miss Ledbetter. You're nice and all, and we hated to have to do it, but it is a Willow Falls tradition. And you can't break tradition."

"No, I suppose you can't break tradition."

On one hand, she was grateful she wouldn't have to worry about a chicken coop built next to her desk when she returned the next morning, and she would have a hilarious story to share with Hetty. On the other, the entire experience had been a bit of a discomfiture.

Annie started to laugh then. "I admit I found Franklin a bit suspicious."

She glanced up to see Franklin—or Caleb as he was truly known—watching her.

Heat crept up her cheeks. Why did she have to blush so easily?

Could be because the man who oversaw the prank traditions was handsome, rather than homely with a boorish disposition.

"I'm sorry too, Miss Teacher," Caleb said, causing a round of laughter from his family.

"I guess I've survived my initiation. And you are all quite sure that there will be no more pranks?"

The chicken coop image once again loomed in her mind.

"These two pranks will be the only ones as far as the tradition goes." Caleb's eye caught hers and she blushed all over again. "It's only for the first day and then school will return to normal."

"Although some of the students might play other pranks on you," Charlotte surmised.

"Let's see to it that none of the Eliason children are in on any other pranks," Reverend Solomon said in a stern voice.

"Yes, sir," John Mark and Charlotte chorused in unison.

Everyone resumed eating, and Annie noticed how quickly the episode at school had been forgotten by the Eliason

Family. There was no doubt in her mind she would remember it for years to come.

A comfortable camaraderie filled the air, one that welcomed Annie to partake in. She took a bite of the meal and did her best to ignore the fact that the handsome Caleb Eliason continued to look her way. Every now and again those dark and handsome blue eyes caught hers.

Eyes that seemed familiar.

Chapter Six

Life in the Eliason household was far from dull. Annie discovered that on her third evening in Willow Falls, when a loud shriek distracted her from the letter she was writing to Hetty.

"Ma, Pa, help!"

Annie emerged from her room to see Charlotte standing outside her own room, wringing her hands.

Lydie attempted to calm her daughter. "What it is, Charlotte?"

"It's—it's John Mark."

"John Mark? Is he all right?" asked Reverend Solomon.

"Yes, he's—he's fine, but..." Charlotte covered her face in dramatic fashion and began to wail.

"John Mark?" Reverend Solomon summoned his son while Lydie comforted Charlotte.

"Yes, Pa?" John Mark stepped from his room, his eyes darting from person to person.

"Something is amiss with Charlotte. Do you know what happened?"

"Yes." John Mark stared down at his bare feet and tapped his toe on the floor.

"Well?" prompted Lydie.

"Ma, it was the most ghastly and loathsome thing that has ever happened to me." Charlotte's wail was muffled as she nuzzled her face into Lydie's nightgown.

"It wasn't the worst thing that's ever happened to you, Charlotte. You're so dramatic," grumbled John Mark, still directing his gaze to the floor.

"He put a frog in my bed and it's still there!" Charlotte's wails grew louder.

"Ah, shucks, Charlotte. You like frogs. Remember how we like to race them during the frog race at the ice cream social every year?"

"But I don't like frogs in my *bed*. They're slimy, slippery, and abhorrent."

Reverend Solomon cast a warning glance toward his son. "John Mark Solomon Eliason, I will meet you in the barn."

"But, Pa—"

"In the barn."

"Yes, sir." John Mark shuffled toward the door and followed his father outside.

Lydie wrapped her arms around her daughter and planted a kiss on her head. "Charlotte, Miss Ledbetter and I will help you remove the frog from your bed."

"Thank you, Ma. Far be it from me to cause a disturbance at this time of night, but this episode truly is dreadful."

"You'll find, Annie, that Charlotte reads many books and has a rather extensive, yet exaggerated, vocabulary."

"Well, reading can take one on adventures they might never go on otherwise. I love to read too, and this entire episode reminds me of past times with my older brother, Zeb."

"That's right, I forgot you have an older brother," muttered Charlotte. "My deepest, most sincere condolences to you, Miss Ledbetter."

Annie thought of Zeb and a sudden rush of homesickness overcame her. Determined to push it aside, she followed Lydie and Charlotte into Charlotte's room where the tan-and-rust-colored amphibian sat, his mouth appearing upturned as if grinning mischievously.

"See, there he is." Charlotte covered her face with her hands again, as if viewing the frog was too much for her to bear.

For the next several minutes, Annie and Lydie attempted to catch the amphibian. About the time they had finally achieved their goal, John Mark returned from the barn full of apologies.

"Sorry, Charlotte. My punishment is that I have to do your chore of clearing the table and washing the supper dishes for a whole week." He folded his arms across his chest and scowled.

"Really?" Charlotte arched an eyebrow.

"It's not fair, it being women's work and all."

As they headed to bed, Annie overheard the words Charlotte mumbled to her brother—words likely meant only for John Mark's ears—"Maybe the frog prank was worth it, John Mark. Supper dishes for a whole week? Won't that be the best thing ever to see you wearing my apron!"

Chapter Seven

THE REMAINDER OF ANNIE'S first week went remarkably well after the prank tradition was settled. Zeb arrived to take her home for the weekend and she apprised her family and Hetty of the happenings—especially the first day of school.

Now it was the Monday of the second week and Annie embraced the idea of teaching her pupils. Most were eager learners who gave her little cause for concern, neither in their studies nor in their behavior. However, there were times Annie had to withhold recess privileges for a few disobedient pupils.

"Younger students, please take out your McGuffey Readers. Older scholars, please continue working on your arithmetic assignment."

"Excuse me, Miss Ledbetter?" Caleb walked in the door of the school. "We are going to be bringing in the new stove. It'll only take us a minute. I'll finish installing it after school is out for the day."

"That would be fine, Mr. Eliason."

Annie hadn't seen much of Caleb since that night at supper when he confessed to being a part of the prank tradition.

Caleb led three men into the school, where they set a potbelly stove on its base in the back of the classroom. It was black and shiny with crafted silver-colored legs.

"That's a fancy stove, Caleb," one of the students remarked.

"Brand new and shipped here all the way from back East. This should keep everyone warm. I'll return after school is out to install it."

※

Annie graded assignments, but her mind wandered. When Caleb had directed a teasing smile at her earlier, her heart had lurched.

"Miss Ledbetter!" Charlotte's panicked tone and waving right hand interrupted Annie's thoughts.

Annie jerked her head up from the task at hand. "What is it, Charlotte?" Surely an emergency had occurred for Charlotte to have overreacted in such a way.

"Miss Ledbetter, I've been trying in vain to capture your attention for the past ten minutes. It's Tobias Hallman. He's being a bother again."

Tobias snorted. "The past ten minutes? More like the past ten *seconds*."

"Is this true that you are being a bother, Tobias?" Annie stood for a better view of the conflict between her students.

"It's possible, ma'am."

"But, Miss Ledbetter, it is true. Tobias just tied my braids together!" Charlotte reached back behind her and pulled a mass of tangled blonde braids above her head. "See?"

"Tobias..." Annie began.

"Miss Ledbetter, you must do something. My braids are wound together in a jumbled clump. I shall absolutely faint away into a hodgepodge of nothingness if something isn't done to relieve this knotted mess!"

Tobias rolled his eyes. "Charlotte, you exaggerate like no one I've ever known. You'll no more faint away into a lodge of nothingness than I'll be on the next stage to California."

Charlotte spun around in her chair and glared at Tobias. "Not a *lodge* of nothingness, Tobias Hallman. A *hodgepodge* of nothingness. You are such an ill-mannered and impertinent boor!"

"You and your big vocabulary. You sling them fancy words around like you're smart or something. Even you don't know what they mean."

Several snickers followed Tobias's insinuation.

"You take that back, Tobias! I do know what every single word I use means. *Every single word.*"

"I'll not take it back. It's your own fault about your braids. If they weren't so long, they wouldn't find themselves on my desk. Keep them in your own space or next time I'll bring my ma's sewing scissors."

Annie pursed her lips and planted her hands firmly on her hips. "Tobias Hallman, may I speak to you at the front of the room, please? Charlotte, you may return to work."

"Thank you, Miss Ledbetter. I regret that you'll spend the next hour with such a disagreeable fellow."

"Charlotte..."

"Yes, ma'am. I'll return to work posthaste." She pretended to focus on her work, but Annie caught her peering their way.

"Tobias? Please come to the front of the room."

Tobias hung his head. "Yes, ma'am."

With the lethargy of a turtle, he removed his long legs from behind the desk and took his thirteen-year-old self to the front of the room. He sighed every couple of seconds as if dragging himself forward to receive his punishment was just too much to endure.

"Why did you tie Charlotte's braids in knots?"

"I don't mean no respect, Miss Ledbetter, but it's like I said before—Charlotte's long, dangly braids were resting on my desk. I'm tired of it. Every day when I look up, there they are, taking up room in my space. I finally had it and decided to do something, so I tied her braids together. But it's nothing that can't be fixed with a little tuggin' and pullin'. Charlotte is such a baby about things. She gets mad every time I play a prank on her."

"And rightfully so. What you did was uncalled for and I'm going to have to issue punishment."

"You sound like Miss Barry."

"I'll take that as a compliment. Now, Tobias, I want you to write on the chalkboard fifty times, 'I will not pester Charlotte.' You won't leave until the task is finished. And I want your best penmanship. "

"Yes, ma'am. And I'm sorry."

"Thank you, Tobias. One more thing: I want you to apologize to Charlotte. And then I want you to apologize to the class for interrupting their study time. You may do that now before you begin writing."

"Aw, Miss Ledbetter. Do I have to?"

"You do."

Tobias's shoulders slumped as if he'd been asked to do something so dreadful it would alter the course of his life forever. He turned toward Charlotte and the rest of the classroom.

"Sorry, Charlotte."

Charlotte fumbled with her braids. "I should hope you are."

"And?" asked Annie.

"Sorry, class."

Annie dismissed her wayward pupil, and he commenced writing on the chalkboard. She returned to her desk, ignoring Charlotte's smug smirk.

Chapter Eight

Later that afternoon, Annie dismissed the children and sat at her desk to prepare the next day's lesson. She was impressed with the children's abilities, especially in spelling. They had far surpassed learning the words on their spelling list.

"Miss Ledbetter?"

Annie saw Caleb stooping next to the new potbelly stove, his manners and clarity of speech a stark contrast from that of Franklin's.

"Yes, Mr. Eliason?"

"I'm going to finish installing the stove now. Don't mind me, I'll try to keep the noise down." He waved a gloved hand at her and began his work. "I don't know if Pa told you, but I'll be making sure you have plenty of wood in the coming months. As you know, it can get mighty cold during a Wyoming winter."

Annie nodded. That was a fact she knew well.

"Thank you."

"I'll also arrive here before you do in the morning and light the stove for you so that by the time you and the students get here, it'll be warm."

"I do appreciate that, Mr. Eliason."

Annie attempted to keep her focus on her papers. His consideration and benevolence in tending to the matters of her and her students' comfort made an impression on her.

"How is your injured hand?"

Caleb held up his hand. "Still painful, but I reckon it's on its way to healing. Helps to keep it covered. How is the teaching going?"

"It's going well now that there are no more pranks."

Thankfully, no chicken coop had been built near her desk and Louie no longer possessed a desire to learn.

Caleb chuckled and began his work on the stove. It was clear Annie hadn't been fond of the prank tradition, but she had taken it in stride. It had been no easy feat to maintain a stoic demeanor, especially while pretending to be Franklin Benjamin.

Never again would he allow himself to be volunteered as the adult in charge. He wasn't good at such things.

Caleb hummed softly as he worked. Things took him twice as long with an injured hand, which frustrated him. Several times throughout the day, he was reminded that his right hand was all but unusable, and the pain searing through it was enough to remind him to give himself extra time to complete his projects.

He sneaked another peek at Miss Ledbetter's beautiful profile. Her intelligence impressed him. He'd heard she was the smartest pupil in her class in Nelsonville. He'd also heard from John Mark and Charlotte about the assignments and how they held much respect for her knowledge.

Annie peered up from her work then, and their eyes connected. "Yes, Mr. Eliason?"

"I—uh, just finishing the stove installation."

What else could he say? That he was admiring her beauty?

Annie returned to her task but intermittently watched Caleb work. He was tall, much taller than her father and broader in the shoulders, although he was leaner. His presence told of his strength—not just physical strength—but strength within him.

Several minutes later, he approached her desk. "I'm finished now, so I'll be on my way. If you ever need anything, anything at all, please let me know. It's my job to make sure the wood is well-stocked and all is taken care of as far as the schoolhouse is concerned."

"Thank you kindly. I'll keep that in mind."

"I'll also be in charge of shoveling any snow off the front steps."

"That's very charitable, thank you."

"You're welcome." Caleb continued to stand in front of her desk.

Awkward silence filled the air.

Annie straightened the bell, shifted the globe slightly forward, placed her Bible in her stack of things to take home, and placed the two extra slate pencils side-by-side.

"Thank you again, Mr. Eliason," she squeaked.

"Yes. Uh, well, guess that's all for now. If I think of something else, I'm sure I can discuss it with you during supper at my parents' house."

Annie knew the heat was creeping up her cheeks at the speed of one of those newfangled trains she'd heard about. "Yes, I'll be there."

She'd be there? Well, of course, she'd be there! Where else would she be?

Caleb placed his hat on his head. "Look forward to seeing you tonight, then."

He would look forward to seeing her?

Her face turned an even brighter red if that were possible. "And I'll—I'll see you as well."

Caleb tipped his hat and turned on his heel to leave.

Annie struggled to return her attention to her duties. True to his word, Caleb arrived for supper at the Eliason home. In the course of five minutes, Annie managed to drop her fork, hit her head on the table while retrieving the fork, and make an utter fool of herself.

Had anyone noticed? She hoped not.

Out of the blue, Charlotte initiated conversation. "That hideous Tobias Hallman decided to tie my braids in knots today."

John Mark provided a sly grin. "It's because he fancies you."

"Does not!"

"Does too!"

"Children, please. This is neither the time nor the place to argue," said Lydie.

"Ma, it was horrid. Tobias said he tied my hair in knots because my braids were resting on his desk. But I suppose it's better than the time he threw my prized dolly in the river." Charlotte paused and took a deep breath as if to calm herself before continuing. "And why did he choose to sit behind me this year? There were three million other places to sit in the classroom, but no. He chose to sit behind me. What are the odds?"

"Like I said," muttered John Mark, "he fancies you. He doesn't do any of those things to any other girl. I should know, he's a good friend of mine. And there are *not* 'three million other places to sit'. Did you forget you live in Willow Falls? It's not like—like New York City or something."

"Don't be absurd, John Mark. And besides, why aren't you coming to my rescue against that despicable Tobias?" Charlotte placed a hand over her heart. "The handsome prince, John Mark Eliason, always coming to someone's rescue…or so the girls at school say. Well, how come you don't come to my rescue?"

"You're my sister. I only rescue other people and injured animals." John Mark straightened in his chair. "Do the girls really say that about me? That I'm a handsome prince?"

Charlotte sliced her piece of steak. "Don't worry. They aren't being serious."

"Well, I *am* kind and thoughtful and always seeking to help others. It's the way I've been raised, to be a gentleman and all."

"Gentleman is hardly the word I would use to describe you. Cheeky and brash is more like it. And I can see why you and Tobias would be good friends. 'Two peas in a pod', as they say. You two and that obnoxious Russell friend of yours." Charlotte paused. "Miss Ledbetter, can you please relocate Tobias?"

"I've already given that consideration, Charlotte. Tomorrow I'll see to it that he is permanently seated at a different desk."

Annie smiled at Charlotte, grateful the young girl had diverted the attention from Annie's lack of poise.

John Mark smirked. "Miss Ledbetter will move him to one of the other three million seats."

"Let's discuss something else, shall we?" asked Lydie. Without waiting for an answer, she continued, "We need to make a few meals for Mrs. Waite. She hasn't been well and I'm concerned for her. Would you mind delivering those for me in the next few days, Caleb? I'll also have Charlotte and John Mark check in on her."

"Sure, Ma. That won't be a problem at all."

That night after everyone else retired for the evening, Annie tiptoed into the kitchen and poured herself a glass of water from the pitcher. The clock on the mantle indicated the hour was late, but Annie couldn't resist staying up after prayers to pen a quick update in her diary.

Dear Diary,
This past week has been somewhat of an adventure.
The man behind the pranks is named Caleb Eliason. He is handsome, twenty-one, has blond hair that curls at the ends beneath his hat, and is strong and lean (not that I have noticed, mind you). He is a generous sort, willing to assist whoever needs him. For some odd reason, he seems familiar, although I can't say why.

Suffice it to say, I did survive the pranks with the supposed Franklin Benjamin and his pet calf, Louie, but only just barely. Never in my dreams of becoming a teacher had I anticipated that towns would have such traditions.

It is late and I best toddle off to bed. Tomorrow is a new day with my students. I am finding them to be an eager bunch with a penchant for learning.

Chapter Nine

THE FOLLOWING DAY, ANNIE stepped out of the schoolhouse and into the fresh Wyoming air. Charlotte and John Mark walked a few steps in front of her, their chatter reminding her of her and Zeb. Homesickness filled her heart.

Caleb slowed his wagon to a stop beside them. "Would you three like a ride home?"

"No thanks, Caleb. Ma asked if we would stop by Mrs. Waite's house and check in on her. She hasn't been well." John Mark shifted his books to his other arm.

"All right, then. Just thought I would check."

"But you could give Miss Ledbetter a ride. It would be a kind gesture considering your part in the pranks," said Charlotte, sounding much older than her eleven years.

"Is that so?" Caleb shot a lazy grin Annie's way.

Under his perusal, Annie nearly stumbled over nothing.

"Yes, that's so," insisted Charlotte. "And it would be the gentlemanly thing to do."

John Mark groaned. "Why are she and Ma always insisting we do the gentlemanly thing?"

"I reckon it's their job," Caleb answered. "And the right thing to do."

He paused then addressed Annie, "Would you give me the honor of giving you a ride home today, Miss Teacher?"

John Mark snickered and Charlotte giggled.

"You may call me Miss Ledbetter, Franklin," Annie retorted, thrilled at her quick wit.

"All right then, Miss Ledbetter. May I accompany you home on this fine Wyoming afternoon?" Caleb removed his hat and attempted to bow from the wagon seat.

"Thank you, but I was contemplating paying a visit to Mrs. Waite with Charlotte and John Mark. Perhaps next time?"

Charlotte shook her head. "You should ride with him this time. It's rather boring at Mrs. Waite's house, although please don't tell Ma I said so. Besides, when John Mark and I are finished, we plan to race home. As such, you would be left all alone."

Charlotte closed her eyes and held her hand to her chest. "Let the man give you a ride home and redeem himself for his role in the pranks, Miss Ledbetter."

"I do believe I see the makings of a stage actress. Very well. If you insist and it's all right with Mr. Eliason, I shall allow him to give me a ride home." Annie figured there wasn't much harm in accepting a ride.

"See you at home," John Mark yelled over his shoulder as he darted off.

Caleb climbed down from the wagon to assist Annie. His hand gently cupped hers and a peculiar tingle traveled up her arm.

"Not sure what to think about Charlotte," said Caleb. "She spends far too much time reading books like *Little Women*. Ma says it behooves her to eliminate Charlotte's reading time when there's a punishment to be had. That sets Charlotte on the right path in no time at all."

He had scarcely beckoned the horses to start their journey home when they were interrupted by a woman walking toward them carrying a bundle of clothing.

"Caleb?"

"Whoa," Caleb said, stopping the horses. "Yes, Mrs. Burns? Is everything all right?"

Mrs. Burns ignored Caleb and instead addressed Annie. "Hello, Miss Ledbetter. We met last week, if you'll remember."

"I do remember, Mrs. Burns. How are you today?"

"Well, besides the rheumatism and my eyes giving me fits, I'm doing as well as can be expected."

"Is there something we can do for you, Mrs. Burns?" Caleb asked.

"Well, I wouldn't just ask you to stop if I had nothing to say. Where is the common sense God gave you, young man?"

Caleb stepped down from the wagon. "Yes, of course, Mrs. Burns."

Annie eyed the woman. She was likely in her early sixties and no taller than five foot, her gray hair styled into a braid that must have wrapped around her head three or four times. Her squinted eyes were covered by thick spectacles and her mouth was downturned. She was thin, but from what Annie could tell, not frail.

"Now, you tell your Ma I need these dresses mended. Tell her not to charge me a penny more than she ought. You know me, I don't have a lot of funds these days. But I'm desperate. With my eyesight the way it is, I can barely see the seams anymore, much less thread a needle."

"I will do that, Mrs. Burns. I reckon Ma is efficient and will have these back to you in no time at all."

"You tell her not to take her sweet time. One of those dresses is my Sunday finery and I can't be wearing this old, dingy dress to church." Mrs. Burns squinted at Annie. "And you, Miss Ledbetter. How are you doing after the pranks that were played on you? I'm proud of you for still being here."

"Do some teachers change their minds and forego their teaching positions after the pranks?"

"Only one. But she was a spineless goat if I ever did see one, so there was no way she was going to stick around." Mrs. Burns rolled her eyes.

"I'm glad the pranks only lasted one day."

"Yes, well, that's all that would be allowed. We don't need a bunch of hooligans with ruthless behavior, mind you. Speaking of which, since you were the adult in charge, Caleb Eliason, I find it only fitting you atone for your actions. So, it's my request that you ask Miss Ledbetter to the ice cream social planned for the Saturday after next."

Caleb cleared his throat. "I—uh—"

Annie looked away.

How embarrassing! Must this really be happening? And what of poor Mr. Eliason? To be placed in such a vexing position?

"Don't stutter about it young man, just do it," barked Mrs. Burns. "And believe you me, come the Saturday after next, I'll be seeing if you followed orders. Now, off with you. The time wasted while conversing is taking time away from your ma getting to my mending."

Without so much as a goodbye, Mrs. Burns darted away with tiny, quick steps.

They rode in silence for a few minutes before Caleb began to chuckle. "That Mrs. Burns is a spunky one."

"She does seem to be a bit on the feisty side."

"Her third husband passed away about two years ago of scarlet fever. I think it's her stubbornness and fortitude that have kept her alive this long. She's somewhat of a bossy woman, but things get accomplished under her direction."

"Speaking of things getting accomplished under Mrs. Burns's direction, Mr. Eliason, you needn't accompany me to the ice cream social the Saturday after next. I realize she put you in an uncomfortable position. Besides, I return home each weekend to Nelsonville to see my family."

"If you decide to remain in Willow Falls, reckon I'm fine with accompanying you to the ice cream social. As Mrs. Burns mentioned, it's the least I can do for being the overseer of the pranks." He offered her a broad grin.

Goodness, he was handsome when he smiled. Speechless, she turned her head and stared at the passing scenery.

And it was on that day, riding home from school, that Annie began to grow fond of Caleb Eliason with his amiable personality and pleasing sense of humor.

Why was he such a dolt when he was around Annie Ledbetter? He spoke far too much and his addled brain spewed whatever came to mind without giving much thought. He rambled, his words uttered at a brisk pace.

Whether at the schoolhouse while fixing the stove, taking her home after school, or seeing her several nights each week during supper at his parents' home, the more time he spent with her, the fonder he grew.

Annie's intelligence, her ambition to be a well-respected teacher, her sweet personality, and her beauty drew him to her.

He'd always admired intellectual folks, even though his time spent in school was sparse. When he became an Eliason, Ma patiently took the time to assist him in the book learning he had missed. Under her tutelage, Caleb learned with impressive speed. After becoming proficient in reading, he devoured every book he could get his hands on, including some, like the Bible, which he read twice.

Now tonight, as his family and Annie finished their meals, Caleb contemplated the upcoming ice cream social. Should he ask if she had decided to attend? Or should he wait and see if she broached the subject again?

Caleb didn't have to ponder his decision for long.

"I am fervently anticipating the ice cream social," Charlotte announced. The girl had an inclination toward making sure there were no silent moments during supper. "Are you going to the social, Annie?"

Annie's face brightened. "My plans are to ask if my family might travel to Willow Falls and attend. I should like for you all to meet them."

"That's a fantastic idea, Annie," said Ma. "We should like to meet them as well."

Chapter Ten

After church, Annie loaded her carpetbag into the wagon for the return trip to Willow Falls.

Ma planted a kiss on her forehead. "We'll see you in a few short days at the ice cream social. I hear several Nelsonville residents will be in attendance this year."

"Sheriff Townsend mentioned at church that he'd invited the surrounding towns."

"I can't wait!" Sadie, with her abundance of energy, had spoken of nothing else since the moment Annie broached the subject at the supper table last night. "And you are sure we are going, right, Ma?"

Sadie rarely possessed the ability to be a lively sort early in the morning; however, she'd been up at sunrise, well ahead of the time church started. She sought confirmation several times since learning she could eat ample amounts of ice cream and not have to wait until after supper.

"Yes, Sadie. We plan to attend the ice cream social with Annie. Now go give your sister a hug so she and Zeb can be on their way."

Sadie wrapped her arms around Annie's neck.

"Just think, Annie, we'll be so full of ice cream on Saturday, we'll barely be able to move!" Sadie unclasped her hands and pretended to waddle. "And then, we'll have some more. I'm not going to eat any food that morning because I'll need all the room I can muster up in my belly for ice cream."

"All right, Sadie Girl," said Zeb. "We need to get Annie back to Willow Falls."

"We'll see you soon, Annie. Safe travels." Pa gave her a hug and assisted her into the wagon.

Once on the road, Zeb decided to bring up an embarrassing topic. "Hetty tells me a young man is accompanying you to the social."

"Hetty told you that?"

Was nothing sacred?

"Only after some prodding. But you know Hetty. No secret is a kept secret."

Annie groaned. "Yes, and it would be futile if I told her to resist divulging such information."

"She knew I would need to be aware of any fellow trying to win my sister's affections. He'll need to pass a full interrogation."

"Zeb, you've been spending far too much time helping the new sheriff fix up the jail."

"A brother can never ask too many questions about his sister's potential beau."

Annie's face reddened. "I'll have you know, Zebediah Walter Ledbetter, that Caleb Eliason is not my potential beau. He is merely my acquaintance—a friend, perhaps—who is accompanying me to my first ice cream social."

"And I'm Thomas Jefferson."

"Nice to meet you, Thomas."

Zeb chuckled. "I do recall, my dear sister, that you were an invaluable part of arranging the courtship between Hetty and me. Should it be said that I returned the favor?"

Annie swatted Zeb in the arm. "You'll do no such thing. Caleb and I are friends. You best not embarrass me."

"Embarrass you? Never."

Annie anticipated attending the ice cream social.

And seeing Caleb again.

From what she knew of him, he was considerate, generous, and had a servant's heart. His sense of humor, even when participating in the prank tradition, had begun to endear her to him.

Annie tucked her cream-colored blouse into her skirt and donned Ma's earrings. She'd never attended an ice cream social before and had only attended an event twice in her life with a young man. Both times had been barn dances in Nelsonville.

Nerves fluttered in her belly and excitement consumed every part of her. Why was it she couldn't wait to see Caleb again? She anticipated each day he offered to give her a ride home from school and always accepted the offer.

It was difficult for her to wait until one o'clock when Caleb would arrive at the Eliason home to retrieve her, and she paced the small area of her room. Her family would arrive soon as well and meet her at the festivities. The day couldn't get any better.

"Caleb's here to take you to the ice cream social," Charlotte announced with hands on her hips.

"Thank you, Charlotte."

"I still don't understand why you can't just ride with us. Pa is fixing to hitch up the team within the hour. We could all ride together."

Annie crossed the room and framed Charlotte's face with her hands. "My dear Charlotte, someday you will understand."

"John Mark says it's because Caleb fancies you."

"John Mark says that, does he?" Annie attempted to hide her embarrassment from the younger girl.

What if what John Mark said was true?

"Yes, he does, and as you know, John Mark thinks he knows positively everything about everything."

Annie giggled. "Charlotte, I have grown quite fond of your resplendent sense of humor."

"It's true. He does think Caleb fancies you and stares at you all wonderstruck during supper."

"Wonderstruck? Surely John Mark has better things to do than examine the expressions of others at the supper table."

"I don't know, Miss Ledbetter. You know John Mark. He's as meddlesome as they come."

John Mark appeared in the doorway of the home. "Are you two gonna just stand there and talk womenfolk nonsense or are you gonna come outside so we can go to the ice cream social?"

"Do you see what I mean, Miss Ledbetter?" Charlotte held a hand to her forehead. "Such nonsense I have never seen, except in my own brother. Whatever shall we do with him?"

"Whatever indeed," agreed Annie. "Such exuberance, Charlotte."

Annie emerged from her room. Caleb stood near the table sampling the homemade cakes Lydie was taking to the social. He wore a crisp gray shirt that accentuated his broad shoulders. Twinkling eyes met hers and a shiver made its way down Annie's spine.

"Hello, Caleb."

"Annie."

"Please, Annie, kindly take this man from my house before he devours all that is left of the cakes for the social." Lydie gently pushed Caleb away from the platter that was holding the decorated delicacies she had painstakingly cut into perfect squares.

"No need to convince Annie, Ma. I'm on my way."

"We'll plan to meet you at the social then." Lydie waved them toward the door.

Moments later, Annie and Caleb began the short trip to Willow Falls. Silence surrounded them most of the way until Caleb finally spoke. "You look beautiful, Annie."

"Thank you." Annie clasped her hands together and began picking at her fingernails.

When had they agreed to a first-name basis? Could he tell she was nervous? She really should polish her social skills.

"Did you know that each year Willow Falls holds the ice cream social as a way to mark the end of summer?"

"Um, yes. I mean, no, I didn't realize that. What a charming tradition." Could she be any more addlepated?

"It is a charming tradition. The entire town shows up for it and people mill around eating ice cream and conversing about the latest news in Willow Falls. Some of the children play games or enter the frog races, and I've even seen a few of the elderly residents napping in the sunshine beneath one of the trees."

"I love trees."

What? She loved trees? What a bizarre statement! Yes, she did love trees, but...Caleb was discussing ice cream and people napping and she said she loved *trees*?

Caleb chuckled. "I love trees too. I'm glad we have our share of them here in Willow Falls. Some places in the Wyoming Territory aren't so fortunate. It's a vast and barren countryside with nothing but weeds and sagebrush. Willow Falls is a nice place to live."

He slowed the wagon as they reached the center of town. A banner stretched between two businesses on each side of the road with the words WILLOW FALLS ANNUAL ICE CREAM SOCIAL. Other businesses boasted various decorations announcing the celebration, and numerous people milled around on the boardwalk and in the street.

Caleb was assisting Annie from the wagon when Mrs. Burns approached them. "I've been waiting for you. It appears as though you did as you were told, Caleb Eliason."

"Yes, ma'am."

"I suppose in the five years I've known you, you've been a respectable young man."

Caleb did his best to hide a snicker. "Much obliged for the compliment, Mrs. Burns."

"Now, now, don't let on that I gave you a commendation because then everyone will expect one, and I'm not too generous with my compliments." Mrs. Burns fanned herself with a folded piece of paper.

"I promise I won't tell a soul."

"Be sure you don't. Now, why don't you take this lovely lady and get her some ice cream? As a matter of fact, you should have already done that. Where are your manners? This *is* an ice cream social. And how are you, Miss Ledbetter?"

"I'm well, Mrs. Burns. Thank you."

"I see you wore your Sunday finest for your outing with Mr. Eliason. Mark my words, it won't be long before the two of you are courting. I'm rarely wrong about such things."

Caleb observed Annie's discomfort. "We best be on our way. Have a good day, Mrs. Burns."

"I hope it will be a good day, although with my rheumatism acting up, I can't be so sure. But enough chitter-chatter. I have other folks to talk with and I'll not show favoritism by only speaking with a privileged few." Mrs. Burns gathered her skirts and walked in the opposite direction toward Sheriff Townsend and his wife.

Caleb tossed Annie a knowing glance and they both laughed.

"That Mrs. Burns," said Caleb. "She's so presumptuous."

"Indeed."

"Eager for your family to arrive?"

"Yes. I've missed them. You'll like Zeb. He's an ornery sort, but I do appreciate his protectiveness over Sadie and me."

An unannounced and fleeting image of Cain flashed through Caleb's mind. Cain might have been considered ornery as a youngster, but as he grew older, he became malicious. And never once had he been protective over his younger brother.

Caleb swallowed hard and pushed aside the thoughts of his brother. Those days were in the past, along with the life he once led. No sense in allowing it to intrude on the present.

"I'll go get us some ice cream."

"Thank you for inviting me. I've only partaken in eating ice cream one other time, but I remember it being delicious."

Caleb grinned. "I don't think I had much of a choice not to invite you, thanks to Mrs. Burns's demands. I wouldn't for a moment want her ire directed towards me."

"Nor would I."

Annie took a bite of her ice cream and allowed it to melt on her tongue. *What a pleasant day spent eating ice cream with the man I'm growing quite fond of. What could possibly go wrong?*

"Not that I wouldn't have asked you to the ice cream social on my own." Caleb's eyes met hers.

And that's when it happened.

Annie inhaled at just the wrong time, causing herself to succumb to a choking fit. Tears streamed down her face and she gasped for air.

"Annie, are you all right?"

Embarrassed, she nodded while attempting to ease the coughs.

"Are you sure?"

The concern in his eyes warmed her heart, but Annie couldn't think of that just now. First, she had to remember how to breathe.

"I can go fetch Doc Garrett."

Annie shook her head. No one had ever died choking on ice cream. Or at least, she hoped not. And she had no ambition to be the first.

"I'm—I'm fine, Caleb."

"If you're sure…"

"I'm sure."

"You had me scared for a minute." Tenderness lined his expression, and he leaned in closer, worry etched in his eyes.

"I've never choked on ice cream before."

"Was it something I said?"

Annie nodded. "Yes—I mean, no."

It had been his comment about asking her to the ice cream social that had started the choking fit, but she wouldn't let on.

She was flustered enough.

Chapter Eleven

Annie's parents, siblings, and dear friend arrived a few moments later, and introductions commenced.

First her parents, then Sadie and Hetty.

Her brother stood, hands on his hips, legs shoulder-width apart, obviously assessing Caleb. While there was a definite size difference between the two, with Caleb being at least six inches taller and much stockier and broader, Zeb's expression gave no doubt as to his fearlessness. He lifted his bearded chin and gave a curt nod. "I'm Zeb Ledbetter."

Caleb extended his left hand, and Zeb clasped it with a firm grip. "Can't shake with my right hand because of an injury, but it is a pleasure to meet you."

Zeb maintained eye contact. "So, you're the son of the folks Annie stays with?"

"I am."

"You should know I'm protective of my sisters."

Obviously, the smaller man took his role seriously.

"As you should be. I'm protective of my sister, Charlotte, as well."

"Hmm. Well, Annie and I are close, and I only want what's best for her."

"You have my word that I'll look out for her while she's in Willow Falls."

Never would Caleb allow something to happen to anyone he cared about. And he was beginning to care about Annie. A lot.

Mrs. Ledbetter placed her hands on Sadie's shoulders. "Are you ready for some ice cream, Sadie Girl?"

"When have I *not* been ready for ice cream?"

"We'll see you in a while, Annie. Pleasure to meet you, Caleb," Mr. Ledbetter said.

"You as well."

After the Ledbetters and Hetty wandered over to fetch ice cream, Annie and Caleb sat on a bench beneath a towering tree.

"Your brother is certainly concerned about you."

Annie laughed. "Zeb warned me he might interrogate you. He reminds me sometimes of one of those loyal collies."

Caleb chuckled at her analogy. "You're fortunate to have a family who cares for you."

Before the Eliasons entered his life, Caleb had no idea what it was like to have someone watch over and nurture him. Ma was the mother he never had with her sweet demeanor and tender heart, and Pa had taught him what it meant to be a godly man, even if those lessons arrived when Caleb had almost reached adulthood.

Sheriff Townsend stood on a platform at the edge of town. "Thank you, everyone, for coming today. I trust you are finding the ice cream satisfactory?"

At this, the crowd cheered. Annie spied Sadie across the way, likely on her third or fourth bowl of the frozen treat.

"A special welcome to our neighbors from Nelsonville who joined us today. And thank you to everyone who took the time to decorate, and of course, to the Mortons for their generous donation of ice cream. Enjoy the rest of your day."

The attendees clapped and disbursed, going in different directions to partake in other activities.

Annie delighted in the camaraderie among the townsfolk and wished she and her family had attended the ice cream social long before this year.

Mrs. Burns interrupted Annie's musings when she again approached, her rushed demeanor indicating an emergency.

"Miss Ledbetter, you must do me a favor." She placed a wrinkled hand on Annie's arm.

"What is it, Mrs. Burns?"

"That man over there, the dashing one with the thick glasses. Do you see him?" Mrs. Burns pointed a gnarled finger across the street.

Annie squinted. "Is that Mr. Ackerman?"

"Yes, I believe that's what he said his name was. Do you know him, Miss Ledbetter?"

"He's the postmaster in Nelsonville."

"Yes, yes. That's what I heard." Mrs. Burns straightened her shoulders. "He's a dapper gentleman, if I do say so myself. And I hear he's unmarried."

Mrs. Burns reached up and tucked a flyaway strand of gray hair into the braid that wound around her head. "I insist you introduce me to him, right this instant."

"Mrs. Burns..." Annie stifled a giggle.

"No, Miss Ledbetter. I insist. Now come along." Without waiting for Annie's answer, Mrs. Burns started toward Mr. Ackerman, pulling Annie behind her.

Caleb grinned. "I'd like to meet Mr. Ackerman too. Right this instant."

"Did someone say something?" Mrs. Burns turned to face Annie and Caleb but kept her firm grasp on Annie's arm.

Caleb cleared his throat. "I was just mentioning that I'd like to meet Mr. Ackerman too."

"Not half as much as I want to meet him. Now come along. The both of you are wasting time."

Mr. Ackerman was speaking to one of the townsfolk when they approached. Mrs. Burns gestured toward him.

"Go ahead," she whispered.

Annie waited for a pause in the conversation. "Mr. Ackerman?"

"Why, Miss Ledbetter, fancy meeting you here. I heard you were in Willow Falls for a teaching position." Mr. Ackerman peered through his thick, round spectacles, his eyes enlarged several times over due to the magnification of the lenses.

"Mr. Ackerman, I'd like to introduce you to someone."

The postmaster raised a brow. "And who might that be?"

"I'm Gertrude Burns, one of Miss Ledbetter's dearest friends." Mrs. Burns stuck her hand toward Mr. Ackerman. "It's a delight to make your acquaintance. I've heard many estimable things about you and what a thorough job you do sorting the mail."

Mr. Ackerman blushed. "I'm Bernard Ackerman, but you can call me Bernie."

"Bernie it is. And you may call me Gertrude."

Mrs. Burns and Mr. Ackerman stood facing each other, seemingly transfixed.

Caleb's gaze traveled from Mrs. Burns to Mr. Ackerman and back to Mrs. Burns.

"Care to join me for a stroll?" he asked Annie.

"That would be splendid."

Caleb offered Annie his elbow and she placed her arm through it.

"I can't say as I've ever seen Mrs. Burns that excited to see someone. She moved here about five years ago and has always been brusque."

They strolled for a while down the street in comfortable silence, waving at those Caleb knew and Annie had recently met.

"I forgot to ask you earlier, how is your injured hand?"

The warmth in Annie's expression tugged at him. "It's doing much better."

"Do you know when you'll be able to have the wrap removed?"

"I reckon in a few weeks."

While Doc Garrett noted his hand improved, it would still be some time before it was completely healed.

He led Annie to a quiet spot near a tree where a bench had been built and donated in memory of Mrs. Burns's most recent late husband.

"May I offer you a seat?"

"Thank you."

Caleb sat beside her and together they watched the passersby. He searched his mind for a topic to discuss, preferably one that didn't include his incessant rambling.

He wanted to know more about her. "Have you lived in the Wyoming Territory for long?"

"I was born in Nebraska and lived there until we lost our farm."

Annie thought about the events that led to their move to Wyoming. The day prior to their leaving, she'd tiptoed out of her room and found a corner in which to perch. Her parents spoke of their plans in hushed tones, and Annie had strained to articulate the words.

Pa had wrung his hands. "I just don't see there being any other choice. The bank has already been more than generous in the time they've given us, and that time has run out. I don't know what else to do, Maria. No one is hiring here and we have no more money after two bad crops in a row."

Annie inched forward, worried about Pa but wanting to hear Ma's response. "We'll be all right, Walter. God will provide. He always does. I heard someone say once that 'home is where your family is.'"

While Annie's uncle invited them to move to the Wyoming Territory, Pa had been hesitant due to Ma's pregnancy. Ma insisted they would need to leave before winter arrived, and while Annie couldn't recall the next part of the conversation, she easily recollected the last words Pa had said.

"What would I do without you, Maria? There's no one I would rather go through life with than you." Then Pa reached for Ma's hands and they sat, their hearts joined through the good times and the bad.

"Annie?"

Caleb's words returned Annie to the present. "Sorry, I was just remembering how difficult it was to leave our home."

How much should she share?

But when he leaned toward her, genuine interest in his eyes, she found it easy to share with him the memories she'd never forgotten.

"Each day before we left, I attempted to commit to memory every detail of every room. But the round table and mismatched chairs in our kitchen that were a gift from Grandpa Ledbetter—I miss that the most out of all of the possessions we had to leave behind. I wanted no part of moving to a new place. Our home, our town where we lived, everything seemed so perfect. I couldn't imagine ever being happy anywhere else."

Annie folded her hands in her lap. "But I've since come to realize that home is not a collection of possessions. As a wise person once said, 'Home is where your family is.'" Annie paused. "Did you ever have to find a new home and were unsure where the changes would take you?"

Caleb reflected on how he'd endured plenty of changes, just not ones he wished to discuss. "I've discovered God's faithfulness through times of uncertainty, yes. You mentioned you'd had ice cream once before. Was that in Nebraska?"

"Yes. My aunt and uncle took us for ice cream one time a few years before we moved to the Wyoming Territory. They are the same aunt and uncle who invited us to move to Nelsonville. We stayed with them until Pa and Zeb could build our home. They have since moved back to Nebraska, but those were fond memories."

Caleb hadn't any fond memories until the past seven years.

"How long have you lived in Willow Falls?"

Her question was innocent enough, but Caleb didn't cotton to talking about himself or his past. The town itself was about fourteen years old, so it would stand to reason he hadn't resided there all his life.

"For many years."

Annie's sister bounded toward them.

"Say, Annie, they are gonna start a baseball game over there." She pointed to a field where several people gathered. "It's Nelsonville against Willow Falls. Wanna come watch? And you too, Mr. Caleb, you can come watch. Or you can play. Zeb is playing."

Caleb chuckled at Sadie's enthusiasm. "I'll come watch. Care to join me, Annie?"

"That sounds splendid, yes."

Chapter Twelve

Annie slumped in her chair in contented exhaustion after her students left for the day. Things were going well. She had arranged a spelling bee and her pupils had eagerly learned their words, Reverend Solomon and Lydie made their home like a second one to Annie, and thus far, she'd been able to return to Nelsonville every weekend to visit her family.

Then there was Caleb, who continuously captured her thoughts. She saw him many evenings when he ate supper at the Eliason home, which according to Charlotte, was more often than before Annie had arrived in Willow Falls. He accompanied her home each afternoon after school, and Annie considered the ice cream social one of her favorite memories. She was fond of Caleb Eliason.

Quite fond.

She closed her eyes and reveled in her blessings.

"Do you always take naps after school or is this a special occasion?"

Annie jumped at the sound of his voice. "Caleb?"

"Sorry to startle you. I couldn't resist." His crooked smile endeared him all the more to her. "May I accompany you home or would you prefer to nap a bit longer?"

Warmth climbed up her neck and onto her face. "I wasn't sleeping, but praying and thanking the Lord for all His blessings."

He assisted her to her feet. She stood close to him, so close that she imagined he could hear her heart pounding in her chest. They stood face to face in silence. Annie feared to even take a breath, unsure if it might ruin the special moment between them.

Caleb stroked her cheek with his thumb, his face now inches from hers. "May I kiss you?"

She willed the words to form an answer to his question. He tilted his head slightly, his eyes fixed on her.

"Yes, you may."

It wasn't a lengthy kiss, but it was warm and tender, and it made Annie's stomach flip-flop.

Caleb took a step back and clasped her hand in his. Would he ask her to court him? She mentally rehearsed her response.

"Annie..."

"Yes?"

Yes, Caleb, I will court you.

"I—"

He rubbed the back of her hand with his thumb, sending a tingling jolt up her arm. Would Pa agree to allow her to court Caleb? What would Zeb say? Would he "interrogate" Caleb again?

An unknown emotion, perhaps concern, flashed through his eyes. "I—I missed you today."

Annie blinked. The words, while welcomed, were not what she expected.

"I missed you too, Caleb."

He gently released her hand. "Reckon I should get you home before Ma begins to worry."

She nearly missed the slight fall of his shoulders.

※

That evening, Annie penned another diary entry.

Dear Diary,

Much has happened since the last time I had an opportunity to write. Mr. Ackerman is courting Mrs. Burns, Zeb and Hetty are considering a summer wedding date, and soon I won't be able to travel home on the weekends, as inclement weather is surely on its way. I am grateful the Lord has blessed me with a fine family to live with while in Willow Falls.

I believe I may be falling in love with Caleb Eliason. He kissed me today at the school. It was unexpected, although not unwelcome. Now I understand when Hetty mentioned her fondness for Zeb.

The curious thing is Caleb does seem oddly familiar, as though I have seen him before I moved to Willow Falls. Perhaps he once visited Nelsonville.

Annie closed the diary and placed it in her bureau drawer. The aroma of freshly baked bread lingered in the air. It was time to assist Lydie with supper.

Caleb shut the barn door and headed into his house. Leaves swirled around his feet and the nip of cold winter air and high humidity foreshadowed rain and possibly snow.

At the supper table earlier, he had found it difficult to take his eyes from Annie. The unexpected kiss in the schoolhouse dominated his thoughts. He was falling in love with her and wanted to court her.

Annie's intelligence, her beauty, and her kindness and compassion toward others drew him to her. Could she be the one God had planned for him? If so, how would he go about telling her about his past?

No woman, especially one as sweet as Annie, would want to court a man like me. A man with a past. She deserves better.

Pa's voice entered his mind as he wrestled with his thoughts. *"You have repented and God has forgiven you, Caleb. He has removed your transgressions as far as the east is from the west. You need to forgive yourself."*

He knew the Psalm by heart, had spoken to Pa about it on numerous occasions, but Caleb struggled mightily to heed that advice. He glanced down at his covered hand and was reminded again of the obstacle that stood in the way of any future between him and Annie. If and when he told her who he really was, and she already had feelings for him, would that change her mind?

Perhaps she wouldn't have to know about his past. Not for a while anyway.

Until he proved to her he was a different man.

Yes, tomorrow, with the Lord's guidance, Caleb would ask Annie Ledbetter to court him.

The following morning, he arrived early at the schoolhouse to light the fire. A layer of snow covered the ground, indicating winter in Wyoming had finally arrived.

As they rode home from school that afternoon, they shared in lively conversation. He told her about Louie's attempted escape from the corral, and she shared with him about her school day. Even in the brisk weather, Caleb was tempted to slow the horses so their ride lasted longer. He cherished these moments with her.

He'd prayed last night that if it was God's will, He would give Caleb the courage to ask Annie to court him. Of course, he'd still need to request permission from Mr. Ledbetter and likely seek approval from Zeb, but would she have him as a beau? He prayed for the opportune time to ask her.

Caleb was about to utter the words on his heart when she continued about her day.

"The pupils shared such entertaining stories today about how long they've lived in Willow Falls. Of course, John Mark and Charlotte were born here, but others, such as Tobias, moved here from Missouri. Russell arrived here from back East…I cannot imagine a journey that lengthy." She shivered.

"Are you cold? If so, you can borrow my coat." Caleb slowed his horse to a stop so he could remove his coat if she needed it.

"Thank you, but I'm fine. I was merely revisiting our migration from our previous home to Nelsonville. It was an adventure I don't care to repeat."

"Oh?" While Annie shared some about her family's move, she'd never before mentioned any unpleasant memories.

She said nothing for a time. Seconds ticked by, and Caleb was pondering whether he should change the topic of conversation when she spoke again, "I haven't told anyone besides my dear friend, Hetty, about what happened that day."

"You're not obliged to tell me, Annie."

"I don't mind. God protected us and delivered us safely to Nelsonville. He provided a doctor just in time so Sadie was born healthy and Ma survived childbirth."

Something in his gut twisted. But no, it must be a coincidence.

But Caleb didn't believe in coincidences. Should he ask her to continue? Talk instead about the weather? Curiosity prodded him. "How long ago was this?"

"About seven years ago."

Tension traveled up his neck.

Annie took a deep breath as if to prepare her words.

Words he wasn't sure he wanted to hear. "Annie..."

"Our wagon train was robbed that day. A man was beaten, another was shot, and my Ma nearly died when she went into labor."

His breath hitched and a foreboding chill ran through his body, although not from the frigidness of the day.

When Caleb's eyes again met hers, he knew without a doubt.

Annie was the girl in the wagon seven years ago.

Chapter Thirteen

CALEB TOSSED AND TURNED, then finally settled onto his back. Staring at the ceiling, he willed himself to fall asleep, but thoughts kept filling his mind—thoughts about Annie.

He'd been so eager to ask her to court him.

Was there a chance he could be wrong about her identity?

No, not after her story corroborated his suspicions.

The memory plagued him.

It was Annie who had been the one to beg him not to take the contents of the small tin box.

Her voice sounded in his ears as if the recollection only occurred yesterday and not seven years before. *"Please, sir, please don't let them hurt us. My ma is going to have a baby soon. Have mercy on us."*

He wanted to respond to her pleading with a promise no harm would come to them, but Caleb hadn't been able to promise her anything.

He hadn't been able to offer her protection; hadn't been able to convince Cain and Roy not to attack her family and friends; hadn't been able to avoid taking what wasn't his.

The scene played over and over in his mind, and he gritted his teeth. Nothing could change what he had done. Nothing could change the way life was altered for so many that day at the hands of himself, Cain, and Roy.

"Lord, please, please forgive me." His voice competed against the howling wind.

He sat up in bed, lit the lamp on the bureau, and reached for his Bible. Caleb's fingers trembled as he flipped through the pages of his well-worn Bible until he came to the Book of First John. He scanned the verses, frantically searching.

"If we confess our sins, he is faithful and just to forgive us our sins, and to cleanse us from all unrighteousness."

Caleb read the verse twice more, trying to shake the guilt. His heart knew his reprehensible choices were forgiven, his inexcusable actions laid at the foot of the Cross. So why then could his mind not reconcile that fact?

It hadn't been just any person whom he'd wronged, but the woman he cared about. The woman he considered spending the rest of his life with.

Caleb plopped down on his pillow. "Lord, guard my mind."

For his mind was always where the battle lingered.

He prayed and prayed again. His heart raced in his chest, the pounding almost too much to bear.

Images of a helpless Annie and distraught wagon train members refused to leave his thoughts.

Finally, he stood again and pushed aside the curtain. Snow blew sideways in the direction of the forceful winds. Air seeped in through the window pane, and his breath fogged his vision.

"Keep your eyes on Christ, Son." Pa's voice echoed through his mind. *"He will see you through this. He will redeem you."*

His second pa. The man who took him in as his own. Gave him a home, gave him his name, led him in the ways of the Lord. The man who never once allowed him to go hungry.

Never once allowed him to question whether or not he was loved. Truly loved.

Caleb inhaled a deep breath. Images of the day his life took a turn for the better blossomed in his memory.

Morton's Mercantile had been a peculiar place to hold a hearing to determine one's future. But the back room had long served as a multi-use area; sometimes as a meeting room and other times as a courtroom.

Judge Halsberg, the circuit judge, sat in the front of the room behind a desk. Facing Judge Halsberg's desk was a row of chairs in audience-style formation.

Today, if Caleb visited the mercantile, the row of chairs would no longer be there unless Sheriff Townsend called a town meeting. And Judge Halsberg hadn't been to Willow Creek in a year.

But seven years ago, Caleb sat before the judge, his future in the hands of a man he'd never met.

"I'm Judge Halsberg and I am here today to determine the fate of Caleb Ryerson in connection with the robbery of the wagon party east of town. This is a closed hearing, meaning that only the people here know of the issue we are about to discuss. Mr. Ryerson, do you have anything to say for yourself?"

Caleb had stood from his place in the row of chairs, trying to ignore the fact that his legs threatened to buckle. He'd deserved whatever sentence they imposed on him, even though rotting in a prison cell or worse, being hanged, had unnerved him.

Caleb walked to the front of the room and took a seat in the empty chair next to Judge Halsberg. He hoped no one would discover that he had cried a time or two after the robbery. What man cried? He imagined Cain's voice in his head criticizing him.

"Stupid fool. Only a clodpoll would allow himself to be such a sissy."

The relief of his old life coming to an end and the fear and frustration of what the future held had wreaked havoc on his emotions. He had stuttered, strained to articulate his words.

"I am truly sorry for my role in the wagon party robbery." His voice sounded raspy to his ears and he struggled to find the right words to say.

The thought of prison had scared him, but the thought of hanging scared had him even more. But he'd deserved whatever punishment they meted out to him.

It was only later that Caleb learned what had happened to Roy when the law had finally caught up with him. Cain's fate included life in the new U.S. Penitentiary at Laramie City. Thankfully they hadn't decided to hang him, but back then, Caleb figured it was pure luck on Cain's side.

He recalled wondering if luck would be on his side as well.

Judge Halsberg stroked his blond beard. "Is that all you have to say? Because I'll be honest with you, I've heard the words of someone being sorry for what they've done so many times that I've become cynical."

Caleb dragged his sweaty palms down the sides of his trousers and cleared his throat. "Your Honor, I wish I could go back and change things. I wish I could go back and make the decision not to be a part of the robbery. But I can't. I also wish I could go back and change the direction my life has taken so far, but I can't change that either."

"No, we can't change the past," Judge Halsberg agreed.

"I wish I could tell the folks in the wagon party that I'm sorry for what I've done. I am truly sorry."

Judge Halsberg said nothing after his statement, only remained in his chair, stroking his beard and eyeing Caleb, as if attempting to discern whether it was truth he spoke. Caleb was dismissed and returned to his seat.

The eerie silence had shaken him.

Caleb exhaled and rested his head in his hands.

He figured folks would stand up and share their feelings about how an outlaw ought to be punished to the law's fullest extent. And when Judge Halsberg called on Doc Garrett to sit in the witness chair and say something regarding the situation, Caleb had assumed that the doctor would say that no one wanted someone like Caleb in their town.

"Thank you, Your Honor. I would like to say that Mr. Ryerson rode through town on the day of the robbery. He was frantic when he found me. Told me there was a woman about to give birth several miles from town. He asked if I could help her." Doc Garrett glanced at Caleb. "Looking back, I thought it was a bit unorthodox that, as a wanted man, Mr. Ryerson showed his face and rode through Willow Falls in search of a doctor for a complete stranger."

"Perhaps he was feeling guilt at the crime he had committed," Judge Halsberg suggested.

"I don't claim to know his motive, Your Honor. I do know he didn't act like a man who cared about being caught. He acted more like a man on a mission to save the life of a woman who was going to die giving birth. Had I not been there when I was, it's likely that woman and her child would not be here today. It is my expert opinion as a doctor of twenty-four years that Caleb Ryerson saved the life of the woman in the wagon party and that of her child."

At Doc Garrett's words, Caleb's mouth had fallen open and he had taken a few shaky breaths. Why had the doctor defended him?

The judge called Sheriff Townsend to testify next. His words that day also astonished Caleb.

"Your Honor, after Doc Garrett assisted the woman in the wagon train with the birth of her child, he returned to Willow Falls. On his way to his office, he stopped to tell me about Caleb Ryerson. He mentioned he was confident the man was one he'd seen on a wanted poster and then proceeded to tell me about Mr. Ryerson's concern for the pregnant woman." Sheriff Townsend paused. "I figured the other men in the wanted poster, Caleb's brother, Cain Ryerson, and Roy Fuller, a fellow gang member, were in the area as well. They are a well-known gang in both the Wyoming and Dakota Territories. I knew then that I would need to ask the men of this community for help in apprehending them, but what I didn't count on was that we would only have to hunt down two of the men."

Caleb appreciated the sheriff's words, but there was no way the judge would excuse his choices. The ramifications of being a member of a gang bent on destroying lives were too great to allow any mercy. Yet, on that day so many years ago, the sheriff expressed his bewilderment that he would only need to hunt for two wanted criminals, instead of three because Caleb had turned himself in.

"Odd as it may seem, Your Honor, I would recommend a lenient sentence for Caleb Ryerson."

Judge Halsberg had reverted his attention to Caleb then and asked why he hadn't run from the law when he'd had the chance. Caleb's words came rushed, pleading for someone to understand.

"I don't want to be a robber anymore, sir. I don't want to run with Cain and Roy and commit crimes just so I can fill my belly. I want to be done with that. I look at Cain and I see what I don't want to become. Even if it means prison or worse, at least I'll be free from the life I've lived."

One final person spoke on behalf of Caleb that day. An honest and forthright man by the name of Reverend Solomon Eliason, who'd spent a considerable amount of time at the jail speaking with Caleb.

That was the best part about that day in the makeshift courtroom—the reverend's words.

Caleb still thought about that conversation from time to time.

"I believe he deserves a second chance." At Reverend Solomon's brief and unexpected announcement, Caleb wondered whether he'd heard correctly.

"A second chance?" Judge Halsberg asked. "Surely you are proposing a preposterous idea."

"Yes, Your Honor, a second chance. There's something about Caleb I just can't explain. Given an opportunity, I believe he could make it in society. He's different from the other two men."

"And you came to this reasoning from spending a few hours with him? It's been my experience that some men will say anything to escape the harsh prison sentence awaiting them."

"I understand that, Your Honor, and I agree with you. There's just something about this boy that leads me to believe that we would be making a huge mistake if we sent him to prison."

"You are a man of the cloth and that does change your perspective."

"I do realize that I attempt to see everyone the way God sees them and that in doing so, my perspective is different from that of others. Still, I am convinced this young man needs a second chance." Reverend Solomon let out a long breath.

"I don't know, Reverend Solomon," Judge Halsberg pulled out his pocket watch. "More than anything, I want to make the right decision. It's an important job to keep the citizens in the towns of the Wyoming Territory safe. I can't just let Caleb Ryerson go."

"What if I offer to be responsible for him?"

"Why would you want to do that? You have a wife and young'uns at home and this boy is a criminal. I have known you for several years and I believe that you want to help everyone. That's likely why God called you into the profession you have chosen. Has Lydie agreed to this?"

"We've prayed about it together and she agreed."

Sheriff Townsend recounted how unruly and disrespectful Cain and Roy had been upon their arrest, and how Roy shot at the deputy and was later killed in self-defense. Before the hearing concluded, the judge recited a lengthy speech about the ramifications for Caleb if he committed a crime, no matter how minor, and how he was giving him a second chance against his better judgment. Caleb couldn't fathom why anyone would desire to show him mercy. Not after what he'd done.

Judge Halsberg called for objections among the five people in the room, but there were none. He then issued his decision.

"One mess up, and I mean it, one mess up, even a meager one, and I will see to it that you are put away in the U.S. Penitentiary at Laramie City for the rest of your life." Judge Halsberg shook his finger at Caleb. As if his large presence wasn't enough to influence the decisions of others, his voice had the boom of thunder in it as well. "Reverend Solomon has a wife and two little ones at home.

You be a good example to them. This town is most often peaceful, especially for a Wyoming Territory town—you see to it that it stays that way. You see to it that no one is robbed of anything they own at your hands. You attend church faithfully and you make it your life's goal to be a productive citizen of society who gives to this community, rather than takes. Am I understood? If not, you'll find yourself in the prison hotel with no chance of ever tasting freedom again."

The men in the room, all who promised to keep this matter between them, encouraged him. He couldn't—wouldn't—disappoint them, nor would he disappoint the judge.

It took Caleb years to fully comprehend and believe God cared about him and wanted to help him start a new life. But he still struggled with understanding God's forgiveness.

The few folks in Willow Falls who knew of his crimes never shared them with the rest of the townsfolk.

"It's like watching God at work," Reverend Solomon had said to Caleb. "To watch the residents of Willow Falls band together in helping you turn your life around, even if ninety-five percent of them don't know about your past."

Over the years, Caleb sat next to the townsfolk in church. He did odd jobs for nearly every resident of Willow Falls and assisted them when a crisis arose. But he knew there was no way he could ever repay their kindness for forgiving him and allowing him to live among them.

Now, with the realization of who Annie was, memories flooded his mind like an overflowing river without a dam. Her frightened face, her trembling voice, her pleading for him to have mercy on her family—it all began afresh in his mind and in his heart. The last thing he needed was to be reminded of the man he once was.

A shot of pain ripped through his hand and reminded him he must not let Annie see the scar.

Nothing was worth the risk of bringing back something Caleb long ago let die. Nothing. Not even his growing love for Annie Ledbetter.

Chapter Fourteen

Swirling peacefully, giant flakes of snow dizzied in the air before landing and melting immediately upon reaching the ground. In a short amount of time, winter would be fully upon them and the weather would no longer be as calm. Blizzards, freezing temperatures, and limited visibility would come in the form of an unannounced storm.

Caleb would arrive any moment and a pleasurable trip home awaited Annie in Caleb's wagon. She anticipated the moments with him when they rode home, sometimes in comfortable silence, other times with words dominating the short ride. She'd become more comfortable sharing with him, especially about matters close to her heart, like the wagon train robbery.

Although recently, Caleb gave the impression of being preoccupied. He didn't speak as much at the supper table, and his posture was hunched as if the world's troubles weighed heavily on his broad shoulders.

The door creaked open and he strode towards her. Annie's heart skipped a beat and she stepped forward from her desk, elated to see him.

"Hello, Annie."

"I was just thinking about our ride home in the snow."

"It's a peaceful snowfall at the moment. I'm not sure how long that will last. Mrs. Burns said she could feel it in her bones that we were in for a snowstorm."

"That sounds like something Mrs. Burns would say. I heard she and Mr. Ackerman set a wedding date for next summer."

Caleb said nothing but now stood so close that Annie inhaled the smell of wood shavings on his clothes. He must have assisted with furniture building today. It still amazed her how diverse he was in the jobs he undertook.

"I've missed going home each weekend because of these winter storms." She smiled at him, hoping to elicit some response.

His eyes locked with hers and Annie thought she could see his very soul in the tender blue. The wariness in his countenance concerned her.

"There'll be breaks in the storms so you can return to Nelsonville. Reckon we should get home before this storm hits."

"Caleb? Is something wrong?"

He shook his head. "Did John Mark and Charlotte have a ride home?"

"Yes, Tobias's father offered to take them so they wouldn't have to walk."

"That's good. Are you ready to go?"

He waited for her to gather her things and bundle up before heading out into the blustery weather.

Caleb opened the door for Annie, then followed her. Annie stepped out onto the first of the three steps. Gazing into the sky, she caught a stray snowflake on her tongue like she had done so often as a child. She absorbed the cool taste on her tongue and closed her eyes. It tasted as snowflakes always had: a delicious introduction to winter. How often had Annie and Hetty stirred together clumps of snow into "snowmeal" with some of Ma's pots and pans? They would sit and eat the snow as if it were an appetizing delicacy. The tradition they started was one Annie hoped someday to pass on to her own children.

So involved in her memory, Annie missed one of the steps. Her ankle twisted, her feet went out from beneath her, and she fell hard to the ground.

Caleb kneeled beside her. "Are you all right?"

A mixture of pain and dizziness filled her mind and tears smarted her eyes. "It's my ankle."

He pulled her gently to her feet, but the throbbing in her ankle demanded she sit.

Caleb removed his jacket and set it on the step for her, then lowered her down and sat beside her.

"I only hope I haven't broken it."

"I'm sorry, Annie. I tried to catch you before you fell. We considered whether to build a schoolhouse that needed stairs, but now I see that it may have been a mistake. I'll take you to see Doc Garrett."

Caleb overheard the conversation between Doc Garrett and Annie in the other room.

"You're lucky," said Doc. "It could have been much worse. Fortunately, you didn't sprain or break it, but it is badly bruised. I'm going to bandage it, but you'll need to keep your weight off of it as best as you can, and I'd like to see you again tomorrow."

"Thank you, Doc."

Her weak tone tugged at Caleb. Having to hide his feelings for her now that he knew who she was pained him. To distance himself and to discount the fondness starting to grow between them caused him great distress. But to know his wrongdoings almost cost her and her family their lives...

Annie, with Doc Garrett's assistance, emerged from the other room into the waiting area. He settled her on the chair next to Caleb's.

"Speaking of injuries, how is your hand doing, Caleb?"

"Much better."

"You're still wearing that bandage?"

"Uh, yes." He couldn't tell Doc the *real* reason he still wore the bandage had nothing to do with his injury. "Reckon I was using my hand a little more than I ought today."

"With overuse, it will take to heal. But I would have thought the bandage would have come off by now. While you're here, it would be as good a time as any to see how the healing is progressing."

"I can wait until tomorrow. Annie needs to get home."

"You're already here and it'll only take a minute."

"With all due respect, sir, it can wait. I'll see you tomorrow."

Doc Garrett took a seat beside Caleb and scrutinized the bandage. "Caleb, you're not usually so argumentative. Now let me see that hand."

He shifted, hoping to block some of the view Annie would have once Doc removed the bandage. The doctor unwound the binding. There was no way Annie could avoid seeing his scar unless she was distracted, but in the stark room, there was nothing else to capture her attention.

Caleb held his breath. Would she notice? Would she recognize the scar she'd seen that day in the back of the wagon? How would she react?

Lord, please, give me a chance to explain it to her before she sees it.

But the instant the bandage was removed, he heard her gasp, a whoosh of breath so strong Doc Garrett likely heard it too.

Not here. Not now.

Lord, please...

Caleb's gaze met Annie's. Would she say anything in Doc's presence? Horror, confusion, and anger filled the depths of her green eyes.

"Annie..." he murmured.

She narrowed her eyes, the shimmer of a tear undisguised. He diverted his own attention to the scuff marks on the floor.

"Let's keep that bandage off for a while. I want you to start some hand exercises, slowly at first." Doc Garrett proceeded to demonstrate exercises to assist in the healing process. But Caleb heard only a minute amount of what he said.

"Now," Doc concluded. "Take this girl right home. She'll need plenty of rest herself with that painful ankle."

"Much obliged, Doc."

Doc Garrett tipped his hat and hurried out the door toward his waiting horse for his next appointment.

Annie limped toward the door without his assistance.

"Annie..."

How could he explain it to her now?

Caleb reached for her, but she continued to inch away from him towards the door. "I can explain everything."

"Take me home. Please."

If only he'd told her before she saw the scar. But all of the "if only's" in the world couldn't heal what just occurred.

Chapter Fifteen

Annie hadn't expected to see the vile scar on his hand. Seeing it sucked the breath from her lungs and his expression told her all she needed to know.

The reason she thought she'd met Caleb before was because she *had*, only not under pleasant circumstances.

A flash of anger coursed through her.

"It was you, wasn't it? You pilfered through my family's belongings and stole whatever you could fit into your burlap sack. You were one of the ones who...why aren't you in jail? Your actions nearly cost more than one life!" Her words tumbled out, accusations from a shocked heart. "Does your pa know his oldest son is a criminal? How many other folks have you robbed in the seven years between now and then? Who are you really, Caleb?"

"Annie, please."

The tortured expression on his face did nothing to quell her frustration.

She shivered, although more from outrage than the frigid weather. "I can't believe you're the one who caused so much pain to so many. Where are your other gang members, especially the one who almost killed Mr. DeGroot?"

The snow fell heavier now and began to accumulate on the road as Caleb steered the wagon toward the Eliason home. "Annie, there's a lot you don't know."

Annie remained short of breath and fought to regain control of herself. "How could you live with yourself knowing you were partially responsible for nearly taking a life? I remember that day. Do you know how long I've struggled to forget those memories? I almost lost Ma and Sadie. Mrs. DeGroot almost lost her husband."

She attempted to ignore the pain shooting through her ankle. The pain in her heart was much worse. She had allowed herself to fall in love with Caleb. How could she not have realized before that he was the one from that day? His familiarity was more than just a random sighting of him on the boardwalk in Nelsonville or Willow Falls. Tears burned her eyes. What if she had agreed to court him before knowing the truth about his past? Was he still a dangerous outlaw? How would she tell her parents and Zeb?

Caleb said nothing as they rode the rest of the way home. Annie bit her lip and prayed the Lord would guard her tongue as questions, disappointment, and shock swarmed through her mind.

Caleb closed his eyes. It wasn't supposed to happen like this.

He loved her.

But how could he have kept his secret from her forever? Realistically, he couldn't. Only now she had discovered it in the most unexpected of ways.

Caleb stopped in front of his parents' home. He climbed down and prepared to assist Annie.

"No thank you." She hobbled off in the snow, and he prayed she wouldn't slip again.

Helplessness engulfed him.

He removed his coat and boots at the door. The aroma of supper temporarily removed from his mind the events of the past hour.

"I'll let Pa know supper will be ready soon. Oh, hi, Caleb. I should warn you about Charlotte. Something has her in a dither." John Mark buttoned up his coat and pulled on his boots.

Charlotte placed her hands on her hips. "I am *not* in a dither. Just because I'm mildly agitated because of Tobias does not mean I'm in a *dither*. He is such a bothersome sort and was exceptionally vexatious today."

Caleb attempted a chuckle at Charlotte's exaggerated statement but fell short. His thoughts about Annie's discovery persisted.

Charlotte wandered toward him. "Poor Annie. Were you there when she injured her ankle today? Ma suggested she recline in her room while we prepare supper."

"Yes, I was there." Although if he could take back the latter part of the visit to Doc Garrett's, he would.

"Is everything all right?" Ma stirred the gravy on the stove.

"Ma, I won't be able to stay long. The weather has taken a turn for the worse."

His mother scooped some food onto a plate. "You're always welcome to stay here overnight."

"I appreciate the suggestion, but I need to tend to the animals anyway." He washed up and then took a seat at the table.

Caleb prayed and ate the food Ma set on the table before him. While his stomach rumbled with hunger, he faced the challenge of eating when his thoughts remained in turmoil.

Ma sat across from him. "Charlotte, would you please check on Annie? I need to speak with Caleb in private."

When his sister left the room, Ma placed a hand on Caleb's arm. "Do you want to discuss it?"

"She knows."

"Knows?"

"About me. About who I am."

Ma blinked. "Who you *were*, you mean?"

He took a bite of supper and a drink of milk. "I need to go. Thank you, Ma."

"Oh, Caleb." Ma's eyebrows drew together. "I'll be praying."

How had he survived before he had a mother who cared about him?

Caleb passed Pa and John Mark as he climbed back into the wagon and headed for home. The drive through the blinding snow gave him time to think.

Seven years had passed since he'd stood in the makeshift courtroom at Morton's Mercantile. Seven years later, he still regretted being a part of Cain's gang. No doubt he would lament it for the rest of his life.

And now, the woman he loved knew the truth about his past before he could share that truth with her. That made two people who were unwilling to forgive him for what he had done—Annie and himself.

Chapter Sixteen

Annie shifted in the bed while ensuring her ankle remained propped on the pillow Lydie had provided. She could hear Caleb's voice in the kitchen, but couldn't articulate the words.

"Hello, Annie. Ma asked me to check on you."

"That's thoughtful of you, Charlotte, thank you."

Charlotte fussed about, adjusting the quilt over Annie's legs and handing her a glass of water from the bureau. "Was it a bad fall?"

"It all happened so quickly. One minute I was walking through the door, the next moment, I fell."

"I'm so sorry. I hope teaching tomorrow won't produce unbearable pain."

Annie would have laughed at Charlotte's word choice were it not for the stabbing ache in her ankle. And her heart.

"Does your ma need help with supper?"

"You are supposed to rest. I'm helping her. Well, after she speaks with Caleb. He's not staying because of the weather. The snowfall has increased in severity."

Charlotte chatted for a few more minutes before leaving to assist Lydie in the kitchen.

During supper, questions continued to swirl through Annie's mind. The Eliason family conversed about their day, with Charlotte adding the most to the conversation. Annie appreciated this family who so graciously allowed her to live with them while she taught school.

How could she tell them the truth about their oldest son?

Did they realize he was part of an outlaw gang that committed crimes? Did they know the money he'd raised to build his own ranch was likely not from his miscellaneous jobs in town, but instead was plunder from innocent families? Could John Mark and Charlotte ever comprehend that their older brother was a thief and a liar?

Annie thought of her own ma. What would she do if Zeb lived the life of an outlaw? Unscrupulously obtained funds? Stood by while someone was shot? Pretended to be an upstanding individual?

Anger, disappointment, sadness, fear, deception, and pain kept her from sleeping that night. That and the continual spasm rippling through her ankle. She attempted to find a comfortable position. When none could be had, she tossed and turned, spending an excessive amount of time willing herself to fall asleep.

Lord, please give me wisdom on how to handle this situation.

Caleb rode his horse to his parents' home the following day. He needed to speak with Pa about the situation with Annie.

She knew nothing about his second chance or how he had changed. She knew nothing about how he'd been adopted, not only by the Eliason family and the folks of Willow Falls, but most importantly into the family of God.

His father sat at the table, his Bible open, as he prepared for Sunday's sermon.

"Pa, I'd be much obliged if we could talk."

"Have a seat, Son. Can I get you some coffee?"

"Yes, please."

Annie, John Mark, and Charlotte were still at school, and Ma excused herself to tend to some mending by the fireplace.

Caleb took a drink of the coffee, allowing the warmth to seep into him.

Pa offered Caleb his full attention.

"Remember how I told you I was in charge of searching the wagons for valuables?"

"Yes."

"Annie's family's wagon was the first one. I think she was ill or something because she was in it when I went through her family's belongings. She saw me up close, even though a bandana covered my nose and mouth. She saw my eyes, and of course, my hand. It startled her that I was the one who—" Caleb choked on the words. "The one who was there that day." Until meeting Annie, hadn't he attempted to remove this chapter of his life?

"I'm sorry, Caleb. I doubt anyone could have foreseen that your paths would someday cross."

Pa's statement bore much truth.

"No, and it came as a shock to her when she saw my hand at Doc Garrett's. I attempted to convince him to see me another day, but he wouldn't hear of it. He figured since we were already there for Annie's injured ankle, he might as well check on my hand."

"Annie is observant to recognize a man from a scar on his hand."

"Truth is, I'll never forget the face of the young girl in that wagon. The terror in her eyes, the pleading that no one get hurt, the begging not to take what meager funds they had..."

How many times in those early years had Pa discussed the matter at length with Caleb? Too many to count. Why then was the topic still a difficult one to broach?

"I do remember you telling me about the girl in the wagon. Would she be the one whose mother was about to give birth?"

"Yes."

"So you saved the lives of Annie's mother and her sister that day?"

"They wouldn't have been in such a predicament if I hadn't been there robbing them."

"Agreed." Pa scratched his beard. "Still, I doubt Annie knows you risked being caught to fetch the doctor to tend to her ma."

"She doesn't know."

"Caleb, you know I don't for a moment condone what you, Cain, and Roy did. I don't for a minute think fetching a doctor eases the pain the three of you caused the travelers that day when you made the choice to rob them. However, you also know that your family, the handful of Willow Falls townsfolk who know of your crimes, and especially the Lord, have all forgiven you. Your sins that day were wiped clean in the eyes of the Lord when you repented. I have no doubt in my mind you are not the same man you were seven years ago."

He'd heard it dozens of times before, but he yearned to hear it anew. That God really did forgive him. That Jesus really had died for his sins, even when those sins included burglaries and being an accomplice to murder.

Pa put a hand on Caleb's shoulder. "The integrity and honesty you have displayed these past few years prove to me that Christ lives within you now and that you have made good on the second chance that God, Ma and I, Judge Halsberg, and the townsfolk have given you."

"I know, Pa, and I'm grateful beyond words for that forgiveness, but that doesn't stop Annie and the rest of the travelers from feeling the way they do. I caused them a lot of pain that day. I can't imagine what it must have been like to watch one of the men get shot right before their eyes. Annie was just a young girl then, much like Charlotte. I would do whatever it took to protect Charlotte from enduring such a thing."

"You've been a wonderful big brother to both Charlotte and John Mark." Pa pulled his handkerchief from his pocket and handed it to Caleb. "Son, someday the time will be right to explain it all to Annie and possibly her family. Then you will be given the opportunity to seek their forgiveness."

He paused as if to choose his next words carefully. "You know, Caleb, God allows things to happen for a reason. I don't believe that Annie being here is by accident. When did you first recognize her as being the girl in the wagon?"

"A few days ago. But I couldn't tell her, Pa. I just couldn't. Not yet. I'd been praying for an opportune time and for the words to say. I know she has every right to be angry after what I did."

"She does have a right to be angry. It was a horrifying experience for her and her family and friends. No one should have to endure such a thing."

"And I was a part of it."

"Things have a way of working out with God's help." Pa folded his hands, and Caleb knew he was about to pray. He did that often. Gave wise counsel, then sought the Lord's guidance.

"Let's pray. Heavenly Father, please put peace in Caleb's heart and help him to forgive himself for what went on that day. We know, as You say in Second Corinthians 5:17, *'If any man be in Christ, he is a new creature. Old things are passed away; behold all things are become new'.*

"In your perfect timing, please guide Caleb to seek Annie's forgiveness and that of her family's. Give them forgiving hearts. Thank you, Father, for the privilege of being this young man's father and for the changes You've made in his life. In Jesus' Name I pray, Amen."

Caleb swallowed the lump in his throat.

Pa stood and Caleb hugged the older man. "Thank you, Pa."

"I love you, Son. I am always here for you, and so is your ma. I forget so often that you aren't my own flesh and blood, that we didn't have you from the start."

"I wish you had. My life would have been so different."

"As do I, but I thank the Lord we have had you for this long. I wouldn't have missed these past seven years for anything. And you have a testimony that could change the life of another."

Pa took a step back. "I'm proud of the man you have become. I know it's only by God's grace that you fought against the odds life stacked against you. But always remember how much God and your ma and I love you."

Caleb bit back the emotion so close to the surface. Only one other time had he felt so undeserving of the mercy shown him by so many, especially the mercy of his Heavenly Father. He'd promised that day that he'd turn from the life he'd been living and turn toward a life that would glorify the Lord.

By God's grace, he had.

Now he determined once again to forget the past, but he knew it would be difficult with the reminders Annie was sure to put in his way.

Chapter Seventeen

That weekend, Zeb arrived to take Annie home. The thin layer of snow on the ground had begun to melt in places, but not enough to allow wagon travel. They would need to ride horseback in order to travel to Nelsonville.

The door opened, and Caleb entered. "Look who I found outside." Zeb stood next to Caleb, and Annie noticed a new and apparent camaraderie between them as if they had been friends for years. What happened to Zeb being protective?

"Reckon we've been discussing cattle prices outside, and I almost forgot to retrieve you and take you home." Zeb's brown eyes twinkled. "But I'm here now."

Her emotions warring, she decided to let the excitement of Zeb's arrival overrule her thoughts about her brother befriending Caleb.

"What's this? No hug for your favorite brother?"

"I would if I could but unfortunately, as I was attempting to leave the schoolhouse, I had a minor accident."

"I wouldn't call it minor," interjected Lydie. "She bruised her ankle pretty badly."

Zeb shook his head. "I leave you alone for a couple of days and you injure yourself?"

"God will heal it quickly. It's truly no cause for concern." The heartache she struggled with overrode the persistent pain in her ankle.

"Zeb, I have some food leftover from breakfast. Would you care to have some before you leave? It would only take me a moment to serve you up a plate." Lydie started toward

the stove.

Zeb took a seat next to Annie. "Much obliged, Mrs. Eliason. Thank you."

"How have things been since I last saw you, Zeb?" Reverend Solomon carried his plate from the table.

"Just fixin' to build a home for myself next spring on a piece of land Pa recently gave me. I've already started to do what I can, but with the lengthy Wyoming winters, it'll be a while before I can make much progress."

"May I tell them why you want to build a home?" Annie asked.

"Sure." Zeb shook his head. "Nothing is a secret with a sister."

John Mark elbowed Charlotte. "I can agree with that."

"Or a brother," Charlotte said, returning the ribbing he'd given her. "You can't tell a brother much of anything because he's a blatteroon."

"At least I'm not a flibbertigibbet." "You take that back right this instant, John Mark!"

"That's enough, you two," Reverend Solomon admonished. "We have a guest here today. Please be on your best behavior."

Charlotte tossed a smug look at her brother, and he returned a similar expression.

And Lydie gave a warning glance to both of them. "Please do continue, Zeb."

Zeb cleared his throat. "I plan to ask Hetty Milstrap to be my wife."

"Congratulations!" Caleb, Lydie, and Reverend Solomon chorused.

Charlotte rested her chin in her hands and swooned. "That's so romantic."

"Ewww, that's loathsome." John Mark's proclamation brought laughter from every corner of the table. "I'm never getting married. Ever."

Charlotte leaned toward her brother. "We'll remember you said that, John Mark, when you fall in love someday."

"Zeb has only adored Hetty for about three years. And now that they've been courting for a while, it's understandable he'd finally ask her to marry him," said Annie.

"I haven't asked her yet, but plan to in the next month. That is, if Annie doesn't ask her for me first."

"Never fear, dear brother, I'll hold my tongue just this once," Annie giggled, then sobered for a moment. She'd thought she'd been in love just days ago.

Until the truth about Caleb came to light.

Caleb observed the exchange between Annie and Zeb. He never had a close relationship with Cain. As a matter of fact, their relationship had been quite the opposite. And although he was close to John Mark and Charlotte, their age span didn't afford him the solidarity that existed between Annie and Zeb. For a moment, envy stabbed at him for the brother he could have had in Cain.

Zeb's concern and protection over Annie prompted Caleb to regret Cain had not been the same to him. But someday, John Mark would be the same protective big brother to Charlotte as Zeb was to Annie and the thought made him smile.

"Thank you, Mrs. Eliason, for the grub. Annie, are you about ready to go?" Zeb placed his silverware on his plate and stood.

Caleb caught Annie's eye for a minute and held her gaze. *I'm so sorry, Annie, for the pain I caused.*

Could she see the apology in his eyes?

But she redirected her focus onto Zeb.

"I think we've worn Annie out this week," said Lydie. "Between the busy days at school and the hustle and bustle of the Eliason home, I believe she's downright tuckered. Will you be all right riding that far with your ankle?"

"I should be. Zeb says we plan to take it slower than usual, and we'll stop a couple of times along the way."

Lydie handed Zeb a packed lunch. "It helps the weather is much more conducive to traveling today."

Zeb assisted Annie onto her horse and Caleb handed her her carpetbag. "Have a safe trip." He and Zeb shook hands. They'd built some sort of bond after discussing fishing, home building, and cattle prices. Ironic how Caleb earned Zeb's respect *after* he no longer needed it to court Annie.

Nonetheless, he was appreciative of the new friendship he'd formed.

"Thanks, Caleb. Don't forget what I said about going fishing in Nelsonville Creek. Those fish will be biting come spring."

"I'll look forward to it."

Annie avoided his farewell and instead fussed about adjusting herself comfortably on the horse, avoiding placing her injured ankle in the stirrup.

When Zeb returned, would they still be friends? Or would Annie tell him what she'd discovered about Caleb's past?

If so, there may not be any fishing plans in their future.

Regret once again held a firm grasp on his emotions.

Annie struggled to ignore the continuous discomfort in her ankle as she rode to Nelsonville. It had already been a long day and she wanted nothing more than to crawl into bed and sleep for the next several hours. Fortunately, by horseback, the trip to Nelsonville was considerably shorter than by wagon.

Zeb slowed his horse and rode alongside Annie. "How are you doing?"

"I'm glad it's not much farther."

"We can stop again if you need to."

Annie shook her head. "I'm fine. I'd rather continue so we'll arrive sooner."

They rode several more minutes side-by-side before Zeb spoke again, "The Eliason family sure seems nice."

"They are." Should she tell him what she'd learned about Caleb? "I noticed you and Caleb have become friends."

"We have a lot in common. He even offered to help me build my house come spring."

Annie attempted to reconcile the fact that Caleb had a servant's heart with what she now knew about him.

"You're deep in thought. Care to share?"

It was a saying she and Zeb had used often. When younger, they reminded Annie a lot of Charlotte and John Mark, but in recent years, she and Zeb had become close.

"It's just something I learned about Caleb. I'm not sure if I should say anything, since you're so protective."

"You know you can tell me anything, Annie."

"I know I can tell you anything, but this is something Pa mustn't find out."

Zeb exhaled a deep breath. "Must be something serious if Pa mustn't find out. But you and I rarely keep secrets from each other. Remember when you were the only one I told about asking Hetty to be my wife?"

Her brother's reminder evoked an image of the day Zeb had told her. Her brother, in his usual energetic fashion, nearly wore out the barn floor pacing while he waited for Annie to finish her chores. However, as similar in Zeb's mind as that example may be, what she had to tell him contrasted considerably.

Lord, please give me wisdom. I can't carry this burden alone. "It will anger you."

"Now I'm really curious."

"I'll tell you when we're not riding." The issue demanded his full attention.

"Whoa." He pulled back on the reins.

"Zeb, we don't have time to stop. It's almost dark."

"We do have time to stop when it's something important. Besides, we're less than a mile from home." Zeb climbed down from the horse to stretch his legs. "Now out with it, Annie."

"I don't know, Zeb. You have to promise me you won't say anything to Pa."

"I promise."

"In that case, Caleb is one of the men who…" She paused.

"Yes?" Zeb's forehead furrowed. "What is it, Annie?"

"Caleb is one of the men who…" Annie shifted in the saddle. "He is one of the men who robbed our wagon party that day seven years ago."

"What? How do you know? Are you sure?"

"Yes, I'm sure. When Doc Garrett examined Caleb's injured hand, I saw the scar."

"What scar?"

"Remember after the robbery, I told you the first man who came into our wagon had a sizeable scar on his hand?"

Zeb nodded, apparently allowing the recollection to settle in his mind. "I do remember. But why isn't he in prison for his crime?"

"I don't know. I doubt his parents even know about his criminal activities. I can only wonder where the other two men are, especially the one who shot Mr. DeGroot and assaulted the other gentleman."

"They could be in Willow Falls, too."

"They could be, although I've never seen them."

"You haven't been there long," reminded Zeb.

Annie shivered and her stomach knotted. The other two men created the impression of being far more sinister than Caleb, especially the one who shot Mr. DeGroot. What if they were in Willow Falls, endangering the community she had grown to love?

"I've invariably prided myself on being perspicacious. Discerning. A good judge of character. But I could not have anticipated Caleb would be an outlaw. Zeb, you cannot disclose this to Pa. If he finds out, he won't let me teach and I love my job in Willow Falls."

Zeb removed his cowboy hat and tugged on his beard. "Truth is, I worry about you too. If his own parents don't even know…what if he harms you?"

"I've pondered that many times, although I don't fear him. From what I know, he's not dangerous. I just…" How could she tell Zeb she was falling in love with Caleb and that changed everything?

"Be careful, Annie. Caleb may not be dangerous, but if he is in cahoots with the other two men who shot Mr. DeGroot, you could be in danger."

"I've never heard him speak of the other two, but then, I never knew about his secret until recently."

Zeb put a hand on her arm. "Promise me you'll be careful."

"I promise. And please keep your promise not to tell Pa."

"I do promise. But I think it might be best to talk to the sheriff in Willow Falls about your discovery."

Zeb's suggestion had merit. "I plan on speaking to Reverend Solomon when I return. He'll know what to do, although it will break his heart when he hears the truth about his son."

"Do you want me to have a talk with Caleb?"

Annie appreciated his concern and his protectiveness. "No, I'll be fine."

"If you're sure... because I can talk to him or I can ride over to Willow Falls mid-week and check on you."

"Thank you, Zeb, but you have work to tend to. Although I do appreciate your concern."

"Why would those men hang around after what they did? And why weren't they caught?"

Annie shook her head. "You can't believe the questions that have been swarming through my mind since I saw Caleb's scar."

"And you're sure it's him?"

"He all but admitted to it."

Zeb nodded toward the sun beginning to set. "Reckon we should be getting on our way. Thanks for telling me. I promise not to tell Pa if you promise to be extra careful."

"I promise."

If only Caleb had been a different man. If only he'd been the man she was beginning to love.

Chapter Eighteen

CALEB APPRECIATED HIS BUSY workload on Saturday. It offered him a distraction from thinking about Annie.

Mrs. Burns predicted no snow in the foreseeable future due to the lack of aching in her bones, and this provided an opportune time for him to busy himself constructing a new fence around his land. The previous fence had been built some time ago and wasn't large enough to accommodate his growing herd. He took in his surroundings—the house, the corrals, and the livestock—and his heart overflowed with gratitude.

Caleb pounded in several more fence posts, pleased he'd dug the holes weeks ago before the ground froze. Pa would arrive later this afternoon to lend him a hand.

Pa. What would Caleb have done if a stranger named Solomon Eliason hadn't offered to take a wayward orphan into his home? An almost full-grown wayward orphan? And not only that, but made Caleb his own son through adoption?

Prior to coming to Willow Falls, Caleb lacked a godly man after whom to model his life. Alvin Ryerson had certainly been anything but a positive role model. And Lydie—could Caleb have asked for a kinder, gentler woman to be his mother? Charlotte and John Mark completed the members of a family he loved—and who loved him.

A forever family.

Would Annie's knowledge of who Caleb was threaten all he had been blessed with and all that he had become? Would she share her newfound knowledge with the town of Willow Falls and tarnish the reputation Caleb had tried so hard to earn?

The memory of that July day when he, Cain, and Roy robbed her family and friends impacted her even more than he had realized.

Clouds of doubt filled his mind. Maybe Caleb didn't believe he truly had changed, either. Maybe he'd been naïve in thinking he was any different now than he was seven years ago. After all, Caleb Eliason was *really* Caleb Ryerson from a bad seed—the son of a drunken gunfighter and the brother of a murderer.

Some things would never change.

He kicked a pebble on the ground. No. That couldn't be right. He was a changed man. The Lord *had* changed him.

Caleb chastised himself for having doubts. God was all-knowing and all-powerful. He created the entire earth and everything in it from nothing. He performed a miracle in Caleb's life. Surely he could perform a miracle in Annie's heart.

Couldn't He?

He had followed Reverend Solomon home the night of his release from the Willow Falls jail, a few months prior to the day he would be adopted into the Eliason family.

"I wish we weren't so cramped in the house." Reverend Solomon led Caleb to the barn. *"We'll start tomorrow on an*

addition so you can have your own room. I've been meaning to add on some space for a room for John Mark anyhow."

Caleb figured he wouldn't be staying long, especially if Reverend Solomon changed his mind or Caleb made a mess of things. He was just thankful to be out of jail and to have shelter. Too many nights he'd been rained on, snowed on, hailed on, and pestered by wild creatures.

Caleb perused the barn and inhaled the smell of hay. It might as well have been a fancy hotel in the city. "Thank you, sir. Reckon it's hard enough for a man to provide for his own family, let alone have another mouth to feed."

"God always provides."

Caleb hadn't known anything about God or whether or not He provided anything to anyone. He sat down on the bed, which had been covered by a blue-and-red patchwork quilt. He ran his fingers along the seams of the quilt, realizing he'd never before owned one.

"Lydie made that quilt. She's quite a gifted seamstress. Have a good night's sleep, Son, and we'll start on that addition tomorrow."

"Uh, sir?"

"Yes?"

Caleb appreciated the way Reverend Solomon called him "son." He knew it was only a formality, but still, it made Caleb feel as though he belonged to someone.

He hung his head. "Why are you helping me?"

"Because I believe you deserve a second chance." Reverend Solomon took a seat next to him.

"Why would you think that? I was part of a robbery and an attempted murder, and you have no idea what else I've done."

"The robbery, yes," Reverend Solomon said, "but I don't believe you were part of the attempted murder."

"How do you know that? You don't know me; you don't know my past. Why would you trust me?"

Reverend Solomon sighed. "I'll be honest with you. I can't recall a time in recent years when I've had to step out in such faith. Although I trust the Lord with all my being, there are times in life, such as now, when I struggle to relinquish control. I have a wife and children to think about. I can't put them in danger. But I do believe the Lord has a plan for you, Caleb, and that He desires for my family to be a part of that plan."

Reverend Solomon spoke of God as though he knew Him personally. As though God cared about His people. It only made sense that a reverend would refer to God constantly but with such familiarity? Caleb couldn't grasp it.

"You don't know Him yet, but I pray He will someday draw you to Himself. That you will turn from your sins and place your trust in Him."

Caleb knew nothing about turning from his sins and putting his trust in God. He didn't trust people. Why would he trust Someone he couldn't even see? He also lacked trust in himself. He was Alvin Ryerson's son. Nothing good ever came from that man.

"What if I make a mess of things?"

"I don't think you will, not in the sense you're thinking, anyway. Oh, you'll make plenty of mistakes because we all do. But you won't mess up in a way that will jeopardize this opportunity you've been given. Besides, I believe you want a second chance too." When Caleb nodded, Reverend Solomon continued, "And I believe that the Lord is calling me to help you gain that second chance..."

Caleb mindlessly stared at the land before him. He'd made minor mistakes over the years, things he regretted.

Things he repented of and with the Lord's help didn't repeat. But nothing that disappointed Pa or landed Caleb in jail.

Several months later, on Christmas day, Reverend Solomon announced the family had a special gift for Caleb. A blizzard raged outside, while inside, the fire warmed the cabin. Gratitude swept over him. He'd already been given so much in recent weeks. He had a permanent room, he'd attended school, and he always had a warm meal in his belly.

"You can decline this present," said Reverend Solomon, "but we hope you won't."

Caleb couldn't understand why they had another present for him. He was already wearing the new shirt Lydie made for him. And why would he ever decline a gift? He'd been given so few in his life.

"'Nother pwesent for Caleb?" Little Charlotte patted him on the head.

Caleb grinned at her. "I'll share it with you, whatever it is."

"Will you share it with me too?" Six-year-old John Mark's eyes widened.

"I sure will."

Reverend Solomon cleared his throat. "Lydie and I would be honored and privileged if you would allow us to adopt you."

Adopt him? Hadn't they done enough? Why would they want another child and such an old one at that? He was nearly grown, for goodness' sake! He watched as John Mark stacked his new wooden blocks and Charlotte played "baby" with her new doll. They had two perfect children. Why would they even consider an imperfect one?

"You don't have to make a decision right now, Caleb. Take some time to think it over. I know it's sudden. Lydie and I were thinking what a nice Christmas gift it would be, especially in light of the fact that this is the day we celebrate Christ's birth."

"Why would you want to adopt me?"

"We have grown to love you." Tears shimmered in Lydie's eyes.

Caleb's head swirled like the snow outside. A variety of emotions filled his heart, from disbelief to gratitude.

"But..."

"We would be honored if you would join John Mark in carrying on the Eliason name. Of course, if you don't feel comfortable with that, you are welcome to keep your given surname. We just want you to know that this is how serious we are about adopting you," said Reverend Solomon, tears in his own eyes.

Words had stuck in Caleb's throat. What if they adopted him and he tarnished their good reputation? Finally, he had uttered his ever-present fear of making a mistake that would cause them to regret their choice.

Lydie patted him on the arm. "Does a day not go by when we don't all do something, no matter how small, that requires forgiveness? Besides, a parent loves their child always, and you would be our child. And you don't have to earn that love. It's already yours. But you think about it, Caleb. We don't want to pressure you. We only want you to know that we love and care about you and want to make you part of our family."

Surely it was a dream and he would awaken at any moment. But after the realization of reality, he agreed to the adoption and vowed to never do anything to cause the Eliason family to regret their decision.

Reverend Solomon patted Caleb on the back. "Welcome to the family, Son."

"Does that mean he's my big brother?" John Mark asked.

"Yes, it does," Lydie answered.

"I've wanted a big brother my whole life." He jumped up and hugged Caleb.

The church threw Caleb a welcome party, complete with his favorite kind of cake. With the exception of only a few, the townsfolk didn't know about Caleb's past any more than Annie had. They thought he was someone Reverend Solomon and Lydie Eliason adopted out of the kindness of their hearts.

Caleb assisted the Eliasons in any way he could, from helping on their ranch to visiting the ill and infirm with Pa. He took on miscellaneous jobs after school and began his lifelong dream to someday own his own ranch. He tried his hardest to stay out of trouble, even though there were days when the teacher had to meet with his new parents about a shenanigan he had pulled. Through every error and lapse in judgment, his new parents continued to love him.

A year later when he was fifteen, Caleb made Jesus Christ his personal Savior. While he himself wasn't perfect and his life wasn't perfect, the plan God had for him since the beginning of time *was* perfect.

Chapter Nineteen

Annie thumbed through her diary to the next blank page and began to pen the words on her mind.

Dear Diary,
It has been some time since I've written, as I'm not sure how to articulate the thoughts flowing through my mind. I discovered, quite by accident, that Caleb is the one who robbed our wagon train as we entered the Wyoming Territory.
When I saw the scar on his hand, I knew. And he didn't deny it.
Before that day, I found myself falling in love with him. We shared a kiss and I knew what my response would be should he ask me to court him. His kindness, delightful personality, his charming smile, and handsome and rugged appearance drew me in. He loves his family and serves others in the community.
A part of me wonders if that is all a façade. How could a man who has those traits also be an outlaw? If I didn't see it with my own eyes that day, I wouldn't have believed it. Is he still involved in such crimes?

She placed the diary in the bureau drawer and prayed again for wisdom and the words to speak.

Later that morning, she left for school in the hopes of arriving before her pupils. Her mind had been scattered as of late, and she needed to tend to some lesson plans before the day officially started.

Annie hobbled up the stairs and into the schoolhouse. Caleb had obviously been there already, as warmth flooded her the second she entered. She sat at her desk and began her tasks when she heard the door open.

"Annie?"

Caleb strolled toward her with slow, plodding steps.

"I made this for you. For your ankle." He set a homemade crutch on her desk. "Reckon it doesn't possess the professionalism of a crutch found at the mercantile, but it's sturdy, and there's a piece of fabric to reduce the soreness of where the crutch will rest under your arm."

Annie stood and gripped the desk for stability. "Thank you."

Silence permeated the air. Caleb rubbed the back of his neck and shifted from side to side.

Annie struggled for words. So instead, she fingered the crutch, noting the precision and excellent workmanship with which it was crafted. What was his reason for presenting such a gift to her?

Before her knowledge of who he was, she would have reacted far differently. But now? She bit the inside of her cheek. "I appreciate this." Her voice sounded tinny in her ears.

Something flashed in his eyes, something akin to... sorrow? Disappointment? Defeat?

"Annie..."

Would he explain the truth? Was she ready to hear it?

"I…"

Several students filed into the room, the sound of joyous chatter in their voices. They greeted Caleb, and Annie noted how his countenance changed when he interacted with the children. A smile lit his face, and she missed what had begun to bloom between them.

She fought the melancholy thoughts and instead prepared to share with her scholars their latest assignment.

Caleb said nothing more to her and left the schoolhouse moments later.

Caleb prayed about whether to set things to rights with Annie. He'd attempted to do so that morning when he'd delivered the crutch, but lost his nerve. No doubt she was hurt, and rightfully so, by what he had done to her family and friends. He wanted to prove to her he was no longer that man. To apologize. To ask for her forgiveness.

Pa's most recent advice lingered in his mind. *"Annie must know the truth when you seek her forgiveness. It is up to you to inform her of the man you really are—the man you have become. It is up to you to show her that Caleb Eliason has taken the place, by God's grace, of Caleb Ryerson. You can't force her forgiveness, but you can pray for God to soften her heart and to be open to your apology."*

When was the proper time to speak with her? The supper table offered no privacy, and he couldn't expect her to limp to the cold barn.

He finished a job in town and rode to the schoolhouse just as school was out for the day. Before she knew who he really was, he would have given anything to see her so many times in one day. But now, dread overwhelmed him.

For the second time, he strode toward her desk. "Annie, there's something I need to speak with you about."

When Annie didn't respond, he continued, "I need to talk to you... about that day."

"Caleb, I'd just like to go home. I neither wish to discuss nor re-invite the memory into my mind."

"We need to talk about it. I need to tell you what really happened."

Dark circles under her eyes indicated her lack of sleep. Her painful ankle surely wasn't conducive to peaceful rest.

"Maybe another time."

"Please. It's not what you think."

"How do you know what I think?"

"I know what kind of man you think I am."

She folded her hands in her lap. "Answer me one thing."

"Anything."

"Where are the two other men from your gang?"

Sheer determination forced him to stand there before her desk and answer her inquiry. "Cain is in prison and Roy is dead. You needn't worry about either of them."

Relief flooded her pretty features. He wanted to ask for her forgiveness, take her into his arms, and continue where they'd left off before she saw his hand.

But with her next words, it was clear their conversation was far from over. Part of him wanted to settle the matter fully, while the other part desired to run from the pain.

"I figured you to be an upstanding and law-abiding citizen."

"I am."

She wasn't prone to temper, but the words and accusations flowed with no end in sight: "Would an upstanding and law-abiding citizen steal from people? Take their hard-earned money? Cause so much turmoil that a woman went into labor and nearly died? Stand by while one man is beaten and another is shot?"

"I couldn't..."

"Couldn't or wouldn't? That was my ma who nearly died. She was already having a difficult pregnancy. What if she died in childbirth? What if the baby died?"

"Annie, you don't understand." He balled his hands into fists and his broad shoulders drooped slightly. "I left the tin box with the money in your wagon. I could have taken that."

"I appreciate that you hid it in the wagon and didn't steal the money and coins inside, but is that supposed to make it better? Do your parents know about you? Does Sheriff Townsend? Do you still commit crimes? Do you have any idea what it was like to watch all of this unfold? There were children younger than me who witnessed this attack. I was a year older than Charlotte. A year older than your sister. What would you have done if Charlotte was in danger?"

"She's my sister. I would have defended her. Laid down my life for her, if that's what it took."

"But you wouldn't come to the aid of other innocent people?"

"You saw my hand and everything changed. I thought we cared for each other. I was going to ask you to court me."

Tears clouded her vision and she wrapped her arms around herself. "I would never consider courting you."

As soon as she uttered the words, she knew she'd wounded him. His chest rose and fell with rapid breaths, and emotion lurked behind his rugged exterior. Caleb opened his mouth, presumably to say something, but clamped it shut again. After a short moment, he turned and left.

Chapter Twenty

After she assisted Lydie with supper dishes, Annie asked if she might speak with Reverend Solomon in the barn.

Oh, Reverend, if only you knew the truth about your son. I feel I must tell you what I know. I regret that it will cause you such pain.

"Please don't tell me John Mark has orchestrated another prank at school." Reverend Solomon's eyes crinkled at the corners. He took his place across from her on another bale of hay and gave her his full attention.

"No, Reverend, I'm afraid it's not that." She shifted uncomfortably on the hay bale.

What would Reverend Solomon do once he knew the truth? It would devastate him and Lydie. *Lord, I ask for your aid in this matter. Give me the words.*

"Please know how much I appreciate you and Lydie allowing me to board here while I teach school. You have become a second family to me and I treasure you both. I've also become quite fond of John Mark and Charlotte."

"You're not thinking of resigning from teaching, are you?"

"Oh, goodness, no."

"I'm relieved, Annie. You are a gifted teacher and we would miss you if you were no longer here."

"And I, too, would miss your family and the entire town of Willow Falls. I've grown to care for the people of this town and look forward to becoming better acquainted with those whom I don't yet know well." She paused and again prayed for guidance. "I wish I didn't have to tell you this as I want in no way to hurt you or Lydie."

"It is best to get these things out in the open."

Annie thought of how Reverend Solomon's name fit him well. She admired his wisdom and attempted to picture the man across from her as a young reverend, as he had been when Lydie first met him. Annie doubted he looked much different then. Well into his thirties, he had thick, sandy brown hair and deep-set hazel eyes that were partially hidden by spectacles. He and Lydie made a perfect match and complimented each other in so many ways, although in many ways they were also opposites. While Reverend Solomon was outgoing and gregarious, Lydie was shy and soft-spoken. While Reverend Solomon was tall, Lydie was barely five feet. Yes, in this short amount of time, Annie had grown to love the Eliason family, and she hated to disappoint them with the news that she felt she must share.

"Reverend, I have discovered something about Caleb that I must tell you. I don't know how to say this, but... Caleb is an outlaw."

"An outlaw?"

"I am so sorry to have to be the bearer of bad news."

Was she shaking because she was cold or had the anxiety overtaken her? Explaining the situation to the reverend transported her back in time.

"When my family and I were moving to Nelsonville seven years ago, we were traveling in a wagon party of five families. As we were just about to reach Willow Falls, we were robbed by a gang of three men. Caleb was one of those men." Annie closed her eyes, trying to shut out the harrowing memory.

"Annie..."

"I'm sorry, Reverend. So, so sorry."

Annie began to sob then. She dropped her head into her hands and allowed warm tears to fall freely down her cheeks. She cared deeply for the feelings of others, always had, and despised that she had to be the one to tell Reverend Solomon his son was not what he seemed. It would be difficult for any man to take, but especially a preacher who lived his life for Christ and brought his children up to do the same.

Reverend Solomon moved from his position to sit by Annie. He placed his hand on her shoulder.

"Annie, it's all right. I know about Caleb."

Annie's head jerked up from its place between her hands. "You do?"

"Yes."

"And it's all right with you?" Annie found it difficult to believe that someone of Reverend Solomon's integrity could condone such behavior. "What if he is still involved in stealing from others?"

"I don't condone any criminal activity. Having said that, Caleb is no longer involved in such things. He hasn't been for quite some time. He is honorable and forthright and is working extra jobs to build his cattle herd, money he earned doing honest pay for honest work." Reverend Solomon's voice held no condemnation, only a gentle, reassuring tone. "Not from money he has stolen from others. The jobs enabled him to purchase the land, the home that was on it, and the animals. It has always been his dream to own his own ranch. He's worked hard for what he has, but not in the profession you think."

"But it was he who robbed our wagon and was an accomplice to the gunshot wound that nearly took the life of my mother, sister, and Mr. DeGroot, not to mention the vicious assault on another man. I witnessed it, Reverend."

"I know you were there, and I know Caleb was a part of the gang."

Reverend Solomon's calm voice soothed her nerves somewhat. She was relieved he knew about Caleb, but the questions churned through her mind.

"Then why is he not in prison? He did a terrible thing. And besides, he likely robbed other wagons, as well. The gang seemed so experienced; I doubt it was their first robbery."

"No, it wasn't their first robbery," said Reverend Solomon, "but it was Caleb's last."

"So you trust him to not be engaged in robbing people anymore? How can you be so sure?"

"I absolutely do trust that Caleb is a different man than he was when he robbed your wagon train."

"But how could you know that for certain?"

"Because of the way Caleb lives his life."

"But, Reverend, I mean no disrespect when I say this, but what if you are wrong? You have Charlotte and John Mark to think about."

"Caleb loves the Lord. He is a different man now. Praise God for second chances." Reverend Solomon paused as if to think over his words carefully before speaking again. "When you look at Caleb, what do you see?"

"I see the man who came into our wagon and pilfered through our things, looking for anything of value to steal." Annie dabbed at her eyes with her handkerchief, as she once again relived that day. "I see a man who stood by while an innocent man was beaten, another one shot, and then who rode off with two other men, never to be seen again. Caleb never cared about what he did. A wife nearly lost her husband that day. My mother nearly died in labor, and what if Sadie hadn't been born?" The contemplation was nearly too much to bear. "That is what I see when I see Caleb."

"I can only imagine what you went through at the hands of Caleb and his gang that day. It must have been very traumatic for you."

"I have had nightmares many times since that day. I hadn't had them for a while. In fact, I had, with the Lord's help, thought I'd put that day behind me. That was, until I saw Caleb's scarred hand and I knew it was him."

"Caleb told me you recognized him. Annie, you have every right to be angry with Caleb for what he did that day. His actions and choices caused great pain for you, your family, and your friends." Reverend Solomon paused for a moment and closed his eyes as if to pray. "Stealing is wrong and Caleb should never have engaged in unlawful behavior. Standing by while someone is nearly murdered is unacceptable. I won't make excuses for Caleb, but I will tell you that he was trapped in that lifestyle and had nothing to do with the attempted murder of Mr. DeGroot."

"How can you be so sure?"

"Because I know my son, and I know he is incapable of such a crime. Yes, he did partake in the robbery, and for that he is to blame. But not the attempted murder. I'm not excusing Caleb's role in the robberies, and I'm not excusing his role in being a part of the gang. But I am saying that since that day, Caleb has made the choice never to engage in such activity again. While he's not perfect, I truly couldn't ask for a son I am prouder of."

Annie's chest hitched. "I don't know what to say."

"It was inevitable that you and Caleb would someday cross paths again. But I had no idea it would turn out the way it has. I pray you will see him through God's eyes. See the man he is now, not the man he was. A man willing to help others, even if he hasn't the time or the resources."

Tears flooded her eyes. She thought of the crutch he'd fashioned for her. The times he tended the fire in the schoolhouse to ensure its warmth for her and the students. The assistance he offered when she fell.

"I know this is difficult for you. It would be for me, too. He knows he has hurt you deeply, Annie, and someday, you'll be able to forgive him."

"I don't think I can." Her choked words caught in her throat.

"Allow the Lord control of this situation, and He will enable you to forgive Caleb. It may not be right away, but He will prepare your heart with a forgiveness that wouldn't be possible without His intervention."

Annie squeezed her eyes tight to prevent the flow of more tears. "What happened to Caleb's hand? The scar, I mean."

"That is something to ask Caleb. He can make the choice to tell you about the scar on his hand, about the robbery, and about his life before the robbery. Those are things best told to you by him. In time, I pray you'll feel comfortable enough to speak with him."

Her emotions remained in an upheaval.

Reverend Solomon checked his pocket watch. "We best go back inside—it's getting late and mighty cold out here. Lydie and I are here to talk whenever you need us. I know we aren't your parents, but we care about you. Please, talk to us whenever something weighs heavily on your heart. And, Annie, please speak to Caleb about the robbery."

She nodded, not sure if she could keep the promise Reverend Solomon expected her to make.

That night in bed, Annie pulled the quilt to her chin and thought of her conversation with Reverend Solomon. Could he be right that Caleb had changed from all those years ago? She had no reason to doubt the reverend's honesty. And if Caleb had changed, was forgiveness possible?

She wounded Caleb with her words earlier in the schoolhouse. If only she'd known the truth. If only she'd asked him and allowed him to explain.

He was well-respected in the community and seemingly liked by all the townsfolk. He also had a family who adored him. Reverend Solomon and Lydie took the chance to make him a part of their family.

And what of her feelings for him, feelings that had become much more than friendship? Jumbled emotions and wondering what might have been conflicted with her need for sleep.

Lord, please help me forgive Caleb.

Chapter Twenty-One

Caleb restocked the supply of logs by the wood stove at the school. He took seriously his task to keep the pupils and Annie warm during the winter months.

Annie hobbled from desk to desk with her crutch, answering her students' questions. Caleb admired her ability to teach. She cared for her students and used creativity in her teaching. He'd noted before how she explained things in unique ways to Charlotte and John Mark when they hadn't understood, and she took extra time with Jack Parsons, sometimes even staying after school, if necessary, to tutor him. After the death of his parents, Jack struggled even more with his schoolwork. But Annie provided the perfect antidote: compassion, patience, and clever learning ideas.

In a soft voice, Annie explained to Jack how to work an arithmetic problem. Jack frowned and shook his head, and with patience, Annie again explained, this time using a box full of buttons. "If you have ten apples and you have to share them equally between students, how many will you give each person?"

After a couple of wrong guesses, Annie proceeded. "Pretend you are going to share with Russell. Here is one apple for Russell."

Annie took a brown button from the box and placed it on the left-hand top of the desk.

Jack grinned. "That's not an apple, Miss Ledbetter. It's a button."

"Yes, you are correct, Jack, but let's put on our imaginations and pretend these buttons are apples."

"All right." Jack retrieved the button.

"Now, here is one apple for Jack." Annie placed another button on the right-side top of the desk. "Let's go through all of the ten apples until we have divided them equally."

One by one, she handed Jack the buttons, and one by one, he split them between Russell and himself.

Jack beamed, evidence he grasped how to work the arithmetic problem. "Thank you, Miss Ledbetter! I understand now."

"You're welcome, Jack. Now try to work the next one on your own and if you need help, I'll be back in a few minutes."

Annie continued to make her way around the classroom. Several of the pupils already finished their arithmetic and were allowed to read or draw pictures on their slates. When she reached Charlotte's desk, she began to giggle.

"Oh, Charlotte, what an endearing picture."

"It's a family portrait. I heard in big cities a device known as a camera produces photographs. Since we don't have a man with a camera in Willow Falls, I thought I'd sketch my own photograph."

"You definitely captured the essence of the Eliason family with your artistry."

Charlotte viewed her sketch from different angles. "Thank you, Miss Ledbetter. I realize the smiles are a bit crooked and John Mark really isn't as tall as Caleb and Pa, but maybe someday he'll grow."

"I am growing," John Mark muttered.

"But I'm nearly as tall as you. You're woefully stunted."

The class laughed at Charlotte's obvious exaggeration.

"Just wait, Charlotte. I'm gonna be tall someday. Taller than both Pa and Caleb."

A smile tugged at Annie's lips and her merriment did not go unnoticed by Caleb. Her head tilted slightly back and she giggled as if smiling toward the heavens. Her laugh was delicate but spirited, and he wished it had been him who'd made her laugh, just like in the past. All those times they'd spent in each other's company, chatting and teasing each other would forever remain fond memories.

But the unfortunate occurrences marred the good memories that he had of them at the ice cream social and the kiss they'd shared. Who knew a distinguishing mark would someday come between them?

If only Mr. Yager hadn't punished him in such an abusive way. Maybe then Annie would never have learned the truth. But would deceit be any way to start a relationship? One he had once dared to hope would include more than friendship?

Remorse seared his heart. What if she divulged what she knew to the townsfolk? Surely some of them wouldn't want an ex-outlaw living among them, no matter how his life had changed. For years after the incident, Caleb feared someone other than the few who already knew would discover his secret.

Annie tucked a wisp of hair behind her ear. He'd fallen in love with her, and he longed to re-establish what began between them; to seek her forgiveness and promise never to hurt her again.

The pain in her eyes stung his heart. He desired nothing more than to take that pain away, and he hoped that by redeeming himself through the small things, he might be able to do so.

Chapter Twenty-Two

Caleb arrived at the schoolhouse to take Annie, John Mark, and Charlotte home. Annie said a reluctant "thank you" as he assisted her into the wagon.

The snow had long melted, but the air remained crisp. The sun, while shining, shared no warmth.

Charlotte folded her arms across her chest. "It hasn't snowed for the past week and a half."

"We need the moisture, and I miss the snow," John Mark added.

Halfway to the Eliason house, Caleb noticed it.

The orange glow lit the surrounding area and the smell of smoke filled the air as flames engulfed Mr. and Mrs. Dixon's home.

"Whoa," he called to the horses and pulled up beside the Dixon home. A handful of townsfolk hauled buckets of water.

Because of the chaos, no one else noticed Mrs. Dixon running to the door and attempting to re-enter the burning home. Caleb jumped from the wagon and sprinted toward her.

"Mrs. Dixon, what are you doing?"

"My Stuart is in there!" The woman's arms flailed frantically.

"Are you sure?"

"Yes! He just ran back in to find the dog! I tried to stop him, but I couldn't. It's all my fault. Once I noticed the fire, we ran outside, but before—before I could stop him, he—he ran back inside. I must save him! Oh, Caleb, what if he's already..."

"No, Mrs. Dixon, don't think that way. You wait out here. I'll go in and get him."

Puppy, Stuart's dog, dashed through the door, his fur covered in soot. Caleb waited a fraction of a second to see if Stuart would follow him.

Annie limped toward the home with a water bucket.

"Annie?"

"Yes?"

"Please take Mrs. Dixon over there." He pointed to a clearing not far from the house. Without awaiting her answer, Caleb dashed inside.

Smoke swirled around him and he gasped for air. "Stuart?"

On his hands and knees, Caleb crawled through the cabin. He'd been in the house so many times, he knew his way around it with his eyes closed. He just needed to find Stuart.

Quickly.

The smell of charred wood greeted him, and a popping and sparking of something near the stove—cooking fat, perhaps?—sounded in his ears.

A quivering voice emanated from a far corner. "Cawub?"

"Stuart? Where are you?"

"I over here, Cawub," Stuart's muffled voice competed with the crackling sounds of the fire.

Caleb's eyes stung and his lungs burned. "Keep talking so I can find you." While his vision wavered, his sense of smell and his hearing became more acute.

The boy began to sniffle. "But I can't find Puppy."

Caleb followed the direction of Stuart's voice. He groped his way forward until he reached the boy. "Take my hand, Stuart. Puppy is waiting for us outside, but we must hurry."

A loud snapping sound and a shower of embers preceded a falling beam that crashed in front of them.

Please, Lord.

Caleb firmly grasped Stuart's hand just as Stuart went limp. Resisting the temptation to fear the worst, he lifted him and forged his way toward the door, struggling to carry Stuart.

Disoriented, he lost his way twice. Time moved slowly, almost as if he spent a lifetime edging his way toward an exit. Smoke blurred his vision and he sought the Lord's guidance to save the young life entrusted to him.

Minutes ticked by, and finally, he emerged from the house seconds before a beam fell and blocked the doorway.

Annie settled Mrs. Dixon into the safety of the clearing when she spied Sheriff Townsend.

"Sheriff!"

"What is it, Annie?" Clutching a bucket, Sheriff Townsend hurried toward the creek to retrieve water.

"It's Caleb. He went inside to find Stuart and hasn't returned yet."

"All right, don't you worry." Dropping the bucket, Sheriff Townsend ran toward what was once the front door of the house. "How long has he been inside?"

Annie searched her mind, but the passage of time was muddled. "I don't know."

"I'm going in to get him." Sheriff Townsend prepared to enter the burning home.

At that moment, Caleb staggered across the threshold and just beyond the front of the home. As he did, flames consumed the remainder of the building and threatened to spread to the barn.

Sheriff Townsend took Stuart from him, and Caleb collapsed to the ground.

Annie's knees buckled and she crouched beside Caleb. "Are you all right?"

His breath came in rapid spurts, followed by coughs. Soot covered his entire face, arms, and legs, and a sizeable tear spanned his shirt. Fear tore through her and tears slid down her cheeks. Annie removed her bonnet, wiped the soot from Caleb's face, and covered him with a quilt Mrs. Talbot handed her. What if he had perished in the fire?

"Annie?"

"Yes, Caleb, I'm here." She held his hand in hers.

He choked the barely audible words: "Is Stuart all right?"

"I believe so."

"John Mark and Charlotte. Are they...?"

"They are hauling buckets of water."

After tending to Stuart, Doc Garrett rushed over to Caleb. "This is the fourth time you've saved someone's life, Son."

Had Annie misheard Doc Garrett's comment? "The fourth time?"

Doc Garrett continued checking Caleb's vitals. "Yes. Some years ago, he saved the lives of a woman and her child. The woman was in labor, and it was possible she and her child wouldn't have made it had I not been alerted of her condition by Caleb. A man in her wagon train had also been beaten and another shot. The latter would have bled out had this young man here not informed me of his wound. And now Stuart. Once again, Caleb, you're a bona fide hero."

Annie exhaled a few shaky breaths and squeezed her eyes shut. Had she heard correctly? Could it be? Was that why the doctor arrived at the wagon party just in time? Sure, she recognized Doc Garrett from that day, and had thanked him profusely on a couple of different occasions, but... Her head swam and she yearned to inquire for more details but refrained. She wanted nothing to impede the care he provided Caleb.

Doc Garrett's words echoed through her mind. *"The woman was in labor, and it was possible she and her child wouldn't have made it had I not been alerted to her condition by Caleb."*

He saved the lives of her ma, her sister, and Mr. DeGroot?

"Annie?"

"Yes, Caleb. I'm here." She held his hand in hers.

She needed to thank him. Needed to apologize.

"I'm sorry."

A sob rose in her throat. "Caleb..."

"I needed you to know." His voice rasped, the pain it took to speak apparent.

She cradled his face in her hands and allowed gratitude to flood her heart.

Caleb, Stuart, and Puppy would make full recoveries, but the Dixon home was a loss and would have to be rebuilt.

As John Mark steered the wagon toward home, Annie sat in the back with Caleb, who rested peacefully beneath a mound of donated quilts. She thought of the burning home and his sacrifice to save Stuart. What if Caleb hadn't gotten out of the home alive? She swallowed hard.

What if he had died before she had forgiven him?

Chapter Twenty-Three

A RAGING BLIZZARD NECESSITATED an early release from school a few days later. After an unseasonably dry and warm start, winter had hit with vengeance.

Caleb arrived to accompany Annie, John Mark, and Charlotte home. Annie huddled against him as they rode double toward the Eliason home. Her cloak and wool stockings failed to protect her from the harsh winds. The stinging snow and bitter cold caused her eyes to water, and she wondered how Caleb could see two feet in front of them when she could barely see her own hand.

Caleb led John Mark and Charlotte's horse, lest they become estranged and lost in the white-out, and the tedious journey gave Annie time to think. She'd not had an opportunity to speak to him after the fire, had not yet thanked him for saving Ma and Sadie, nor discussed what the reverend had relayed to her. An awkwardness between them persisted, and she hoped to rectify it. Reverend Solomon's words again entered her mind about the change in Caleb. He'd been given another chance to be a law-abiding citizen, and Annie had been given another chance to fully forgive him.

Caleb intermittently spoke, but the whistling of the wind interfered with Annie's ability to hear his words. Finally, after a considerable amount of time, he stopped near a cabin.

"We'll stay here until the storm clears. Annie, get everyone in the house while I put the horses in the barn."

Annie willed her frozen legs to move. Her ankle was mostly healed, but the cold made her limbs unresponsive to her prompting. She stumbled to the door and held it open for John Mark and Charlotte. Gratitude enveloped her at their safe arrival.

"Whose home is this?" Annie asked, inspecting the rustic log cabin that was like so many others in the Wyoming Territory.

Charlotte's teeth chattered and she rubbed her hands together. "It's Caleb's."

"Caleb's?"

Annie had never seen Caleb's house but knew he resided within a short distance of Reverend Solomon and Lydie. She inspected the tidy home, noting its simplicity. A worn table with four chairs, a fireplace, and a four-legged stand with a stack of a few mismatched dishes completed the front room.

John Mark commenced building a fire in the stove and Annie prepared the coffee.

Moments later, Caleb opened the door and slammed it shut behind him.

"It's downright cold out there," he said, removing his coat and gloves.

Annie handed him the hot coffee and he wrapped his hands around the cup. "Thank you. I told Ma and Pa we'd likely have to stop here and wait out the storm."

John Mark rubbed his stomach. "Except there's nothing to eat here."

"Oh, poppycock, John Mark. You're always hungry." Charlotte rolled her eyes.

"Not *always*...just most of the time."

Caleb chuckled. "I'll see what we can find to eat, but be warned, this isn't Ma's house."

"That's the truth. If we were at home, I would be inhaling the aroma of freshly baked apple pie." John Mark closed his eyes and pretended to inhale.

"I'll wager Caleb has a few crackers or crusts of bread."

"I hope you have more than that." John Mark's eyebrows came together in a look of concern. "I may just starve to death."

Charlotte stood up straight and cleared her throat. "Here lies John Mark Solomon Eliason. He died a tragic death after starving at his brother's home. According to verifiable witnesses, the young man was flummoxed by the lack of sustenance available after a laborious journey from the schoolhouse in a precarious snowstorm. John Mark will be remembered as a nincompoop who engaged in multiple shenanigans. He leaves behind his family and a horse."

"You're the nincompoop, Charlotte. For one, I'm not flummoxed by the lack of sustenance available at Caleb's house. If Ma didn't feed him, he'd be the one dying a tragic death."

"You forget I do provide for myself for two out of three meals," said Caleb. "I'm not entirely dependent on Ma and Pa to feed me every meal."

Charlotte jabbed a finger at her oldest brother. "You mean to say you feed yourself two of three meals, with one of those meals being leftovers Ma sends home with you each evening."

"All right, you two!" Caleb pretended to chase after them with a clump of snow he'd removed from his coat. His siblings easily escaped around the other side of the table. "I suppose you're safe this time, but just wait until my feet thaw."

Annie observed the camaraderie between Caleb and his siblings. No doubt he was a doting older brother. And while she struggled with the forgiveness she knew was due, so much of what Reverend Solomon had said made sense. His words echoed in her mind. *"I'm not excusing Caleb's role in the robberies, and I'm not excusing his role in being a part of the gang. But I am saying that since that day, Caleb has made the choice never to engage in such activity again. While he's not perfect, I truly couldn't ask for a son I am prouder of."*

She thought of the fire and how she'd almost lost him. Perhaps today the Lord would give her the opportunity to make things right.

After a hodge-podge noonday meal, Annie took a seat by the fireplace. Even after two hours in Caleb's warm home, Annie still could not shake the chill permeating through her after their ride. The storm showed no signs of stopping and it appeared they were trapped, at least for the time being.

Charlotte and John Mark played a game at the table at the other end of the room, and Caleb pulled a chair up beside Annie. He added a log to the fire and stoked it.

"Reckon it's been an adventurous day."

"That it has. I've known several folks who've been caught in blizzards, but I never imagined I'd be one of them."

Silence followed for several minutes, as they both watched the flickering flames. Should she broach the topic of her discussion with Reverend Solomon? Tell Caleb she'd come to a new conclusion about his past?

Caleb appreciated the fire's warmth after their bone-chilling ride from town. He studied Annie's profile. She'd softened toward him since the ordeal at the Dixon house. He recalled how she had cared for him in the aftermath. Was it possible she would someday forgive him for his role in the robbery? She turned toward him, and he searched her face for any signs of hope that there may be a chance to reconcile their friendship.

A wisp of hair had escaped her bun, and her cheeks were flushed from sitting so close to the fire. She rested her dainty hands atop the quilt, and he longed to hold them in his, to rekindle what had begun between them, and to pretend his past and her discovery of it had never happened.

They spoke no words, but Caleb welcomed the stillness since the appropriate thing to say failed to come to mind.

Charlotte's squeal about winning hers and John Mark's most recent game interrupted his thoughts. John Mark replied with an offer to challenge her to yet another round.

Caleb searched his mind for the best way to broach the topic, but he'd never been an eloquent speaker. He prayed that his words would reflect his sincerity.

"Annie..."

"Do you two want to join us?" Charlotte stood beside them, her chipper voice competing against the sounds of the howling wind and crackling fire.

Annie tucked the quilt more tightly beneath her. "I appreciate the thought, Charlotte, but I'm still trying to get warm."

"Maybe later." Caleb wanted—needed—this opportunity to talk to Annie.

Charlotte returned to the table, and Caleb prayed for courage. "Annie, I need to talk to you about that day."

"Caleb..."

He threaded his fingers through his hair and lowered his voice. "I need you to understand that I didn't want to rob wagons or stagecoaches."

She slipped him a questioning glance, and he took a deep breath and attempted to clarify his statement. "We mainly robbed stagecoaches, but we also robbed lone travelers, a mercantile here and there, and whatever other opportunity presented itself."

Caleb detested the admission that rolled off his tongue. Had he really been a thief? A kidnapper? An outlaw?

"You don't have to tell me these things."

"Please, Annie. It's necessary. Not to make excuses for what I did, but to show you that by God's grace, I'm not that man anymore. You have to believe that." The hesitancy lingered, and he wrestled with where to begin.

A slight nod of her head encouraged him to continue.

"My ma died giving birth to me," he whispered. "The last words out of her mouth were that she wanted to name me Caleb, or so that's what my pa said."

He could see only the back of the chair where John Mark sat. From the sounds of it, he and Charlotte were immersed in their game. Relief flooded Caleb. He didn't want his brother and sister to hear about his life before becoming their brother.

"I thought you were an Eliason? You have me completely confused."

"I wasn't always an Eliason. I have an older brother named Cain. He's three years older than me and just like my pa. Not Reverend Solomon, but the pa I had before I became an Eliason."

Caleb paused to again make certain Charlotte and John Mark couldn't hear him. "Anyhow, Pa was heavy into drinking and didn't care who he hurt in order to have what he wanted. He was a mean man and an outlaw. He would take us on his jobs sometimes and I think Cain took pride in learning the tricks of Pa's trade."

The story weighed on him, and he pondered whether he'd really lived that life at all. Or if it was merely a bad dream.

"I'm thankful I don't remember much of Pa or those times, only that I didn't want to be like him and I hated accompanying him on his jobs. He died when I was eight and Cain was eleven. Most boys want to be just like their pa, but I never did."

Chapter Twenty-Four

NOT ONLY WAS CALEB *not* an Eliason, but he was an orphan? His father had been a horrible man, and apparently, he had a brother who was just like his father. Annie closed her eyes and attempted to imagine the life Caleb had led so long ago. She struggled to comprehend the new information.

Caleb stared absently into the fire, his voice low and restrained. "After he died, we went to an orphanage for a while. The lady there kept telling us that someone would come and adopt us, but we knew it wasn't true. No one wanted a Ryerson boy. We were from a bad seed and no one adopts that kind of youngster. Even I knew that."

"Caleb, if this is too painful to recall…"

"No, Annie, I need to share this with you. You have to know." He sighed. "Pa had a reputation in town no one wished to emulate. For anyone to want to adopt a child that came from him, they'd have to be crazy, especially since Cain was just like him and folks assumed I was, too. Cain learned from an early age that if he did things a certain way, he'd escape consequences. He and Roy kidnapped someone once in Colorado." Caleb winced. "He met Roy in a saloon. Roy was a few years older, and even though Cain was too young to be frequenting a saloon, he looked older than he was, so no one questioned him."

If only Annie had known. Known his past. Known the odds against him. "They kidnapped someone?"

"And never got caught. The victim didn't survive."

"How long did you stay in the orphanage?"

Annie couldn't imagine living in an orphanage. She couldn't imagine her parents passing away when she was a youngster.

"A couple of years. The headmistress disliked children, especially Cain and me. I've never met a harsher or more hateful woman. So Cain persuaded me to escape with him, said he promised Pa he'd look after me."

Tears pricked Annie's eyes. *If only I had been quicker to ask for the entire story instead of being judgmental and making hasty conclusions.*

Her voice wavered, "So you left the orphanage?"

"We left during the night unnoticed. Cain always escaped punishment until..." Caleb paused and peered at Charlotte and John Mark, who remained engaged in their game. "Until we robbed your family. You see, Annie, some orphanages have nice people working there; this one didn't. I was never so glad to leave in all my life. There was no love there and no compassion. It was as though the employees had been forced to work there, and they took that bitterness out on us."

Annie's heart ached. Caleb had never known his mother, had an unloving and odious father, and received no love, much less attention, at the orphanage. No wonder he followed the only family he had left when that family member demanded it.

"I could have stayed at the orphanage, but it's strange. As mean as Cain was, I loved him. I looked up to him and wanted to please him. When he said 'let's go', I went. For all his faults, he seemed so wise, at least to a young boy like me. When he wanted seconds at the supper table at the orphanage, the staff told him there wasn't any food left. It was that way a lot—there never seemed to be enough food. Cain didn't take 'no' for an answer. He took the bowl of the child beside him—just traded his bowl for that child's bowl."

As if lost in the memory, Caleb stopped and looked down at his hands.

"Caleb?"

"I was just remembering things I haven't remembered in a long time."

"I'm so sorry. For all you went through."

"I want to tell you, not for your pity, but so that you know why I did the things I did. I don't want to hide anything from you anymore."

"But if it's too painful to recall..."

The pain in his eyes grieved her. How could she have believed the worst about him?

"After Cain and I left the orphanage, we begged for money on the streets. One day, Cain told me that we needed to go out West because that's where the gold was. We needed to earn some money first, though, so we could afford horses and other supplies for the trip." He ran his fingers over the scar on his right hand. "That's how this happened."

It was Annie's turn to gasp. "I feel awful now thinking you received the scar from a botched robbery or knife fight or something. But that's not the case, is it?"

"No, not the case at all. Cain and I worked for a man who was a blacksmith. If my pa ever had a man who resembled him in dishonesty and lack of integrity, it would be this man. His name was Mr. Yager. He favored Cain but was as mean as they came and had no qualms about letting that meanness show. We were assigned some difficult work, stuff only men should do. I worked my hardest for Mr. Yager, but it was never enough. To earn his respect was something I endeavored to do." Caleb nodded toward Charlotte and John Mark. "They don't know about all this. No one does, except Pa...and you. Ma knows some, but not all of it."

"Thank you, Caleb, for trusting me enough to tell me."

"One day, Mr. Yager asked me to do something I couldn't do. No matter how hard I tried, I couldn't do it. I wasn't strong enough. That's when he found it fitting to punish me."

Annie cringed when Caleb confirmed her suspicions.

"Mr. Yager burned my hand as a punishment. Sometimes, I relive that pain searing into my flesh, and...I've never felt anything so painful."

"And you rescued Stuart, despite the fact you could have been burned even worse?"

"Never a hesitation on Stuart. Never."

Guilt and remorse washed over her. To think she had judged this man as a callous criminal. Without having given him a chance to explain himself, without watching him risk his life for the life of another, without really knowing him, she had imagined the worst.

"I am so sorry, Caleb. I'm sorry about your hand and about the life you lived before coming to Willow Falls."

※

Her words emboldened him. Encouraged him to share with her the most difficult part of his past. The part that included her. His pulse quickened and he spoke before he could change his mind.

"We started robbing stagecoaches and wagons when I was about twelve, and the last robbery was your wagon train when I was fourteen. In those two years, I saw the worst side of humanity that a young boy can see. Cain and Roy showed no mercy, especially Roy. Cain was bad enough, but Roy...he was just plain evil. His pa had died in prison and he was destined to a life of crime."

Charlotte and John Mark were trading witty barbs, hopefully ignoring the conversation between Caleb and Annie.

"Please don't think less of me for everything I've told you."

"I don't. I respect you more for sharing your painful past."

"I honestly didn't think I had a choice that day we robbed you. Now I know there is always a choice."

Chapter Twenty-Five

When Caleb finished, Annie sought to mention the words weighing heavily on her mind. "Caleb, there's something I need to tell you about that day. Something I didn't realize until Doc Garrett mentioned it after the fire."

"Yes?"

Could she maintain her composure while thanking him for saving the lives of her mother and sister? For alerting Doc Garrett to the situation? "That day, a doc..."

Her words were interrupted when John Mark scooted his chair from the table, and he and Charlotte wandered over to where Annie and Caleb sat. "Looks like the storm has cleared," said John Mark.

Charlotte placed her hands on her hips. "We need to return home posthaste before John Mark gets hungry and finishes eating all your crackers and crusts of bread."

John Mark playfully jabbed his sister. "Let's not lollygag. We need to leave before Charlotte prattles on and continues to share her gibberish with us. Me? Eat all of Caleb's food? Pshaw. I wouldn't get my fill anytime soon with the slim pickins' here."

"My gibberish? Really, John Mark. For pretending you don't appreciate vocabulary, nor those who fastidiously study it, your use of it is improving."

John Mark's mouth fell open, and Charlotte declared herself the winner in the most recent debate. "Have I rendered you speechless?"

"Before you two have another of your squabbles, let's retrieve the horses, John Mark." Caleb paused and faced Annie. "Much obliged if we could continue this conversation later."

Their eyes met and she nodded in agreement. There was still much that needed to be said.

The wind had calmed, the snow had stopped, and the evening was clear. The abundant snow on the ground, including tall drifts, were the only indication a blizzard had swept through the area.

While grateful to be nearing the Eliason home, Annie regretted she and Caleb didn't have the chance to continue their discussion.

School resumed the following day. While no opportunity presented itself for him and Annie to continue their talk last night after supper, Caleb offered to accompany her home after school.

And she had accepted.

Now Caleb stood before her desk as she prepared to leave. He fiddled with the brim of his hat and shifted his feet. Never had he shared so much about himself as he had yesterday. What must she think of him? She said she respected him for sharing about his past and that she was sorry for the life he lived, but did she believe he had changed?

Could they rekindle their friendship?

Should he have been so forthright with divulging nearly everything about himself? Insecurity flooded through him.

"Caleb, there's something I need to tell you."

He braced himself for the unknown and attempted to ascertain the emotions in the depths of her pretty eyes. "Yes?"

"Doc Garrett mentioned something after the fire. Something for which I'm indebted to you for."

Annie was indebted to him for something? After all the pain he caused her?

"After..." she took a deep breath. "After the robbery, we weren't sure if my ma would survive. The turmoil caused her to go into labor."

She squeezed her eyes shut. Was she recalling that day?

"Annie, I'm sorry."

"I—we—weren't sure Ma or the baby would survive. We knew if a doctor didn't arrive soon, we may lose them both. I felt so helpless. So powerless. The women did what they could, but we didn't know if it would be enough. We thought it a miracle when Doc Garrett arrived from nowhere." She paused. "But he didn't come from nowhere. It was you who sent him."

Caleb stared at the floor. The vivid memory rushed to the forefront of his mind. "I couldn't bear the thought of you losing your ma in childbirth the way I lost mine. I rode through Willow Falls like a madman searching for a doctor."

"And in doing so, you saved their lives. Doc Garrett told me Stuart was the fourth life you'd saved. Then he proceeded to share a story about a woman and her child and a man who'd been shot, and how you saved their lives by fetching him."

"It was the least I could do on account of the mess I'd made."

"Thank you for saving them." Tears shimmered in her eyes and he took a step toward her.

"But if I hadn't been robbing..."

"That's how you were caught, isn't it?"

"Yes. I was arrested, but the judge and several of the townsfolk, the reverend included, gave me a second chance. When I found you in the wagon that day, pleading with me not to hurt your family and not to take the cash inside that box...I can't imagine being in your place. Having someone climb into the back of your wagon and pilfer through your personal belongings, three men threatening the lives of those you care about..."

Annie shuddered. "The fear of not knowing if we would survive was unimaginable. The memories for the longest time were unrelenting. Worrying about Ma and knowing the heartache that would come to Mrs. DeGroot and her daughter should Mr. DeGroot not survive..."

Caleb's gut twisted. How many other people's lives were ruined at the hands of him, Cain, and Roy? The amount of times they interrupted the lives of the innocent and left them to pick up the pieces in the wake of destruction.

No matter how much he wanted it to not be so, the grief he caused would persist in the memories of those he hurt.

A barrage of emotions welled within Annie, and her throat tightened. Would enough time ever pass until the memories were forgotten?

One of the men who caused her, her family, and her friends pain stood before her now. A man repentant of his actions; a man who heroically saved the lives of others. A man who needed to hear her words of forgiveness.

Caleb took a step closer to her. "I never meant to hurt you." He lifted his hand and tenderly caressed her cheek with his thumb.

His touch caused her heart to skitter and the feelings she once had for him threatened to resurface. Pain lingered in his expression as his eyes searched hers.

"Please, Annie," he said, his voice husky with emotion. "Please forgive me for that day."

The words came from deep within her heart; words of truth. Words she'd wanted to say since the fire. "I forgive you."

Caleb blew out a deep breath and his shoulders slumped. "Thank you, Annie."

Chapter Twenty-Six

CALEB, WITH CHARLOTTE IN tow, offered to take Annie home on Tuesday for the upcoming Thanksgiving holiday. The weather finally cooperated and the snow from the blizzard two weeks prior had melted, leaving no sign of being replaced anytime soon.

Things had improved between Annie and Caleb, and they began to slowly rebuild their friendship. With the past behind them, there was no place to move but forward.

Busying herself with packing her carpetbag and penning a diary entry, Annie almost didn't hear Lydie announce Caleb's arrival.

"Hello, Annie."

Warmth filled her chest. "Hello, Caleb."

The moment was interrupted by Charlotte's proclamation. "I'm going to be slightly delayed. Perhaps you'd like to escort Miss Ledbetter on a stroll while I tend to preparations."

"Don't dally, Charlotte. We need to reach Nelsonville before sundown." He offered his arm to Annie. "Shall we?"

The winter sun shone brightly, and from a bare tree branch, a robin chirped. They ambled along the road in comfortable silence.

At the top of the ridge not far from the house, they stopped. "If you look through those trees, you can see my place. Never thought I'd own a home and a fair-sized plot of land."

Annie directed her gaze where he pointed. From her peripheral, she saw his satisfied smile.

He faced her then and took her hands in his. "I'm glad things are better between us."

"Me too."

Caleb caressed the back of her hand with his thumb and leaned closer. Her breath caught. Would he kiss her? She remembered that day in the schoolhouse when their future held so much promise. Was it possible to return to that again?

"Caleb? Annie?" Charlotte's voice echoed through the still air.

"Reckon we should get you to Nelsonville." Caleb let go of one of her hands, but his right remained holding hers as they meandered back toward the house.

Annie glimpsed his hand with its raised scar. How could someone have been so cruel as to abuse another in that manner? The torment Caleb withstood at the hands of his father, brother, and Mr. Yager was unconscionable. How had he grown to be such a gentle man with a tender heart?

When they reached the Ledbetter home hours later, Sadie's face, nose pressed up against the window, drew Annie's attention.

"Sadie's been waiting for us."

A few minutes later, Sadie darted out the front door to greet them. "Annie!"

Annie lifted her sister and swung her around. "I have missed you so much, Sadie Girl."

"I've missed you even more."

Annie set her sister down and planted a kiss atop her head. "Are you sure about that?"

"Very sure." Sadie offered a near-toothless grin.

"Have you grown while I was away? You seem taller." Annie took a step back and eyed her sister with suspicion. "You're not supposed to grow when I'm not here."

Sadie giggled. "I maybe grew just a little bit." She held up her forefinger and her thumb to show a small space between them to accentuate her point.

"Sadie, do you remember Caleb and his sister, Charlotte?"

Caleb took a step forward and shook Sadie's hand. "Nice to meet you again, ma'am."

Sadie giggled again. "I'm not a ma'am, I'm just a little girl!"

Caleb chuckled. Sadie was a miniature Annie in appearance and charisma. Her long blonde hair was fixed in two braids and she had the same deep green eyes. She was petite, small for her age, with thin arms and a wispy body. Charlotte stood next to Sadie and dwarfed her by a foot.

So this was the girl who almost didn't make it through her birth. Time passed quickly. While he was attempting to start over in his life, Sadie was just beginning hers.

"Annie, thank you so much for bringing my new friend for a visit. Would you like to see the new baby puppies?"

Sadie clasped Charlotte's hand and pulled her toward the barn.

"I love puppies," declared Charlotte, following Sadie.

Mrs. Ledbetter emerged from the house. "I was wondering what all this commotion was about. Annie, we've missed you something terrible." She hugged her daughter. "It's not the same without you here, especially when you weren't able to come home these past few weekends due to the weather."

"I've missed you too, Ma. You remember Caleb from the ice cream social?"

"It's a pleasure to see you again. Would you both care for some supper?"

"I'd be much obliged, thank you." Caleb followed Annie and Mrs. Ledbetter into the house. While he'd met Annie's family at the ice cream social, no recollection occurred as to when he'd seen them during the robbery. The woman with child, the man tending her, and the young boy beside them were a blur in his memory.

Charlotte bustled in with Sadie and took a place at the table beside Caleb.

Mrs. Ledbetter prepared a plate for the three of them. "We've already eaten. Walter and Zeb left on an errand but should be back any minute. I appreciate you bringing Annie home, Caleb. She and Zeb both speak highly of you," Mrs. Ledbetter remarked after Caleb blessed the meal. "I recall that your pa is the reverend in Willow Falls. What type of work do you do?"

"I do a lot of odd jobs. I've been saving money to expand my ranch. So far I've done pretty well with the few cattle I have, but I hope to continue to purchase more as the funds allow."

Caleb's words sounded odd to his own ears. Was it really true that his dream of owning a ranch was getting closer to fruition with each passing day?

"*He* brought you home?" The first words from Zeb's mouth as he entered the home attested to the fact that Annie had spoken to him about Caleb's past.

Caleb extended his hand and Zeb reluctantly shook it. "If you have a minute, Zeb, I'd be much obliged if you could show me that river where all the good fishing is."

"It's frozen over. Still too cold for several months yet to fish."

Caleb recalled the first time he'd met Zeb. His protectiveness reminded Caleb of his own watchful eye over Charlotte. The second time they'd met, he and Zeb realized how much they had in common and became fast friends. He hoped this third time would mirror the latter, but Zeb's tone and wary expression indicated otherwise.

"Would you be willing to show me the river? It would also give me a chance to speak to you about a matter of importance."

Zeb scrutinized Caleb, much as he had the first time they met. Finally, he spoke. "All right. I'll saddle the horses, but we'll need to hurry. It's close to nightfall."

The ride to the river took less than ten minutes. Zeb's words were few until they stopped. "You need to know that if you hurt my sister..."

Caleb held a hand up. "I would never hurt Annie."

"But you were there that day when the wagon train was robbed. She told me how she recognized you. Your scar." Zeb balled his fists at his sides and raised his voice. "Why has Annie allowed you to bring her to Nelsonville after what you did? Why are you free to walk the streets of Willow Falls? Or has no one ever caught you? Is that it?"

The tension in Caleb's neck and shoulders increased. "Zeb, I appreciate your concern for Annie. I'm the same way with Charlotte." He paused. Where to begin? "Yes, I am one of the men who robbed your wagon train. And yes, I'm a free man. Annie has allowed me to bring her to Nelsonville because we've reconciled."

"Reconciled? How? A free man? Why?" Zeb took a step toward him.

"I'll explain everything."

"See that you do."

Caleb figured Zeb a force to be reckoned with, despite his thin and wiry stature.

He began at the beginning of his story. "My brother, Cain, and I..."

Once Caleb finished, Zeb narrowed his eyes at him. "So, you're telling me you never wanted to be involved in the gang?"

"Right."

"And you're telling me you're no longer an outlaw?"

"Yes. Haven't been for over seven years."

Zeb kicked a pebble on the ground. "That's quite the yarn."

"Not a yarn. The truth. I will never return to that life again. God has given me a second chance. And I would never do anything to hurt Annie. I care about her."

Zeb rubbed the back of his neck. "Reckon there are only two choices here. To believe you and leave the past where it belongs or to not believe you. It's difficult for a man to know what to do."

"I hope you'll choose the former."

Zeb sighed. "I've made mistakes myself and need God's grace every day. Since Annie believes and has forgiven you, I'll do the same." He gestured toward the river. "This here Nelsonville River is the best in these parts for fishing. Come summer, what do you say about catching us some trout?"

"I can taste it now."

Zeb chuckled. "Did I ever tell you about the fish I caught last year? It was this long." He used his hands to indicate the length of the fish.

"How long was it the first time you told the story?"

"About half that length."

"Did I ever tell you about the fish I caught a few years back?"

After Caleb and Charlotte left for Willow Falls early the next morning, Annie accompanied Zeb for a ride into Nelsonville to purchase a few items for their Thanksgiving meal from the mercantile.

"I spoke with Caleb yesterday about the robbery."

"Did he tell you he was the one who fetched the doc?"

Zeb shook his head. "He didn't mention that."

"If it hadn't been for him, I shudder to think of what may have happened to Ma and Sadie. And Mr. DeGroot."

"I'm indebted to him for that. Guess I never gave it much thought about how the doc arrived so quickly." Zeb stopped the wagon in front of the mercantile. "Ma wants us to see if there's any mail while we're in town. She's expecting a letter."

Mr. Ackerman, always his exuberant self, greeted them at the post office. "Annie, such a pleasure to see you. How have you been?"

"I've been well. And I hear congratulations are in order for you and Mrs. Burns."

"Ah, yes. Mrs. Burns. I've never known a more exquisite and comelier woman." A rose-colored blush covered his wrinkled face. "I plan to make her my wife next summer."

"Congratulations."

"Thank you. I've waited a long time for true love."

Annie's eye caught Zeb's and her brother grinned. "I've never known you to be such a romantic fellow."

"Well, I have been known to pen a poem or two. Mrs. Burns says they're eloquent and well-written." Mr. Ackerman handed Annie a letter. "This here came for your ma. Likely it's the one she's been waiting for."

"Thank you. Will you move to Willow Falls after you and Mrs. Burns marry, or will she move here?"

"We've debated that topic. For now, it seems most advantageous for Mrs. Burns to move here. Of course, she'll miss all of her friends in Willow Falls—that woman is highly-regarded and esteemed there—but she says she'll have no problem making friends here. And I hear congratulations are in order for you and Hetty, Zeb."

"They are. We plan to marry next summer as well."

"Perhaps we could have a double wedding. Saves on having to invite folks twice."

Zeb's terrified expression caused Annie to giggle. "That suggestion certainly has merit," she said, amused at the predicament in which her brother found himself.

After ho-humming for a few seconds, Zeb answered with what anyone else would view as confidence. But Annie knew her brother well. Mr. Ackerman's words alarmed him.

"I'll see what Hetty thinks. You know how womenfolk plan weddings for months on end. She may already have every detail organized, and who am I to argue with her?"

Well said, Zeb. Well said.

Chapter Twenty-Seven

Sunday evening after returning to Willow Falls, Annie sat down and penned an entry in her diary:

Dear Diary,
There is much to tell from this past weekend. Because of a break in storms, I was able to finally travel to Nelsonville. Thanksgiving with my family reminded me once again of all that I am grateful for.

Zeb and Caleb settled things between them. I pray my parents don't discover Caleb was one of the outlaws. It would worry them both to no end.

Caleb and I have spent more time together as of late. Our camaraderie has returned.

<hr>

Lydie arranged food in the basket. "Please tell Mrs. Waite we will stop by after church on Sunday for a visit. Your pa has an idea that might work for her living arrangement. Mr. and Mrs. Talbot have an extra bedroom in their home. They are willing to take her in if she'll agree."

"Hopefully she's amenable to the suggestion. She can't continue living there by herself." Caleb took the basket from Lydie and carried it toward the door. "I plan to chop some more wood for her while we're there."

"And I'll mend the curtains and do some cleaning," said Annie.

"Thank you, both of you. I know she'll appreciate all you do for her."

Annie and Caleb arrived at Mrs. Waite's house to find the woman resting in a chair by a waning fire. The shawl bunched around her shoulders and a thin blanket on her lap failed to keep the elderly woman's teeth from chattering.

I'll have it warm in here in no time." Caleb set about tending to the fire while Annie cared for Mrs. Waite.

"Mrs. Waite, have you eaten today?" Annie kneeled to the woman's height.

"Not yet. I'm just too weak to prepare regular meals." Her usually bright eyes were dull and her thin skin an unhealthy pallor. Prominent cheekbones protruded from her angular face, and she stared absently into the fire.

"Should we fetch Doc Garrett?"

Mrs. Waite shook her head, the motion appearing to exhaust her. "He was here yesterday. What with losing my dear husband so recently and all my aches and pains, there's not much he can do."

Annie covered Mrs. Waite with the quilt she'd brought from the Eliason home and prepared a sandwich from the contents of the basket Lydie had provided.

"You two are just such precious folks to care for me." Mrs. Waite took a bite of the sandwich, slowly chewing, as if every movement was an effort.

"We were concerned for you."

The woman washed the bite of sandwich down with the milk Annie poured for her. "It's so cold and lonely here. When my husband was alive, it was never this forlorn. I miss him." Tears glistened in her eyes. "He's been gone four months and three days."

Annie wrapped an arm around Mrs. Waite's shoulders. "I'm so sorry."

"What I wouldn't give to have him back, even for an hour." She paused and bit her lip. "We had many wonderful years together, but they went too fast. It does my heart good to see you young folks so in love." She dabbed at her nose with her handkerchief. "Appreciate every moment you have and don't allow disagreements to fester."

Annie and Caleb traded a glance. Mrs. Waite's words were full of wisdom.

While the elderly woman finished eating, Annie cleaned the humble home and mended the curtain. Caleb chopped more wood and ensured the woman had an ample supply until she moved into the Talbot home.

"My parents will be here after church to visit with you. Before we go, is there anything else you need?"

Caleb's tender care of the woman impressed upon Annie. More than ever, she realized her error in believing he was the same man who had robbed the wagon train.

A week later as Caleb drove Annie, Charlotte, and John Mark home from school, an idea formed in his mind. "Would you care to join me for some ice skating?"

"Ice skating?"

He was amused by Annie's stunned expression. "Have you ever ice skated?"

She shook her head. "I haven't. Although Hetty told me how enjoyable it is."

Charlotte piped up. "You'll take great delight in ice skating, Miss Ledbetter. Ma and Pa discovered it while courting and still skate each year when the pond freezes over. They taught us several years ago. Can't say that everyone is as competent on ice skates as some of us are, though."

"Miss Ledbetter, you'll be proud to know I'm about to use our new vocabulary word in a sentence." John Mark paused. "Balderdash, Charlotte! You're such a braggart."

"Not a braggart, John Mark. Just honest, candid, and forthright."

A smile lit Annie's voice. "Well done, both of you, for utilizing an assortment of this week's vocabulary words in a sentence."

"Thank you. I do make it my goal to be diligent about ensuring I know how to use each word properly and befittingly in a sentence," Charlotte gloated. She paused as if to wait for John Mark's rebuttal. When there was none, she continued. "So, Miss Ledbetter, would you care to familiarize yourself with the art of ice skating? Caleb would be ecstatic to offer his assistance."

"Ecstatic for certain." Caleb tossed Annie a broad grin. He'd missed these times of playful banter with her. Annie's face flushed a rosy red and the gentle breeze blew a few hairs loose from her bun.

His breath caught and he couldn't help but stare.

"Caleb, you drove right past the pond!" John Mark's panicked voice interrupted Caleb's notice of Annie's beauty.

Charlotte giggled. "Mayhap you ought to concentrate on the road, rather than Miss Ledbetter."

"And perhaps you two forgot we have to retrieve the ice skates from home first. So, Annie, would you care to try ice skating if your ankle no longer pains you?"

"I suppose I'm a bit skeptical. It's not so much the ankle that concerns me, as I rarely have any pain with it now that it's healed. But falling while skating doesn't sound pleasant."

"What if I teach you and stay by your side the entire time? Ma has a pair of skates you can borrow."

"You should try it, Miss Ledbetter," urged John Mark.

"All right. You've all convinced me. I'll try it."

Several minutes later, Caleb and Annie meandered toward the pond, skates in hand. A slight breeze rippled through the otherwise comfortable winter day. Harsh temperatures would arrive within the next several weeks, restricting most outdoor activities, and he aimed to take advantage of the weather and spend as much time with Annie as possible.

Things were progressing well between them. Since reconciling, they spent more time together, and thankfully, had rekindled their relationship. It was almost reminiscent of the days before she discovered his scar—a mutual fondness for each other Caleb hoped would develop into more.

Charlotte and John Mark threw snowballs and chased each other around the nearby trees while Caleb aided Annie in fitting Ma's adjustable wooden skates over her own shoes. He then fitted Pa's skates over his boots.

Annie stood, teetering precariously on the thin metal blades. "Goodness, I'm unsure I'll be able to maintain my balance walking, much less skating."

He extended his arm. "Don't worry, I won't let you fall. And before long, you'll be gliding across the ice."

She giggled at his statement and gripped his arm tightly as if her life depended on it. She tilted her head back, her radiant expression entrancing him. The tip of her nose was bright red from the cold air and he leaned forward to plant a kiss on it. She closed her eyes, and his breath hitched.

A gander around the area confirmed Charlotte and John Mark were preoccupied with who could hit the other with the most snowballs.

Caleb pulled her to him and embraced her, his mouth meeting hers. He hoped she could sense the love and adoration in his heart for her.

They drew apart, his eyes searching her expression. Was it too soon to ask? Too soon to hope for things to progress? He enfolded her hands in his.

"Annie..."

Did she know what he was about to ask?

Charlotte ran toward them and hid behind Caleb. "Save me from Sir Nincompoop!"

"Caleb won't save you, Charlotte. Now quit lollygagging." John Mark dodged around the tree and hurled a snowball, hitting Charlotte in the arm.

"You'll have to excuse me," said Charlotte, "as I must leave now and prepare an arsenal of snowballs to use as recompense on our beloved brother. Are you two ever going to ice skate?"

Charlotte dashed off after John Mark, snowball in hand.

"Those two. I think they'd die of boredom if they didn't have each other to harass." Caleb shifted his feet. He again mustered the courage to ask Annie the question on his mind. "Would you do me the honor of courting me?"

"Caleb..."

"If you say 'no,' I'll understand."

But he wouldn't. Not really. Not when nearly every moment of his day was filled with thinking about her and the possibility of spending his life with her.

"Yes, Caleb, I would be honored to court you." Her uttered words were so quiet, he wondered whether he'd heard them at all.

"May I steal another kiss?"

She examined his handsome face. Rugged. Eyes the color of a summer sky. Blond hair swept over his forehead. He stood so close, she feared if she breathed the moment would end.

"Yes," the words left her mouth in a breathless whisper.

How could she not say 'yes'?

His lips met hers with the gentleness and affirmation of the love that had once again begun to blossom between them.

When the kiss was over, Caleb took a step back and reached again for her hands. "Reckon I'll ask your pa next time for his blessing."

Charlotte reappeared, slowly walking toward them with a cache of snowballs cradled in her arms. "Are you going to teach Miss Ledbetter how to skate, Caleb?" she asked, inserting herself into the conversation. Her brow furrowed. "You two dawdle more than John Mark does."

John Mark sauntered toward them with his own hoard of snowballs. "You and Tobias will be like Caleb and Miss Ledbetter someday, Charlotte. Holding hands and pondering whether or not to ice skate."

"You take that back, John Mark Solomon Eliason. I will *never* hold Tobias' hands. Nor will I ponder whether or not to skate with him." Charlotte shivered in disgust to add effect to the seriousness of her words.

Annie and Caleb shared a laugh at Charlotte's announcement before stepping onto the ice. He skated backward while holding her hands and guiding her forward.

She willed her feet to cooperate as she attempted to avoid falling. She cautiously shuffled her feet, while Caleb steadied her each time she nearly slipped, pulling her to his chest. She rested in his tender embrace before trying again.

"See, Charlotte, that will be just like you and Tobias, only you'll be the one making sure Tobias doesn't slip and fall."

"How repulsive." Charlotte beaned him with a snowball.

Annie laughed at their antics. "Those two are quite amusing. Zeb and I bickered the same way years ago when he was a much more vexatious fellow."

She peered again at the antagonistic siblings while maintaining a firm grip on Caleb's hands. So far she hadn't fallen once, thanks to his vigilance. "I appreciate you persuading me to try ice skating. We'll have to do it again sometime."

Chapter Twenty-Eight

Annie returned to Nelsonville for the weeklong Christmas vacation. Caleb and Charlotte took her home each weekend between Thanksgiving and Christmas when the weather allowed, and Caleb and Zeb continued to build their friendship while making more definitive plans for fishing and the building of Zeb's home.

Two days after Christmas, Mr. and Mrs. DeGroot came for a visit.

Ma invited the DeGroots into the house. "May I get you some coffee?"

"That would be delightful." Edith DeGroot removed her bonnet and coat and sat at the table in one of the chairs Ma offered.

"Seems we may yet receive an adequate amount of snow," said Pa, settling across from Horace DeGroot and Zeb.

Annie and Ma joined them at the table while Sadie rushed off to the barn to play with her puppies.

"We need the moisture. Seems a drier year this year overall," said Horace.

He and Pa continued to discuss the weather and cattle prices until the discussion shifted to Annie and Zeb.

"Annie, it's good to see you, dear. How do you like teaching in Willow Falls?" Edith's severe countenance hadn't changed in all these years.

"I quite enjoy it now, but at first I wasn't sure. They have a tradition in Willow Falls where the students play harmless pranks on the new teacher the first day, and I had the privilege of having an old student and a calf named Louie in my classroom as part of those pranks."

Edith's hand flew to her bosom. "Well, I never. That sounds dreadful! I'm glad you survived that first day. I'm not sure I would have put up with such nonsense."

"Not only did she survive them, but she has since begun to court the one behind them," teased Zeb.

"And what about you and Hetty?"

Ma clasped her hands together. "Oh, yes. Zeb, do tell Edith and Horace about your upcoming wedding."

"We've set the date for June twentieth."

Annie couldn't resist adding, "They are contemplating a double wedding ceremony with Mr. Ackerman and Mrs. Burns."

"Oh, my, but whyever would you contemplate that?" Edith's expression could be likened to that of one who ate the sourest raspberry.

"Annie and her tomfoolery. Hetty and I declined Mr. Ackerman's request. They'll marry on June thirteenth."

"Congratulations. It's about time you started thinking of settling down." Horace squinted at him. "Do you have a place of your own yet, boy?"

"Yes, Pa and I have been building a home on some land about a quarter of a mile from here."

Pa patted Zeb on the back. "Zeb has been working hard on his new place. I'm proud of him."

"I recall our first home. Remember that, Edith? It was a soddie."

"I do. It wasn't a bad home as far as sod houses went, and it boasted two rooms. It stayed warm in the winter and cool in the summer."

"I reckon I'm thankful for the home we have now," chuckled Horace. "Ain't nothin' fancy, but it beats that old soddie."

"We'll remember the wedding date. We wouldn't want to miss such a momentous occasion." Edith's smile tugged on the permanent frown lines of her severe disposition. "Now, Annie, dear, tell us more about this young man you are courting."

"His name is Caleb. He's the son of Reverend Solomon Eliason and Lydie. I've been boarding with them in Willow Falls."

Edith shot Horace a stuffy glance. "It's difficult to remember those days when we were courting, isn't it, Horace?"

"I don't remember them at all, Edith. Reckon, it's been thirty years and then some since that day."

"Time sure does have a way of passing us by." Ma's voice was a welcome sound in the midst of Edith's harsher tone. "Before we know it, Sadie will be old enough to go courting."

Horace folded his arms. "What do you think of this Caleb fellow?"

"Maria and I approve of him. He seems strong in his faith and a hard worker. He's been working on building a ranch for himself."

"You mentioned that he was the one who was a part of the pranks at Willow Falls, not that I can understand why any adult in their right mind would consent to such a thing." Edith shook her head.

Annie did her best to remain patient with Edith's condescending tone. She'd never much cared for the woman or her husband. Judgmental and pompous were the first words that came to mind when she thought of the couple. Not that she shared that with Ma, who always saw something good in everyone. Annie sat up straighter in her chair, lest Edith accuse her of slouching.

"It's a tradition in Willow Falls, as silly as it is, and by having an adult in charge, it prevents the tradition from getting out of hand."

"Pshaw. Absurd, if you ask me," said Edith.

"But no one did ask you, Edith, now did they?" Horace picked at a scab on his thumb.

"I'm sure you think the same, Horace. I'm just the first to say it."

"Mebbe so," muttered Horace.

Annie struggled to retain her pleasant disposition. *I wish I could be like Ma, not allowing my ire when Edith and Horace are in our company.*

"How is Helvina?" Ma was always adept at charitably changing the topic of discussion.

"She's doing well. She and her husband recently had their fourth child." Edith beamed. "There's nothing like being a grandmother. It's a shame you haven't yet had that privilege, Maria."

Ma graciously ignored Edith's remark. "Are they still living in Elmer Creek?"

"Yes, and Elmer Creek has been growing lately, much like Willow Falls."

Horace peered from the left to the right. "Just makin' sure the young'un ain't within earshot. We have something we thought you might ought to see. When they built the new jail, I was the one who moved the box of important items from the former one. Out of our concern for Annie, we thought it prudent to tell you what I found. It's one of the reasons we came for a visit."

"That and we wanted to bless you with our company," Edith added.

Pa leaned on the table and steepled his fingers. "Go ahead."

Horace stood and reached into the pocket of his trousers for a crumpled piece of paper. "I came across this old wanted poster that I found in the box. Never thought much of it until Edith told me about Annie teaching in Willow Falls." Unfolding the yellowed paper, he read: "C. Ryerson: wanted for multiple robberies; C.A. Ryerson: wanted for armed robbery, kidnapping, murder, and attempted murder; and R. Fuller: wanted for several counts of armed robbery, kidnapping, murder, and attempted murder."

He pressed the creases in the folded paper. "This is an old paper and likely the first one printed as it doesn't contain their full names, but it does contain sketches of the men and a physical description of each."

Annie's heart drummed in her chest and she willed her countenance to remain stoic.

"These are the ones who robbed us that day seven years ago, and there's a chance one is in Willow Falls." Edith's haughty air did little to assuage Annie's fears.

Ma gasped. "To this day?"

"From my understanding, C.A. Ryerson is serving time in the U.S. Penitentiary at Laramie City. They caught him after the robbery and sentenced him to life in prison. R. Fuller was shot in a shootout with the law."

Pa nodded. "I remember hearing something about that. After the incident, we wanted to put it all behind us and had faith that justice would be done. The memories have been bad, as you both know. We figured the best way to attempt to forget those memories was to not give the men involved any more thought, even though it was difficult."

"It has been difficult," agreed Edith. "I can't tell you how many nights I lost sleep wondering if they were going to come after us again. And to see my beloved Horace shot before my eyes. I shan't ever forget that day."

Pa's brow furrowed. "What happened to the third man?"

"That's what I need to speak with you about." Horace scowled, his double chin becoming more prominent. "From what I heard, the third man was never caught. He's still on the loose. If he had any smarts about him, he wouldn't stay anywhere near where the robbery took place, but with your daughter off by herself in another town, Edith and I thought you should be aware."

"We just assumed Annie would be safe since she never travels alone and is staying with a nice family in Willow Falls," Ma said.

"And surely, as you mentioned, Horace, the fugitive wouldn't be so foolish as to stay in the area," added Pa.

"I would certainly hope he wouldn't stick around, but even so, it's still wise for Annie to heed my advice and use caution when traveling between here and Willow Falls. I'll pass this around so you all can see the men. Like I said, the first two ain't gonna be a problem since one is dead and the other is spending the rest of his life in prison. But that third man..." Horace gritted his teeth.

Annie held her breath as the room started to spin. Her heart pounded loudly in her ears. Zeb met her gaze, the apprehension in his expression unmistakable.

Lord, please, don't let Pa and Ma recognize Caleb from the poster.

Edith's high-pitched voice added to Annie's trepidation. "It's a miscarriage of justice this man was never caught and convicted of those robberies. It would suit us well to look at the poster and make sure we are aware of his appearance should we ever come across him. Especially you, Annie."

"Perhaps he's long gone and in another state or territory by now. We can only hope." Ma's gentle voice contrasted Edith's harsh tone.

"That could be, but these criminals sometimes aren't too bright. 'Sides, I've always prided myself in erring on the side of caution. Reckon I keep thinking about that day. I can describe that R. Fuller from a mile away. You don't take a bullet and not remember who's responsible. You don't ever forget those hard-as-stone eyes. The other man, the one with the gun and the one I assume is serving time in prison, I'm not so sure I could recognize him, or the younger fellow who searched the wagons if I saw them on the street. But maybe I could." Horace shook the paper causing it to rattle with an uncanny eeriness.

Pa stroked his beard, as he always did when in deep thought. "Our first priority is that Annie is safe. While you do travel between the towns with Zeb or Caleb, there are times in the school day you're likely by your lonesome. I don't know that as an unmarried woman teaching in a school in a different town, it's safe when a criminal has been on the loose for seven years."

"But, Pa, I love teaching in Willow Falls."

Ma rested a hand on Annie's arm. "We know that, Annie, but we don't want anything to happen to you."

"I don't think anything will," argued Annie. "This man hasn't been seen for seven years. Why would he suddenly reappear? That doesn't make sense."

A devious expression crossed Edith's face. "Unless he doesn't think he'll get caught."

What would Annie do if they decided she could no longer teach in Willow Falls? The DeGroots had a way of bringing rain to a picnic. She peered from Edith to Horace and willed her voice not to tremble as she attempted to change the topic. "Are you preparing for spring planting, Mr. DeGroot?"

"Why would you ask such an absurd and unrelated question while we are discussing an important matter?" Edith shook her head and grimaced, causing her pinched face to become even more pinched.

"I was just thinking about spring and how pleasant it will be to start planting the garden and such. Besides, all this talk of the outlaws from that day dredges up memories I'd rather forget."

"I tend to agree with Annie. What's the use of rehashing this matter?" Zeb leaned back in his chair.

Edith drummed the table with her gnarled fingers. "Goodness gracious, child, we're not even thinking of spring planting yet."

"Not in the least," Horace agreed.

Pa reached for the well-worn paper in Horace's hand. "Can I see the wanted poster?"

Annie held her breath.

"This man looks familiar." Pa stared at the yellowed paper. "I can't say that about the other two, but this one here, this C. Ryerson...he's familiar."

He passed the paper to Ma. "I've seen him before, too."

"Maybe he's visited Nelsonville. If so, that's even more frightening." Edith shook her head. "Best we alert the sheriff. Perhaps call a town meeting."

"Annie, may I speak to you in the barn please?"

Annie shuddered. "Yes, Pa," her own voice squeaked in her ears.

"Do excuse us, please, Edith and Horace." Pa stood and pushed the chair toward the table with a little too much force.

"Surely Annie doesn't know him." Edith's eyes grew large and she gave Annie one of her famous condescending glares.

"I'm not sure," said Pa. "But it's best to exercise caution and speak with our daughter about the importance of staying away from this man, *whoever* he is."

Annie slipped into her coat and boots and followed Pa to the barn. She dreaded what her father would say.

Lord, please, You tell me that You will never leave me. Please don't leave me now.

Chapter Twenty-Nine

Pa sent Sadie to the house and handed Annie the wanted poster. Below the sketch of Caleb it read: *C. Ryerson, age fourteen, light blond hair, blue eyes, lanky build, six feet tall, wanted for multiple robberies.* Although the sketch of Caleb was from years earlier, the resemblance was striking and she cringed. A chill rippled through her when she viewed the sketch of R. Fuller, the one who shot Mr. DeGroot. The sketch of Cain was frightening, as well. He held no resemblance to Caleb.

"Do you recognize C. Ryerson?" Pa's stringent tone made her flinch. She'd only seen him this angry on one other occasion.

"Pa, I can explain."

"Do you recognize C. Ryerson?"

"I—I do, Pa. C. Ryerson is really Caleb Eliason." Annie choked the words.

"I figured as much when I saw the sketch." Pa flung the poster onto a hay bale and paced the area, hands behind his back as if contemplating his next words.

"Pa..."

"Did you know you are courting an outlaw?"

"Caleb is *not* an outlaw. Yes, he was a part of the robbery that day, but..."

"It says here he is wanted for multiple robberies. I reckon that means the attack on our wagon party was not his first?" Pa retrieved the paper and snapped it, causing a loud crackling noise.

"Yes, he was involved in the robbery. Yes, he robbed some stagecoaches with his brother, but that was in the past. He's not the same man he was."

"Not the same man?" thundered Pa. He shook his head. "You were there that day! Your ma and Sadie almost lost their lives, as did Mr. DeGroot. Out of respect for our guests, we will go back into the house and bid them goodbye. Out of respect for you and our family, I'll not share any of this with them. But I must forbid you to see Caleb again. He's a dangerous criminal and the Willow Falls sheriff needs to be alerted that a wanted man lives in his town." Pa paused. "And we'll need to discuss your position as a teacher in that town as well."

Pa discovered the truth about Caleb in the most awful of ways. If only Annie had told him before he'd had a chance to find out from Edith and Horace.

Annie choked back the sobs. Pa would never change his mind about his decision.

What was she to do? She loved Caleb and now she was forbidden to see him. And Pa mentioned contacting Sheriff Townsend. Nothing could be worse for Caleb than the town of Willow Falls discovering his past. He'd endeavored to start over and forge a new life. Would the townsfolk realize Caleb was nothing like the man who once robbed stagecoaches and wagon trains?

And what of Edith's and Horace's assumptions if they discovered Annie knew Caleb and had courted him? Surely they had to be suspicious when Pa asked to see Annie in the barn.

After their discussion, Annie went for a long walk in the chilly December air. She didn't know how or if Pa had attempted to smooth over the situation with the DeGroots, but if he hadn't, the news would be all over the entire Wyoming Territory by tomorrow.

Annie's restless anxiety plagued her and her stomach ached. An old wanted poster shared by two pretentious people had the possibility of ruining more than just one life.

She'd always believed and known from Scripture that God heard her prayers and answered them according to His will. He was faithful even when His children doubted. But how would God answer her prayers about Caleb, their relationship, and her teaching job in Willow Falls?

The wind whipped around Annie and she pulled her cloak tighter. Soon she'd have to return home and face her father.

But not yet. First, she needed more time to think. And pray.

Annie rounded the corner of the road that led to her parents' home. How many times in the past seven years had she run up and down this road with Zeb on their way to and from school? How many times had they traveled in the wagon or on horseback? The dormant trees, void of leaves and their summer color, eagerly awaited the freshness and new life of spring, which was still several months away. A stray snowflake swirled on the breeze and fell peacefully to the ground. Would things be better in a few months? Or would her life have taken the turn of finality that Pa decided it must take?

Her father had always been protective of his family. Even in the midst of hardship, Pa, with his dedication and determination, ensured those he loved were cared for. Never had she once doubted his love for her. Or his decisions.

Until now.

That night, Annie tossed and turned in a futile attempt at sleep. She prayed for guidance. For words to speak. For a softening of Pa's heart toward Caleb.

The next morning after breakfast, Ma took Sadie to collect eggs and Zeb left to visit Hetty, with a promise he'd speak to Pa about the issue when he returned.

Pa sat at the table across from Annie. Dark circles beneath his eyes and more wrinkles than Annie remembered lined his tired features.

"Annie, you must know how much I love you and how I don't want to be harsh with you, but I must do all I can to protect my family. To protect *you*."

A wave of frustration surged through her, and Annie took a deep breath before responding, "I once felt the same way you do about Caleb. I believed he didn't deserve to freely walk the streets of Willow Falls."

"But since then, he's changed your mind. He coerced you into thinking he's a man of honor."

"Not coerced me, but I do believe him."

"I wish I didn't have to discuss this matter at all. Do you realize the seriousness of Caleb's crimes?"

She fidgeted and wrung her hands together. Had she truly believed her father would never discover the truth about Caleb's past? She'd been naïve in believing it would remain unknown to her parents. "I changed my own mind about Caleb for many reasons."

"And what are those reasons?"

"For one, I had a long discussion with Reverend Solomon. He and his wife, Lydie adopted Caleb after the robbery. Many of the townsfolk and the judge wanted to give him a second chance. Believe me, Pa, when I first discovered Caleb was the one who robbed our wagon party, I reacted the same way you are reacting now." Annie's words tumbled from her mouth, so she attempted to slow her speech. Pa needed to hear each word slowly and clearly. "Caleb helped me when I hurt my leg leaving the school. It was at Doc Garrett's when I noticed the scar on his hand, and I knew right away he was the same one who had stolen the things from our wagon because I'd seen that same scar that day."

She paused to catch her breath.

"After I spoke with Reverend Solomon, the Lord began to open my eyes to see that, yes, while Caleb had committed crimes, he had also, by the grace of God, changed his life into that of a respectable citizen. It took me time to realize this and I regret I didn't do so sooner. Caleb's reputation in the community is one of integrity and honor. He even rescued a boy from a burning home. Remember when I told you about that?"

"I remember. While such an act is commendable, I reckon it doesn't change a man, much like the stripes on a zebra can't be changed."

"But Pa, people *can* change, and they *do*. Reverend Solomon preached about Paul of the New Testament last Sunday."

Pa rested his head in his hands. When had his hair started to gray? He sat up again and folded his arms across his chest. "We all know most courtships lead to marriage. I cannot give you my blessing."

Would hers and Caleb's courtship lead to marriage? No one knew for sure, but if it did, Annie surely wanted Pa's blessing.

"Caleb was the one who fetched the doc for Ma, Sadie, and Horace. He also could have taken our small metal box that held our life's savings in it, but instead, he hid it under some of our other belongings so his brother wouldn't find it."

"That all may be the case, but my decision stands. Please stop courting him, and please ask Reverend Solomon to begin looking for a replacement for you at the school."

"But I love him and I don't want to give up teaching in Willow Falls! Is there nothing I can say to make you change your mind?"

"I'll be in prayer about the situation."

The finality of the matter hung in the air.

Chapter Thirty

Caleb arrived the following day to retrieve Annie. He missed her during the days they'd been apart and couldn't wait to see her again.

But he was not ready for the reception or the news he would receive.

"Hello, Caleb." Tears welled in her eyes.

"Annie?" He took a step forward and opened his arms to her. She shook her head and increased the space between them.

Confused by her reaction to him, Caleb dropped his hands to his sides.

"Hello, Caleb," said Mrs. Ledbetter. "Please, come sit down."

A heaviness stalled in the air. Something wasn't right.

Mr. Ledbetter looked up from his place by the fire where he was cleaning his rifle. He spoke no words but narrowed his eyes.

"Mr. Ledbetter, it's nice to see you again." Maybe he could fix whatever problem occurred in his absence. Had there been a death in Annie's extended family? Had someone been injured? Caleb took a seat.

Mr. Ledbetter avoided Caleb's eye. "Would you please join Zeb in the barn, Sadie?"

"Yes, Pa. Is Charlotte here, Mr. Caleb?"

"She is. She was hoping to see the puppies."

Sadie barely had her coat on before dashing outside.

Mr. Ledbetter spoke again, his tone stern, "I take it you came to fetch Annie and take her back to Willow Falls?"

"Yes, sir."

Surely Annie's father knew his reason for being there.

"I'll get straight to the point, Caleb. Over the Christmas holiday, we discovered some things about you we didn't take kindly to."

Caleb sucked in a deep breath. Who had told Mr. Ledbetter? Annie? Zeb?

"Pa, please…"

"Annie, I understand and respect your position on this matter, but this discussion is between Caleb and me." He stood and joined Caleb at the table. "Is it true that you were a part of the gang that robbed our wagon train?"

Caleb swallowed hard. Mr. Ledbetter did know. "Yes, sir."

"And you weren't apprehended by the law?"

"I was given another chance to make something of my life."

The interrogation from Mr. Ledbetter was almost worse than that day so many years ago in the back of Morton's Mercantile in front of the traveling judge.

"Unbelievable."

The impact of that one word punched him in the gut. He struggled to remain calm.

"I want the courtship broken off immediately."

"But, sir, I love her."

Mr. Ledbetter either didn't hear or chose to ignore him. "Zeb will return Annie to Willow Falls. She will resign as a teacher there once the reverend finds a replacement."

"That would be unjust. She loves teaching."

"I'll not have my Annie's life in danger."

"With all due respect, her life is not in danger. I love her and I would never harm her or allow anyone to harm her." How could he convince Mr. Ledbetter he spoke truth?

"Is that why you allowed your gang to rob our wagon party and put Annie's life in danger?"

"I did all I could to protect her, even then." He tamped down his anger. It would benefit him none to lose his temper. To do so would only confirm Mr. Ledbetter's lowly opinion of him.

"My word stands. I'm sorry you drove all this way, but you may leave now."

Caleb searched the faces of Annie and Mrs. Ledbetter. "Annie?" he whispered.

She said nothing, and his heart ached to see the muted tears that slid down her lovely face.

Annie and Zeb spoke few words on the ride back to Willow Falls. Zeb had tried to convince Pa that Caleb was a changed man as well but to no avail.

Caleb left as Pa had ordered. In the far distance, she saw the back of his wagon and his broad deflated shoulders.

Her heart ached. To not be able to spend time with him again bored a hole in her heart that could never be repaired.

What must Caleb think of her? Did he think she was the one who told her parents about him? He'd spoken of his love for her during the discussion with Pa, but would he still love her and wait for her while a mess that showed no signs of ever being repaired was remedied?

That night, Annie settled into bed, her diary in her hand. While tears blotted the pages and smeared her writing, she continued to pen what was in her heart.

Dear Diary,

The past few days have surely been the worst. Pa has forbidden me to see Caleb. How can one have such an unforgiving heart? But as I ask those words, I must look inward. I too harbored those exact feelings of unforgiveness a short time ago.

Pa wants me to relinquish my teaching position. But alas, I cannot do so. If I am here, I hold on to the flicker of hope that I will someday be able to be reconciled to Caleb. For how can I forget the man I love?

The days passed and the pain in Annie's heart refused to lessen. Although she prayed faithfully, the Lord had not yet provided an answer.

A blizzard prevented Annie from returning home for the next two weeks. While she missed her family, she saw the inclement weather as a blessing and a way to avoid seeing Pa until things were set to rights. Ma and Hetty both wrote letters, although their words did nothing to ease the pain.

Annie sat at the supper table that night, her mind miles from the meal in front of her. Not that she was hungry, anyway. She'd been unable to eat much since arriving back in Willow Falls.

"Miss Ledbetter?"

She saw the concern in Charlotte's face. "I'm sorry, Charlotte. What did you say?"

"I was saying how delightful it is that we both received letters today. I received one from my great aunts, Fern and Myrtle. They're Ma's aunts and they also live in the Wyoming Territory. They always have so many wonderful things to say, and someday I'm going to pay a visit to them." Charlotte continued to chatter about her great aunts and Annie struggled to listen.

"And you received a letter too, Miss Ledbetter. Have you read yours yet?"

John Mark shook his head. "Charlotte, you are so nosy."

"You're just jealous because Aunt Fern and Aunt Myrtle didn't send you a letter."

"Why would I care about letters? I'm a boy. Reckon boys don't care about letters and such. We only care about fishing and baseball and climbing trees and stuff like that. We don't care about letters."

"No, only sophisticated womenfolk such as myself would give a concern to the written word." In an exaggeratedly hushed tone, Charlotte declared, "John Mark is such a boor." She then dismissed the conversation as over and continued eating her supper.

"Speaking of the aunts, Charlotte, how are they?" Lydie asked.

"They're doing well, Ma. Just the other day, they purchased a home. Finally, they no longer reside at the boarding house. They described their new house, and I must say it sounds resplendent!"

"What a blessing to hear they're doing well. It's been some time since we've seen them."

"I'm going to visit them someday, aren't I, Ma?" Charlotte shot a stuffy glance toward her brother.

"Yes, I think the aunts would delight in having you for a visit."

"They don't know Charlotte very well if they think they'd delight in having her for a visit," muttered John Mark.

Charlotte returned her attention to Annie. "So, Miss Ledbetter, did you open Hetty's letter? How is she doing?"

"Charlotte, perhaps we should allow Miss Ledbetter to eat."

"Yes, ma'am." Charlotte took a bite of her mashed potatoes.

"I haven't yet read my letter from Hetty, Charlotte." Annie prodded at the potatoes on her plate with her fork.

She couldn't remember the last time she'd had such a profound lack of appetite, as had been the case these past few days. While the Eliason family carried on in a somewhat typical fashion, it wasn't the same at the table without Caleb. More nights than not, he didn't arrive for supper.

Nothing really mattered right now. Not even a letter from her best friend.

Annie sat on the bed and unfolded Hetty's letter. She stared at the words without really seeing them. Finally, she forced herself to read:

My Dearest Annie,

I was dreadfully sorry to hear about your Pa's decision not to allow you to see Caleb. Zeb told me some of what happened. I cannot imagine the pain you must be experiencing. I don't know what I would do if Pa told me I could no longer see Zeb. Such a thought is too awful to entertain. Know that I am praying for you.

Zeb and I have begun making plans for our wedding. There are several relatives from back East I long to invite, as well as Ma's family in the southern part of the Territory and some cousins, as well. I'm not sure I have seen such an elegant dress in all my years as the one Ma is sewing for me. Zeb is anxious to continue working on our new home, but spring is still so far away. I daydream often about the new life Zeb and I will share. It seems June can't come soon enough.

Something is amiss with Mr. Ackerman lately. He doesn't seem to be himself. Rather than constantly attempting to see the contents of the letters, he instead is courteously relinquishing any correspondence without much inquisitiveness. No fuss, no nothing. Just a grin and a "Have a good day." Lately every time I visit the post office, he's humming. I never knew Mr. Ackerman to hum. And he sure is smiling an awful lot. Do you think he's not well?

I best go for now. Hoping the weather improves soon so you can return to Nelsonville posthaste. I miss you.

Much love,
Hetty

Annie placed the letter on the bureau. The despondency crushed her. She knew now why she'd not been eager to open Hetty's letter. In the past, Annie yearned to hear about Hetty and the updates on the upcoming wedding.

But not today. Not now.

Now the joy of Hetty and Zeb's upcoming wedding tore at her heart, and Annie fought the envy daring to rear its head. Yes, she was thrilled for them, but she also grieved that her plans for a future with Caleb were dashed based on Pa's inability to see reason.

No words would come even if she could write a return letter to Hetty, which she couldn't. Not now. Not when her heart ached.

Annie reclined on her pillow and folded her hands across her stomach. One topic in Hetty's letter did strike her as interesting—Mr. Ackerman's change in disposition. Could it have something to do with Mrs. Burns? Annie allowed the slightest of smiles to tug at her lips. Yet another couple who was allowed to express their love toward each other and plan a future.

Unlike her and Caleb.

Annie found her days lackluster and she herself lethargic. She couldn't even find the energy to write in her diary. It seemed a struggle to accomplish anything, even teach her students—a job she treasured.

True to Pa's instruction, Caleb kept his distance. Reverend Solomon and Lydie were apprised of the situation from Caleb, and Annie was appreciative of their prayers.

One day after school, Annie sat at her desk watching out the window as each of the children left for home, waiting for Reverend Solomon to retrieve her.

Caleb no longer accompanied her home and she realized how much she missed even something so seemingly minor as riding with him.

Was this the way her life would be forever? Full of regret of what might have been?

Chapter Thirty-One

Loneliness filled every part of him. He no longer dared to frequent his parents' house for supper, both because it proved too painful to see Annie, and because he had no wish to cause further strife between her and her father. So instead, he sat at his own table with his own meal, eating by himself.

When he could eat.

Caleb bowed his head in prayer and debated eating the sandwich on his plate. Part of him wanted to go to Mr. Ledbetter and let him know, in no uncertain terms, what he thought about the refusal to allow him to court Annie. But Caleb wasn't sure he could restrain his words.

So instead, he muddled through the days, praying for God's guidance and trying to take his mind off of Annie by continuing his jobs in town and growing his ranch.

But his plan wasn't working. He couldn't stop thinking about her.

Questions plagued him. Why had Annie told her parents about his past? Did she think they would understand why he had done the things he'd done during the robbery? Apparently, they hadn't. Mr. Ledbetter's reaction proved that point.

A knock at the door brought Caleb's thoughts to the present.

Pa stood in the doorway. "Your ma thought you might like a slice of apple pie, right out of the oven."

"Thanks." Caleb motioned for his father to step inside the house.

"How are you doing, Son? Your ma and I have been concerned about you." Reverend Solomon set the plate with two slices of apple pie on the table.

"I'm not sure what to do about the whole situation."

Reverend Solomon placed a hand on his son's shoulder. "It's a difficult position, no doubt about that. We sure have missed you at supper."

"I can't bear seeing Annie when I know her pa forbids us to see each other. I'm not even allowed to speak to her."

"From what I've seen, Annie is struggling with this as well."

"I just don't understand. I'm not the man I once was. How can I convince Mr. Ledbetter of that?"

"If you'd like, I can go with you to Nelsonville and talk to him. Remember Annie's feelings when she first realized you were the one in the robbery?"

"I do. Why does it have to be so hard, Pa? Why is my past a constant reminder?"

"Things that are worth it aren't always easy."

"I had hoped she would be in my future forever. That I would someday ask her to..." Caleb stopped and took a deep breath.

"Annie is worth it, Caleb. She's worth the fight."

"I know she is."

Pa took a seat at the table. "I'm not sure if I ever told you this story, but my parents had a similar situation. My ma resided in Minnesota and my pa emigrated from Scotland with his family. Poverty-stricken and alone in a strange land, my pa's family didn't measure up to what my ma's father had in mind for a potential suitor. My grandfather did about all he could to keep them apart. Ma told me many times how difficult my grandfather could be. His lack of compassion and refusal to see past outward appearances didn't exactly make him the kind of father most children wished they had."

"I never knew that. But they did marry?"

"Only because they eloped. They were married for many years before they both passed away from influenza. Now, I'm not suggesting you and Annie elope—that's not the answer you should seek."

"We won't elope, Pa."

"I'm relieved to hear that. I'm only telling you this because others have faced similar situations. Now, my grandfather was a difficult man with a lack of benevolence toward most people. I don't think Mr. Ledbetter has that in common with my grandfather. He seems like a godly man. From a father's point of view, I reckon he's only trying to protect his daughter."

"I agree. I doubt Mr. Ledbetter is anything like your grandfather, and I know he's only trying to protect Annie, but he's not listening to the entire story."

"Someday, Lord willing, you'll have children, Caleb. You might even be blessed with a daughter or two. When a man thinks his daughter is threatened in any way, he knows he has to do all he can to keep her safe. I know that's what I'd do for Charlotte, without even thinking twice. I love her more than I can express, and I'm sure Mr. Ledbetter feels the same about Annie."

Caleb nodded. "It still isn't fair."

"No, it's not. But I'm going to have faith that Mr. Ledbetter will see your true character and God will use that to convince him he's making the wrong choice when it comes to you and Annie. And remember, Caleb, your ma and I are here for you. We love you."

The words "I love you" still shook Caleb after all these years. Love from a man and his wife who hadn't given birth to him and hadn't even raised him until he was nearly an adult. Love for a boy who had no future until God stepped in.

"Thank you, Pa. I mean it, thank you for everything."

"You're an easy boy to love, Caleb. Now, what do you say we dig into this apple pie? Your ma will have my hide if she finds out all her hard work baking went to waste."

That thought brought a smile to Caleb's lips. Ma did take her baking seriously and thought of it as an act of love toward those who meant most to her. "You're right. No sense in having Ma mad at us."

Speaking with Pa about his predicament helped Caleb put things into perspective. Maybe Caleb would consider his offer to pay a visit to Mr. Ledbetter.

Maybe then Annie's father would realize his mistake.

Separating her blonde hair into three pieces, Annie braided it, then twisted the braid into a bun at the base of her neck.

Sitting apart from Caleb at church had not been easy, and now Sunday had arrived once again.

"Annie? May I come in?"

"Yes."

"Solomon and John Mark are outside hitching up the horses for church and Charlotte is attempting to build a snowman in her best church dress." Lydie paused and her mouth curved into a smile. "That Charlotte. Such a determined young girl. But that's not what I came to speak to you about. I wanted to ensure you were all right. I know your father's decision has not been easy on you."

Annie plopped down on her bed and Lydie took a seat beside her. "It's not easy at all." Tears burned Annie's eyes.

"Oh, Annie." Lydie put her arm around Annie's shoulder, and Annie rested her head on Lydie's shoulder.

"Some things just aren't fair."

Lydie placed a motherly kiss on Annie's forehead. "I'm here for you, whenever you need me. I know I'm not your mother, but I've grown fond of you during your time here and think of you as a daughter. You and Caleb will get through this. Your father will see his error. He *has* to see."

"And if he doesn't?"

"He will. I have faith. God didn't bring you two together to have it end like this."

Annie closed her eyes. Kind and gentle Lydie with nary an unkind word toward anyone. Annie had grown to respect and love Caleb's mother.

"Ma, Annie, Pa says it's time to go."

"We'll be right down, John Mark." Lydie patted Annie on the arm. "Whenever you need to talk, I'm here."

"Thank you, Lydie."

Annie dabbed at her tears with a handkerchief. Things would work out.

They had to.

※

After the service, Reverend Solomon and Lydie visited with parishioners. Outside in the churchyard, Annie caught Caleb's gaze. His eyes filled with the same knowing emotions. She longed for time spent with him, for their comfortable conversation, and for his embrace.

"Miss Ledbetter?" Mrs. Burns approached Annie and interrupted the nonverbal moment.

"Hello, Mrs. Burns. How are you?"

"I'm doing splendidly."

"Your rheumatism isn't bothering you?"

"Rheumatism? Not in the least. And neither are my eyes. As a matter of fact, I'm seeing things better than I have in years."

Annie scrutinized the older woman. Come to think of it, Mrs. Burns appeared healthy and spry. Her once slightly stooped figure stood more upright, her shoulders back, and her posture better.

"That's fantastic to hear, Mrs. Burns."

"Yes, well, I owe it all to you, Miss Ledbetter."

"Me?"

"Yes. If you hadn't introduced me to that delightful Bernard—I mean—Mr. Ackerman, I would never have met the love of my life."

The love of her life? Hadn't Mrs. Burns been married several times prior? "I'm so happy for you, Mrs. Burns."

"I'll be Mrs. Ackerman in a few short months. And Bernard is so handsome and charming, and so respected at his job at the post office. Who would have thought I'd be so fortunate?"

"Indeed."

"I'll be moving to Nelsonville, of course. I know so many here in Willow Falls will miss me. I've been the matriarch of this town, and with my charismatic personality, I dare say things won't be the same around here. Now, I must toddle along. I can't show favoritism by only telling you. There's many of whom to express my ineffable delight."

Mrs. Burns marched toward another parishioner, her visage altered by love.

Across the way, Caleb whispered something to Charlotte. Charlotte gave him a questioning look, then bounded toward Annie. "I'm supposed to deliver a message from Caleb."

"Oh?"

"Why I'm delivering this, I have no idea, other than Caleb promised me licorice from the mercantile. He says to tell you that he thinks of you as Mr. Ackerman thinks of Mrs. Burns. Now why would he say that, Miss Ledbetter? You're nothing like Mrs. Burns and he's nothing like Mr. Ackerman."

Annie blushed. Perhaps having a messenger would ease the struggle she and Caleb faced. "Tell Caleb I think of him as Mrs. Burns thinks of Mr. Ackerman."

Charlotte shook her head. "I might need to ask for two pieces of licorice for this silly shenanigan."

She ambled back toward Caleb, who promptly gave her another message.

"This time Caleb says to tell you he thinks you're the prettiest girl here. Why, when I'm a woman, I'm never going to be all lovey-dovey like you and Caleb." Charlotte shuddered. "I'd love to partake in more messages, but I really must find my friends."

"Thank you, for being an exceptional messenger."

For a moment, Annie forgot about the dilemma she and Caleb found themselves in. For a moment, all was well again with the man she loved.

The next couple of weeks moved at a slow pace. Annie hadn't seen Caleb since church, but his amusing messages did much to give her hope. She missed him.

More than she ever thought she could miss someone.

Annie bid the last student goodbye, then sat in the chair at her desk to wait for Reverend Solomon. Looking out the window, she saw Charlotte and John Mark involved in a snowball fight with several other children.

She thought of Caleb. Where was he right now? Did he miss her too? Was he praying for their reconciliation? Did he know how much she cared for him? Pain struck her again. If only the DeGroots hadn't paid a visit to Annie's parents. If they'd never arrived, none of this would have happened.

The opening door interrupted Annie's thoughts. Caleb strode toward her desk. "Annie, can I speak with you for a minute?"

"Caleb, my Pa said I can't speak with you."

"I know that and I have respected his wishes, but..." Caleb removed his hat. "When love finds you, you don't run from it. I love you, Annie. And I will do whatever it takes to convince your pa I'm worthy of you. I have tried, though it's been nearly impossible, to keep my distance from you for the past several weeks. It has been the worse time in my life—even worse than those days with Cain and Roy and that day when Mr. Yager burned my hand." Caleb raked his fingers through his blond hair.

She stood and walked to the front of her desk. "I just don't want Pa to not allow me to teach here. Then I'll never see you."

Strong arms embraced her and held her.

The arms of the man she loved.

"I don't like disobeying your father either. Believe me, I don't. But this has to be settled."

"Caleb, there's something I need to tell you," Annie said when they separated. She took a deep breath. "Some friends came for a visit to our house, and they told my parents about your role in the robbery."

"I was wondering how they knew."

"You surely know I wouldn't tell them."

When her question was met with silence, Annie repeated herself, "Caleb, surely you know I wouldn't tell them, right?"

"I did wonder how they found out, Annie."

"Some friends of my parents, the DeGroots, paid us a visit. They were in the wagon train all those years ago and Horace is the one Roy shot. He found an old wanted poster. Caleb, it was awful. One minute I was telling Edith about my teaching position here in Willow Falls, and the next minute Horace was sharing about the poster. He said one of the men was still on the loose and that my parents should be careful since the man was last seen in the Willow Falls area."

"A wanted poster?"

"Yes. It had sketches of you and Cain and the other man, physical descriptions. My pa knew right away that it was you. And the look on his face…Oh, Caleb, his expression is one I shall never forget. "

"It seems like what happened all those years ago keeps coming back to haunt me."

Annie's heart broke at Caleb's statement. She had been part of that reminder.

"It's understandable, your pa's take on the situation. I try to think about what I would do if I had a daughter and she wanted to court someone like me."

There wasn't a day that didn't pass by that Caleb wished he could change the past. But he couldn't.

He could only live in the present.

And while Caleb tried to respect Mr. Ledbetter's position, it had brought nothing but turmoil to both him and Annie. What would Mr. Ledbetter think if he really knew how Caleb felt about Annie? That Caleb had more in mind than courtship?

Caleb pulled her to him once again and held her in his embrace. He ached for her pain and his own.

Was it God's will that they have no future together?

"I've missed you, Annie."

"I've missed you too, Caleb."

His lips found hers, and he imagined what lay ahead. What their future held. What could be if only her pa would allow them to again court and eventually marry.

When the kiss ended, Caleb cradled her face in his hands. He would fight for her, no matter what it took. He would not—could not—lose her.

Chapter Thirty-Two

A WEEK LATER, ANNIE prepared to return home for the weekend. She dreaded visiting with her father, but Reverend Solomon had agreed to accompany Caleb on the return visit to retrieve her.

It comforted Annie to know that so many prayed for their situation.

During their trip to Nelsonville, Annie and Zeb rode side by side and had much time to talk. She took the opportunity to share her feelings about the situation in which she struggled.

"Things have been tense at home as well," Zeb said.

"It's my fault, but it's not reasonable that Pa should make the decision he has. I miss Caleb something awful. Can you imagine if he forbade you to see Hetty?"

Zeb shook his head. "I don't even want to contemplate such a thought."

"Have Ma and Pa discussed the issue?"

"They have. Of course, not in front of Sadie and me, but I have heard their muffled voices deep into the night. From what I can tell, Ma agrees you should be able to continue seeing Caleb and that you are a good judge of character."

"At least Ma agrees."

"Don't forget your favorite brother agrees with you too."

"Thank you, Zeb. I don't know what I would do without you." Just knowing Zeb understood her situation reassured her everything would be all right.

The passing scenery was so dull, so brown, and so drab in the dead of winter. The snow had melted and left behind bare tree branches and a stark chill in the air that Annie found difficult to shake. "It was hard forgiving Caleb, Zeb. It wasn't something I could do on my own. I needed to be reminded of how God abundantly forgives us."

"Forgiveness never is something we can do on our own. Reckon it's the hardest thing God calls us to do."

"You're right. But what if Pa doesn't ever forgive Caleb and he never allows us to resume our courtship?"

"I don't know the answer to that. But I do know that worrying about it isn't going to help."

"True. It's just hard."

"I know."

At the Ledbetter home, Annie headed inside, while Zeb left to unhitch the horses.

"Annie!" Ma placed her hands on either side of Annie's face and planted a kiss on her forehead. "I've missed you."

"I've missed you too, Ma."

"Are you all right?"

Ma's regard consoled Annie. The disagreement between Annie and Pa threatened more than Annie's love for Caleb.

Not a day passed when she hadn't prayed for her father to change his mind.

"Annie, I'm going to town to see Hetty. Wanna come along?"

"I'd love to." Anything to get out of the house and away from the tension in the air.

Sadie bounded into the room. "Can I come?"

"You sure can." At least her younger sister was oblivious to the unpleasant happenings around her.

Spending time with Hetty always encouraged Annie, even on the most difficult days. And this day was no exception.

Hetty enveloped Annie in a hug as she greeted them. "I'm so sorry to hear about Caleb. But everything will be all right. It just has to be."

Zeb winked at Hetty. "All right, Sadie Girl, let's go to the mercantile for a few minutes and let these chattering hens converse."

After Zeb and Sadie left, Annie and Hetty took a seat in the parlor. "Have you talked with Caleb at all since the incident with your pa?"

"I have. It's difficult. We only see each other at church, and that's only on the weekends when I can't return to Nelsonville. He hasn't eaten supper with his family as often since Pa spoke with him."

Hetty knitted her dark eyebrows together. "Were you able to tell him how disappointed you were?"

Annie sighed. "Yes, and I was able to share who it was that told my parents about him. I think at first he thought it was me."

"Do you ever wonder if you should have told your parents first before they found out from the DeGroots?"

"After Pa's reaction, I'm confident the outcome would have been much the same, possibly even worse. I know Pa only cares about me and seeks to protect me, but oh, Hetty, what am I to do?"

Hetty placed an arm around her. "I'm not sure, Annie. But your parents have always been levelheaded. Surely your pa will see the error of his ways."

"Enough about me. How are your wedding preparations coming along?"

"Ma has been working diligently on my dress. Would you care to see it?"

Annie followed Hetty into her room. "It's exquisite!"

"Thank you. It's almost finished. Folks tell you to start planning your wedding an adequate amount of time before the actual day. I never understood why until now."

Annie brushed the soft fabric of Hetty's wedding dress. Would she someday know the joy that came with giving your heart to the one you loved?

Pa stood by the barn door awaiting Annie's arrival when she, Zeb, and Sadie returned from Hetty's house.

"Annie, I need to speak with you."

Annie's heart nearly stopped. The moment she dreaded had arrived. She could only avoid her father for so long. But there was something in his face, something other than the harsh defensiveness that had been there before when he'd forbidden her to see Caleb.

A kinder, gentler look in his eyes.

"Shall we go to the barn?"

Annie nodded. Chats in the barn were always serious and this one would be no exception.

"We need to discuss you and Caleb."

Annie took a seat on a hay bale. She'd assumed as much. Worry etched his face and she remembered once again how much she loved him. He'd been a doting father to her in every sense of the word. He'd provided for her, Ma, Zeb, and Sadie, and had been there when they needed him. He'd instructed them in the Word of God and made sure they knew they were always loved.

"Pa, I've attempted to understand why you have forbidden me to court Caleb. I know you are only trying to protect me, but your decision is unfair."

"You're right. I have been trying to protect you. Your ma and I love you very much and want nothing to happen to you."

"I know, and I am grateful you only want what is best for me, but you have to understand how much I love Caleb and how he is a different man now. Do you not trust my judgment?"

Pa remained silent for a few minutes and Annie wondered if he might postpone the remainder of their conversation.

Finally, he spoke, "Annie, I humbly admit that I'm not proud of the way I handled the situation with Caleb. I have had much time to pray about it and to talk it over several times with your ma. I have to turn this matter over to God and trust that He will guide your steps—that He will protect you."

"Please give Caleb a chance. You'll see how he has changed. Once you spend more time with him, you'll come to know the type of man he is. He's not perfect, but Caleb is a godly man with such kindness in him. He regrets what he did that day and wishes he could take it back."

"Yes, well, Caleb will have a chance to prove himself to me. As I said before, this wasn't an easy decision. But I want nothing to come between us, Annie, and I know I need to let go and trust your judgment. You're not Sadie's age anymore."

Tears brimmed in her eyes. "Thank you, Pa. When Caleb and Reverend Solomon arrive to retrieve me, you can spend some time with Caleb and see for yourself the kind of man he has become."

"Yes, I will do that. Now, we best head inside before your ma has our hides for allowing supper to get cold."

Chapter Thirty-Three

Nerves consumed Caleb when he and Pa strode toward the Ledbetter home. Did he have the courage to speak with Mr. Ledbetter about what was on his heart? Did he have the bravery to ask the man to reconsider his choice in allowing Caleb to court his daughter?

Would Mr. Ledbetter ever release the harbored grudge against Caleb for his role in the robbery?

Mrs. Ledbetter greeted Caleb and Pa when they entered the Ledbetter home. Should Caleb request to speak with Mr. Ledbetter immediately? Or should he wait? Should he ask Pa to accompany him?

The answers came within moments.

"Caleb, my husband would like to speak with you in the barn. Reverend Solomon, may I offer you a cup of coffee?"

The barn door stood ajar. "Mr. Ledbetter, I was told you wanted to speak with me?"

"Yes, Caleb, please come in." Mr. Ledbetter closed the barn doors behind him.

Caleb shoved his hands in his pockets and prayed for courage.

"There are some matters of concern when it comes to you and Annie."

Already this wasn't going well, and it had only just started. But Caleb knew what he must do. If he ever wanted to see Annie again with Mr. Ledbetter's blessing, then he had to continue with his plan to convince Mr. Ledbetter he'd changed. "I know that, sir, but I believe in putting the past behind us."

Mr. Ledbetter frowned. "That's all fine and well, but you weren't the victim, Caleb. You caused a lot of grief for my family and the families of others."

"For that, I'm not proud."

Mr. Ledbetter sighed. "With the Lord's help, I will be able to fully forgive you. As of now, while I'm not proud of it, I still hold a bit of a grudge. You changed a lot of lives for the worse that day."

Yes, Caleb had, but when would the past not be allowed to affect the present?

"I realize that. I have many regrets from that time in my life." He gently kicked a piece of hay near his boot. There was nothing he could do about Mr. Ledbetter's choice of whether or not to forgive.

"A father worries that a man might lay an unkind hand on his daughter when that man has a past as you do."

"I understand. But I love Annie and would never hurt her."

Mr. Ledbetter nodded. "I love Annie too. She will always be my little girl and I only want what's best for her. You'll understand one day if you're blessed with a daughter."

This wasn't going well. Was there any hope of convincing Annie's pa? "I know and respect how much you love her. She speaks very highly of you and I have seen for myself that you are a good father. I promise you I would never lay an unkind hand on her."

"And I'm to trust your word?"

"Yes, sir."

"Can't tell you how many times I thought about that day and tried to remember you after the DeGroots showed us that wanted poster. I remember the other two men as if the robbery happened yesterday. But your face—it rarely came to my mind when I thought of that day. It was as if your image couldn't be found within the confines of my memory. But you were there. You took part in the crime and now you expect me to believe you're a changed man." Mr. Ledbetter's voice held no condemnation, just a matter-of-fact statement.

"I want more than anything for you to believe that." His favorite verse came to his mind. "Sir, are you familiar with Second Corinthians 5:17? It states that when a man is in Christ, he's a new creature."

Mr. Ledbetter nodded. "I have read that verse before many times."

"When I came to know Christ as my personal Savior, I became a new man. Yes, the past will always be around to haunt me, and no one will ever be more unforgiving of me than I am of myself. I regret being a part of something that altered the lives of folks in such a negative manner. If I could change that day, believe me, I would. But I can't do the changing, only God can." Caleb sighed. "I am that new creature the verse talks about. The old things in my life—the crimes, the choices—they've passed away. When I came to know the Lord, He changed me in profound ways that I can't begin to describe. Not all at once, but over time. And He gave me a fresh start."

"Reckon you know your Bible."

Was there a slight hint of admiration in Mr. Ledbetter's words? Or was it optimism on Caleb's part? "Guess I better know the Bible, seeing as how my pa is a preacher. Mr. Ledbetter, I humbly ask for your forgiveness for that day. I also ask that I would be granted the privilege to court Annie." There. Caleb had said it. The worst that could happen would be that Mr. Ledbetter would deny both requests.

But what would Caleb do then? After he'd exhausted all of his options?

Stifling silence filled the air. Mr. Ledbetter said nothing for an extended period of time. Caleb offered several prayers heavenward.

Pa mentioned many times that God heard every prayer, no matter the size of it. Surely God heard the prayers of a man seeking the forgiveness of another.

Finally, Mr. Ledbetter spoke. "Maria reminded me many times that the forgiveness that I bestow upon you would not only be for Annie's sake, but for my own sake, as well. I'm ashamed to say I'm struggling with that forgiveness, Caleb."

"I will do whatever it takes to earn your trust."

"Perhaps seeing more of you would set my mind at ease."

"I can arrange that."

"Stay for a while when you deliver Annie and retrieve her. Allow me some time to get to know this man my daughter has grown fond of." Mr. Ledbetter tugged at his beard. "In the meantime, you may again court my daughter."

"I will do that. And thank you." Caleb extended his hand to shake Mr. Ledbetter's. "I won't disappoint you."

A hint of a smile crossed Mr. Ledbetter's face, giving Caleb hope that he might someday fully win the man's respect.

Chapter Thirty-Four

THREE MONTHS LATER

A CASE OF NERVES and jitters jolted Caleb at the thought of what lay ahead of him. The prospect of asking Walter Ledbetter for his daughter's hand in marriage seemed daunting. Three weeks had passed since his proposal and Annie's acceptance.

The day to seek Mr. Ledbetter's blessing had arrived.

"Hello, Mr. Ledbetter. May I speak with you for a moment in private?" Caleb cleared his throat and hoped his nervousness wasn't too apparent.

"Certainly. We can talk in the barn."

Caleb took a deep breath. "Mr. Ledbetter, I am humbly asking for your daughter's hand in marriage. I love Annie. She means more to me than anything, and I want to start a life with her." Caleb paused to take a breath. He was so lousy at speaking his mind when it came to matters of the heart, even if he and Mr. Ledbetter had grown in their respect for each other in the past few months.

"If you're worried about the past—my past—I'm more than willing to court Annie for years, if necessary, until I can fully earn your trust. I have a home, and as you know, I've been saving up to expand the number of cattle I own so that I'll be able to provide for your daughter."

"You've done well for yourself, Caleb. I recall how when I asked for Maria's hand, I was only eighteen and all I had was a horse to my name. Of course, I was still helping my own pa rebuild his life after losing everything to liquor and gambling." Mr. Ledbetter paused as if his mind was deep in the past. "Maria's father was concerned I wouldn't be able to provide for her. I had to reassure him I could, and that wasn't an easy feat.

"But you, Caleb, you have made a life for yourself. And no, you don't have to court her for any length of time to earn my trust. I believe we've made strides in that area."

"Thank you, Mr. Ledbetter."

The older man looked down at his boots. "And I seek your forgiveness for taking so long to forgive you. I only wanted what was best for my Annie. And now, having spent more time with you and having seen firsthand how much you love and care for her, you not only have my respect, but you also have my blessing and my full forgiveness."

"I appreciate that, sir."

"Forgiveness can be a challenge. I can attest to that. But I have been forgiven for much, and so I also need to forgive."

Caleb appreciated Mr. Ledbetter's humility.

"One other thing." Mr. Ledbetter removed his hat and scratched his head. "I never expressed my gratitude for you fetching the doctor that day Maria went into labor with Sadie. I've been told your courageous act saved both of their lives. I will forever be indebted to you for that."

Chapter Thirty-Five

CALEB RECEIVED THE LETTER on a cold spring day in March as he was on his way to meet Annie for lunch at the schoolhouse.

At first, he was shocked and overwhelmed.

Second, feelings of frustration with Cain for meddling in his newfound life entered his mind.

Lastly, Caleb was frustrated that Cain had dared to bring up a past Caleb so diligently attempted to forget.

"What did the letter say?" Annie sat on the steps of the school with Caleb as they partook in their lunches and watched her students play.

"It was sent in care to Sheriff Townsend with a note at the top of the letter to forward it to me. The letter said Cain is dying and that he'd like to see me." In Caleb's own ears, his voice sounded flat and lacking emotion.

Annie placed her hand gently on Caleb's arm. "Cain would like to see you?"

"I know I've spoken so few times about him, and for good reason. I've tried hard to leave that part of my life in the past and now Cain is rehashing all of those memories."

"Are you going to go?"

Even in the chill of the day, sweat beaded on his forehead at the thought of seeing his brother. "I don't know. Maybe. I haven't given it much thought yet. I just received the letter." He removed the tattered piece of paper from the envelope. "I'm not sure how Cain convinced the prison to allow him to send this. But then, Cain has way of manipulating people that I never could understand."

Caleb handed the letter to Annie. "You can read it if you'd like."

"Are you sure? It's a private letter."

"You're going to be my wife soon, Annie. And besides, I don't want any more secrets between us."

Annie unfolded the letter. Uneven edges lined the brown, soiled, note-sized piece of paper. Caleb watched as she read the scribbled words:

Sheriff Townsend, please forward this letter to Caleb Ryerson if you can.

Caleb,
I'm in the U.S. Penitentiary at Laramie City serving time for the robberies. I'd like to see you. I'm dyin' of some illness and my time is short. Reckon it'd be good to see you one last time.
Your Brother,
Cain

Annie rested a hand on Caleb's arm. "Whatever you decide, Caleb, I will support you."

"It's been almost eight years since I've seen him. I've tried so hard to put the past behind me. He wasn't a doting big brother. He wasn't like how Zeb is to you and Sadie or how I try to be to John Mark and Charlotte. He taught me things an older brother shouldn't teach a younger one."

"I'm so sorry, Caleb."

Caleb shook his head. "And then he signs his letter 'Your Brother, Cain', as if nothing ever happened between us. As if everything is fine and he is an upstanding citizen when nothing is further from the truth."

"Maybe he's trying to make amends."

"It's too late for that. Much too late. I'm going to speak to Pa about it and ask him if he'll go with me *if* I decide to go. At this point, I don't want to. But I know I probably should." Caleb paused. "If I do go, would you come with me too?"

"Yes."

"I could ask Ma if she'd be able to teach your class for you while you're gone. I know the trip itself isn't lengthy, maybe a few days, and my visit with Cain would be brief. That much I know for a fact. If I go at all."

"I know it's hard to forgive him for what he did and that seeing him will bring up memories you had long ago laid to rest, but I think you'd regret it if you didn't go."

"Reckon you're right, Annie. I wouldn't know what to say to him. I know what I feel like saying, but those words wouldn't be the words of a man who knows the Lord."

"I'm surprised about the letter. Did you ever think you would hear from him again?"

"No, I thought for sure he'd already died in prison or else maybe he'd forgotten about me. He knows I was the one who turned him and Roy over to the law. Maybe that's why he wants to see me—to tell me what he thinks of me for doing that."

"I hope not, Caleb. I pray the reason Cain wants to see you before he dies is to reconcile."

Caleb shook his head. "I wouldn't count on it. You don't know him. He's heartless and mean. I don't think I ever heard him say he was sorry for anything he did."

Could he pretend he'd never received the letter? Burn it and never think of it or Cain again? Several minutes ticked by.

"Let's change the subject. Have you been giving any thought to our wedding date?"

"As a matter of fact, that's all that's been on my mind. I am looking forward to being Mrs. Caleb Eliason."

Caleb planted a quick kiss on her cheek. "Not half as much as I'm looking forward to you being Mrs. Caleb Eliason."

"What do you think about Saturday, June twenty-seventh?"

"June twenty-seventh? Is there some significance for that day?"

"None at all, I just thought it would be a good time as far as weather goes, and June does seem to be the month of weddings. Zeb and Hetty are getting married on June twentieth inside the church. I thought it would be delightful to be married right outside the church with lots of flowers and..."

Caleb smirked. "This was what Pa warned me about when he told me that women view weddings differently than men. Women are more into the details. Men just want to focus on the ceremony itself."

Annie looked at Caleb askance. "The details are important, Caleb. Lord willing, a wedding only takes place once in a person's life, so it's important to have everything just so."

"I reckon you're right, Annie. You can have as many flowers as you want and June twenty-seventh sounds perfect."

"We'll set the date, then."

"I love you, Annie."

"I love you too."

Scanning the play area outside of the school to be sure none of the students were watching, Caleb gently brushed her lips with his.

Were it not for Cain's letter, the day would have been perfect.

On a Wednesday during the first week of April, Caleb, Annie, and Pa set out to the U.S. Penitentiary at Laramie City by stagecoach.

Although he'd internally fought against going, he knew he must. And after much time spent in prayer and receiving wise counsel from Pa, Caleb knew what he was doing was right.

The stark looming building with a fenced-in yard was surrounded by a barren landscape. It included a lookout tower manned by two guards, and a black prison wagon was parked in front awaiting the next delivery of prisoners.

This could have been where he spent his life had the Lord not had other plans for him. Humility overwhelmed him.

Pa put his hand on Caleb's shoulder. "Are you ready to go in?"

"I don't know, Pa. I don't think I can."

Pa folded his hands and bowed his head. "Let's give this matter to the Lord, shall we? Dear Heavenly Father, we thank You for our safe trip and for the opportunity Caleb has before him to see his brother again. Lord, we don't know what You have in mind for this visit or why Cain felt it was necessary to see Caleb again. But what we do know, Lord, is that You are in control of the situation, and we pray You will guide Caleb and give him the wisdom he seeks. In Jesus' Name, Amen."

"Thank you, Pa."

Caleb struggled to restrain his emotions as they entered the prison and a guard led them toward the warden's office. A pungent odor loomed in the air, and the chill of the crimes of those serving time within the prison walls caused a lump in his throat. This could have been *his* fate.

A man behind the desk scrutinized them. "May I help you?"

"Yes, my name is Caleb Eliason and I was wondering if I could see my brother, Cain Ryerson?"

The man searched through a book of names.

"Yes, here he is. Cain Ryerson." Glancing at Annie and Pa, the man continued, "Two visitors at a time may see this inmate. In some circumstances, the prisoner is able to meet with more than two at a time in the visiting center; however, since Mr. Ryerson is in ill health, he is confined to the infirmary and only two visitors are allowed at a time."

Annie rested her hand on his arm. "I'll wait for you here."

"As will I," said Pa.

Caleb glanced ahead of him, then behind him. Then ahead once again.

Could he do this? Could he really see Cain again after all these years?

Chapter Thirty-Six

Caleb followed the prison guard to the infirmary, a separate building on the grounds. He was thankful he didn't have to pass by the actual prison cells.

The guard waited outside the door. Cain appeared to be the only patient and an additional guard stood nearby, his back against the wall.

"Cain?" Caleb barely recognized his brother. Yes, his hair was still auburn, although much shorter and sparser than Caleb remembered it. His hazel eyes had a yellow hue and were small above the large black circles below them. His mustache was gone, and he lay beneath a white blanket and appeared to struggle to turn his head at the sound of Caleb's voice.

He swallowed hard. It was clear that the end of his brother's life was near. Once again, warring emotions tugged at his heart.

"Caleb?" Cain's voice was weak and barely audible. "Can you help me sit up?"

Caleb stood behind Cain's bed, placed his arms under Cain's, and pulled him to a sitting position. Being in such close proximity to his brother brought about a whole new set of emotions.

He couldn't do this.

"Uh, Cain, maybe this wasn't such a grand idea, me coming here and all."

"Please, Caleb. Have a seat." Cain pointed to the vacant chair beside the bed.

"Cain..."

"Please, Caleb."

Could Cain see the panic coursing through Caleb's entire being?

I can't do this, Lord. I can't stay here and talk with Cain, not after all that's happened. There's too much of a history between us—too many memories.

Cain's hoarse voice interrupted Caleb's prayers. "Couldn't know for sure if you were even still in Willow Falls. Had to take that chance." He paused as if to catch his breath. "I was wondering if you would come."

"I was wondering the same thing," muttered Caleb.

The dismal room boasted plain white walls. There was a window at the far side with bars on it, but from where Cain was, he couldn't see out of it.

Why am I here? What is Your purpose in all of this, Lord?

Cain extended a frail arm toward Caleb. "I'm glad you did come. I wanted to see you before..."

"I know. I got your letter." His clipped response lacked mercy for the brother who'd mistreated him.

"There are some things I need to say to you."

"Then say them."

Lord, I cannot do this alone. I have no love for this man, even though he's my brother. Without Your grace, I can't sit here with this man who wrecked my life and caused havoc in the lives of so many others, including the woman I love.

"I guess I should start with 'I'm sorry.' I'm sorry for the way I treated you, sorry I made you steal, and sorry that I ruined your life."

Caleb looked away. Anger needled its way inside his heart, and he fought the urge to get up from his seat and leave the room. Did Cain think that a mere apology was enough to cancel years of pain?

"If you think an apology will change things, you're sorely mistaken."

"I understand."

"No, Cain, I don't think you do."

Caleb balled his fists in his lap. How dare Cain act as though he knew about the agony he'd inflicted on him during the first fourteen years of his life! Sweat beaded on Caleb's forehead and his heart pounded.

Cain cleared his throat. "Could you please hand me a glass of water?"

Still bossing me around, only at least this time there's a "please" behind it.

Caleb poured water from a pitcher on the nearby bureau and passed the tin cup to Cain. With a shaking hand, his brother lifted the cup to his mouth and drank.

"Thank you." He handed the cup back to Caleb. "As I was saying, I'm sorry for what I done."

Caleb said nothing. The sooner this mockery of an apology was over, the better.

Cain's raspy breathing echoed in the otherwise still room. "I heard you didn't do no jail time. I'm thankful for that, Caleb. I really am. The last thing I wanted to see was you doin' time for a crime you didn't want to be doin' in the first place."

"I thought you would be mad at me since I was the reason they found you and Roy."

"I was mad at you for the longest while. I was even madder when I found out they shot Roy. He was my best friend and I blamed that on you too. I even plotted a way to seek revenge on you. I knew if you hadn't been ridin' through Willow Falls that day, you would have never gotten yourself caught. I heard you were fetchin' some doctor."

"A woman in the wagon train we robbed was in labor and I fetched the doctor for her. That's when they caught me." Aggravation churned inside of Caleb.

"Did she survive the birth?"

"She did and so did the baby."

"Glad to hear that."

Caleb scowled as resentment clouded his thoughts. "You didn't think that when we were robbing them."

"You're right. I didn't. I didn't care about that woman or anyone else in the wagon party. All I cared about was gettin' what I thought was owed us. What a fool I was."

"Do you expect me to believe that you've changed, Cain? Because I'd be the fool to believe that."

Cain inhaled, causing him to wince. Was it from the pain of his illness, the pain of Caleb's accusatory remarks, or both?

Caleb tried not to care. But he did. And more than just a little.

"I do expect you to believe that," said Cain. "I've changed a lot in these past seven years. And believe me, I've been counting the days I've spent here. On my cell wall, I made little marks for each passing day. Lined the whole wall with marks."

He coughed, his pale face becoming red and tears sliding down his hollow cheeks. "Now with this illness, the prison doctor said I don't have much time to live. Reckon that's given me a whole new look on a lot of things."

Caleb doubted what Cain said. How could a man have been so rotten for so long and then claim he had changed? Caleb shifted in his chair and offered another prayer heavenward.

"You know, I've been wantin' to tell you something for a long time now. Our ma was a good woman."

"How would you know that? You were three years old when she died."

"I don't remember her at all myself. But I remember folks tellin' me that through the years while Pa was still alive. There was one woman—her name escapes my mind now—but she worked at the mercantile. She would always tell me things about Ma. How pretty she was, how kind she was, and about her strong faith."

"And I'm sure you cared to listen."

"Caleb, I know this isn't easy for you, but please hear me. I've been wantin' to see you for some time now. I need to tell you things—things that are important."

Guilt flooded him. "Sorry. Continue."

"As I was sayin', Ma was a wonderful woman."

"How did she end up with a man like Pa, then?"

"I don't know the answer to that, but there had to be a reason." Cain lifted a thin arm to scratch his head. "I reckon maybe it was so you could be born. Had she not married Pa, she wouldn't have had you."

Caleb's eyes stung. He should leave the room. Leave the prison. Leave Cain. Pretend he'd never had this painful conversation.

"I sure wished things had been different. I wished I wasn't lyin' in a prison bed waitin' to die. I have so many regrets." Cain cleared his throat. "So tell me, Little Brother, how have things been with you?"

Uninvited memories permeated through him. The only time Caleb had ever called him "Little Brother" was out of disrespect and hatred.

"I need to leave."

"No, Caleb, please. Please don't leave yet. I ain't done with saying my piece."

"It always was all about what you wanted, Cain."

"No, it's not only that. I want to hear about you too."

Caleb drew upon the Scripture verses hidden in his heart. *My grace is sufficient for thee...*

"Tell me about you, Caleb. What have you been doing all these years?"

Did Cain really care to know?

"Cain..."

"Caleb, I want to know all about you. I've missed so much, I have so many regrets."

The pained expression on Cain's face caused Caleb to relent and share a minute part of his life with his brother. "I was adopted by the reverend of Willow Falls and his wife. I gained a whole new family—parents and a brother and a sister. The Lord gave me a new life."

"Well, I'll be." Tears formed in Cain's eyes. "I'm proud of you, Caleb." His smile was weak, but the meaning behind his words was strong.

If Caleb could believe those words.

"Proud of me nothing, Cain; I don't believe you've changed, not for a minute."

There, he'd said it. His tone hadn't been disrespectful or harsh, only firm.

"I don't expect you to forgive me. That's not why I asked for you to come."

"Then why did you ask me?"

"I need to tell you I was wrong for what I done." Cain shifted in his bed. "But I don't expect you to forgive me or to even understand."

"You ruined my life." The terse words flew from his mouth without a thought.

"I'm sorry for that. Please believe me, Caleb. Looking back, I done so many wrong things. I should have let us stay at that orphanage and get adopted. I should have been a good example to you instead of a lousy one. I should have protected you from crime, not led you into it. I can do nothing about the past. The only thing I can change is the present."

Caleb rubbed his sweaty palms on his trousers. The sooner this conversation ceased, the better. "You sound as if you've rehearsed your words several times."

"Nah. But I did hope you'd come."

Caleb bit his lip and tapped his foot on the prison floor. The guard sitting quietly at the desk paid them no mind, but instead immersed himself in a book he was reading.

Moments ticked by.

Lord, let me see him the way You do.

The image of Cain caught his attention, and Caleb looked at his brother—really looked this time. Not a passing glance or an uncomfortable stare. But with intense scrutiny at the man before him. Something in Cain's eyes had softened.

The realization hit him hard. He could forgive Cain as the Lord had forgiven him. But only with the Lord's help.

And the Lord would help him. Of that Caleb was sure.

"I half expected you to be married with a couple young'uns by now," chuckled Cain. "Time has a way of getting away from us."

"I am engaged." Annie's beautiful face flashed before his mind.

"You don't say? What's her name?"

"Annie."

"Tell me about her, please."

"Cain..."

"Tell me about her. Marriage and children is something I'll never get to experience."

"That was by your own choice."

Cain blinked, and his voice hushed to barely a whisper. "I know it was by my own choice. But...well, guess I'm happy to know you are able to have the sorta life I can now only dream of."

"Since when did you want to be married and have young'uns?"

"Since about two years ago, when I really started thinking about how badly I'd messed up. By then it was too late. Even if I was released from prison, who would want to marry me? So tell me about this Annie."

"She's the new teacher in Willow Falls. She's staying with my Ma and Pa. She was in the wagon train that day and..."

"She was one of the ones we robbed?"

"She was. It took her a while to forgive me and realize it wasn't my intention to be leading a life of crime." The second Caleb uttered the words, conviction tugged on his heart. Annie had forgiven him. Her family had forgiven him.

Now Caleb needed to forgive Cain.

"I'm thankful she forgave you, Caleb. Tell me, is she pretty?"

"She has beautiful blonde hair and the most sparkling green eyes you've ever seen. She has a tender heart and loves children."

"Sounds like you've done well for yourself. Do you have your own place?"

"I do. I purchased it a couple years ago and with Pa's help, we've fixed it up."

Cain wiped at his face with the back of his sleeve. "Bet you ain't never seen a grown man cry before." Before Caleb could answer, Cain continued, "I'm proud of you, Caleb. I mean it. I thank the Lord that you've been given a second chance and that you ain't nothing like me and Pa."

"You thank the Lord?" Caleb found it surprising that Cain would mention God.

"I haven't told you yet...I accepted Christ as my Savior two years ago today. I kept track of that too, with a big mark on my cell wall."

Caleb's jaw dropped. He knew God was in the business of miracles, but to save Cain?

"God has a way of changin' folks. He changed me in a mighty way all 'cause someone gave me the Bible and I read it. Until I became so sick that I was bedridden, I was telling my fellow inmates about Jesus. Imagine that—Cain Ryerson spreadin' the Gospel! I know God's hand was in the whole thing because we are under a 'no-talking' rule here. Means we can't talk to no one ever, except if we have a visitor. But crazy thing was, they let me talk to the men once a week, provided it was about the Bible. Soon, more and more men came to our meetin'. Can't say for sure if it was so as they could talk and be talked to or if they really wanted to learn about Jesus. Whatever the reason, I had to know my Bible because they asked a lot of hard questions." Cain shifted, the pain he endured obvious in his expression.

"Don't let anyone ever tell you God don't change people. Don't ever let anyone tell you God don't forgive. That's why He sent His Son to die—for people's sins—yours and mine. Of course, you probably already know that, being a reverend's kid and all."

Caleb's words in response failed to come.

"I reckon it would be difficult to believe, seeing as the kind of man I been. I devoted my life to the Lord and asked Him to use me however He deemed fit. I didn't bank on finding out I was gonna die, though. But it just makes it that much sooner I'll be in the Lord's presence." Cain paused and for the first time, his eyes shone. "You don't know how much I've prayed for you, Little Brother."

Caleb swallowed hard. Cain had prayed for him? Caleb had never once prayed for Cain, nor even considered doing so.

Cain chuckled. "All of that is difficult to believe, I know. But I had to tell you before I died that I was sorry. You don't have to forgive me right this minute. I'd rather you forgive me when the Lord moves your heart to do so."

"God has been merciful to me and shown me grace beyond what I deserve. I came in here madder than all get out, but... I do forgive you, Cain."

In an unexpected moment Caleb could never have foreseen, he knelt down and hugged his brother.

"You and me, we'll always be brothers, right? No matter that you have another brother now, you and me we're still brothers, huh?"

"Yes." He bit his tongue to stop the flow of tears.

But Cain was crying too. "Can we change things today and for the future? Can we put the past behind us?"

Yes," answered Caleb. "By God's grace, we can."

"Thank you for forgiving me."

"Thank you, Cain, for calling for me. I almost didn't come, but I'm glad I did."

"Much obliged for you coming, staying, and hearing what I had to say. Did you bring Annie and your new pa?"

"Yes, but they're waiting for me in the warden's office. Would you like to meet them?"

"Yes. Yes, I would."

Caleb stood to leave the room. "I'll go get them."

"Thank you again, Little Brother."

Caleb realized for the first time he didn't mind if Cain called him "Little Brother."

Cain Ryerson wasn't at all what she expected and didn't resemble the sketch on the poster Mr. DeGroot presented to her parents. Cain's eyes weren't hard and mean like his eyes in the picture. There was no scowl, only a weak smile.

Cain held out his hand. "You must be Annie. It's a pleasure to meet you."

They spoke for the next few minutes with polite conversation until Annie took a step back and stood against the far wall of the room to allow Reverend Solomon time with Cain. Tears misted her eyes as she overheard the conversation between the two.

Moments later, in the warden's office, the tears continued as Reverend Solomon relayed to Caleb his conversation with Cain.

"There's something I need to ask you, Caleb. I desire only your honesty. There is no wrong answer."

"What is it, Pa?"

"How do you feel if your ma and I adopt Cain?"

Caleb's eyes widened. "Adopt Cain?"

"Yes. He asked me if we would. He said it would mean more to him than anything to know he had parents who cared about and loved him."

"I suppose that would be fine."

"I didn't figure you'd mind, but we agreed I should ask you. I'm hoping we can finalize the papers before he passes away."

"That would be right fine, Pa. Right fine," Caleb whispered, his voice choked with emotion.

"Very well then," Reverend Solomon said, gazing upward. "The Lord works in amazing ways. Who knew I'd someday be the pa of three sons?"

Chapter Thirty-Seven

ANNIE SAT ON A log near the river and watched as the water meandered through the landscape. Pulling her diary and her pencil from her bag, she began to write her longest entry to date:

Dear Diary,

Today is June twenty-second, and I have so much to say and am not sure where to begin. Zeb and Hetty's wedding was lovely. We held it at the church in Nelsonville and most of the town attended. I dare say Sadie enjoyed the festivities perhaps more than anyone, except Zeb and Hetty, of course. Ma had tears in her eyes and Pa stood so proud watching his oldest child become a married man.

Mine and Caleb's wedding is fast approaching. To say that I am fraught with nerves is to put it lightly. Ma has nearly completed my dress and Lydie has offered to make our wedding cake using her own mother's prize-winning recipe. Sadie and Charlotte offered to design flower bouquets from an abundance of wildflowers they offered to pick.

We'll be getting married outside of the Willow Falls church and, of course, Reverend Solomon will be conducting the ceremony. I was ecstatic to discover that Ma, Pa, and the Eliasons are going to pay for a wedding photograph of Caleb and me. What a treasure to be able to recall that day, not only in my mind, but also on paper as a permanent reminder. The modern advancement of photography has very much interested me.

I am blessed God has given me a man such as Caleb for my husband. I cannot wait to begin our lives together and am looking forward to helping him realize his dream of one day owning a sizeable cattle ranch. I continue saying my soon-to-be new name in my mind: Annie Eliason. I have even practiced writing it several times.

Silly as it sounds, I have saved much of the meager earnings from my teaching position to purchase a wedding gift for Caleb. I know it's not necessary, and I should really be saving the money for our new life together, but I have instead chosen a gift that I know Caleb will appreciate.

Sadly, Cain went to be with the Lord three days ago. While this is not sad in the sense that Cain will now spend eternity in Heaven, my heart aches for Caleb. He feels there was so much wasted time between them. More than anything, he wanted Cain to be able to attend our wedding. I thank the Lord that they were able to reconcile before Cain's illness took his life.

As I sit here gazing upon God's creation and watching new life spring forth during this season, I have much to be thankful for, especially Caleb, my family, and the Eliasons.

Epilogue
June 7, 1885

ONE LOOK AT THE wagon told her Caleb's siblings and Sadie had taken much joy in tying old food cans to the back of the wagon and decorating it with whatever they could find.

"It looks as though Sadie, Charlotte, and John Mark have been busy."

Caleb chuckled and helped Annie into the wagon. "I guess it's their way of welcoming you into the Eliason family."

He climbed into the wagon and prompted the horses toward their new home. "We'll stop at our home on the way to Ma and Pa's house."

Annie smiled. *Our home.* Not *his* home, not *her* home, but *their* home—the home they would share together forever. Dressed in his Sunday finest, she admired Caleb's handsome appearance. He was even more dapper than ever—if that were possible. She squeezed her eyes tight and offered a prayer heavenward regarding their future and wondered what it might hold: the family they would raise, the ranch they would expand, and the hopes and dreams they would share.

"What's my beautiful wife thinking?"

"I was thinking of our future together. I pray we'll be married for at least seventy-five years. By that time, I'll be ninety-five and you'll be ninety-seven. Hopefully, we'll remember we're married."

"I plan to always remember I'm married to you, even if I'm over one hundred. And even though a hundred years is a long time, I'm going to thank God for every day of those one hundred years."

Without taking his eyes off the road ahead of him, he leaned over and brushed Annie's cheek with a kiss.

"I'm also thinking about my wedding present to you. I can't wait for you to see it. Do you think our family and friends will give us a few minutes before heading to your parents' home for the reception?"

"I hope so because I have something for you inside the house."

A few minutes later, Annie and Caleb came to the road that led to their home. Lest he go further and see the surprise, she asked that he stop for a moment. They both climbed down from the wagon. "Now close your eyes." While Caleb did so, she walked a short distance and peered around the numerous trees. Sure enough, Pa and Zeb had installed the gift earlier that day.

"Keep your eyes closed and allow me to guide you."

Caleb chuckled. "Is this what it means to have complete trust in the one you've chosen to spend the rest of your life with?"

"Exactly, and I'll know if you peek, Caleb."

"Not a chance." He squeezed his eyes tighter and Annie led him slowly toward the gift. "Keep them closed a bit longer."

"Are we walking back to town?"

"Just halfway," she teased.

As soon as they reached the end of the trees, Annie stopped him. "All right. You may open your eyes and look up."

"I'm always looking up."

"Not quite as high as Heaven, silly." She pointed to the tall sign arched on poles ahead of them.

Caleb followed her finger with his eyes. "Well, I'll be..."

"Do you like it?"

Caleb bolted toward the gift. Two large logs on either side supported a finely crafted wood sign. In fancy lettering, the words *Eliason Ranch* had been cut out of the stained wood. Caleb's cattle brand was on either side of the wording and below it were the letters "C&A" etched in to the wood.

"What do you think?"

"I don't know what to say."

"You could tell me whether or not you like it," suggested Annie, although she already knew the answer.

"This makes it official. This makes the Eliason Ranch—*our* ranch—official. Thank you, Annie."

He lifted her in the air, swung her around, and planted a kiss on her waiting lips. Several more followed until it wasn't clear where one kiss ended and the next began.

When they finished, Caleb again peered at the sign. "Reckon God has smiled mighty favorably on me to give me you." He paused. "This means a lot to me, Annie. Thank you."

"You're welcome. I suppose we should continue to your parents' home for the wedding cake."

"Not so quick. I have something for you inside our house."

Taking her hand, Caleb led her to the porch. Opening the door with one hand, he lifted her off her feet and carried her over the threshold.

"It's your turn to close your eyes." He set her carefully on her feet.

"All right, you can open them now."

Annie opened her eyes and gasped at the sight before her. A familiar round wooden table with four chairs sat in the middle of the room. The table and chairs were made of different wood—the table of oak and the chairs of maple. Annie ran her hand across the smooth top of the table. "Caleb, is this the table I think it is?"

"The one and only."

"However did you find it?"

Caleb smirked. "With a little bit of help from your ma and your brother. Zeb told me how much you missed the table that your grandpa made for your family. It wasn't easy to find, especially since I didn't have a whole lot of time. Your Ma helped me place an advertisement in the newspaper where you used to live in Nebraska. She told me who the folks were who purchased the table, and I sent them a letter, as well. The rest of it shall remain my secret. Do you like it?"

Tears clouded her vision, although not tears of sadness. "Caleb, this is the perfect gift. Thank you."

"I figured as much. I imagine someday we'll fill those other two chairs with young'uns of our own. I love you, Annie."

"And I love you." Annie wrapped her arms around her husband's neck and buried her face in his chest.

Caleb had given her a gift she never thought she would see again, a gift that brought back fond memories of her life in Nebraska.

And she'd had no idea of his plans.

Annie thought of how her life with Caleb had started with a memory…and how their lives would continue with more memories to come.

READ A SNEAK PEEK FROM

Dreams of the Heart

SOMETIMES THE HARDEST BATTLES TAKE
PLACE IN THE HEART.

Dreams of the Heart
Sneak Peek

WHY WAS HE ALWAYS watching her? Scrutinizing her? Did he think her a ne'er-do-well? That she was part of the messes her pa found himself in?

Deputy Eliason was a lawman, after all.

Hannah shifted her attention toward the street lined with multiple saloons, a brothel, mercantile, dress shop, the new restaurant, barbershop, and sheriff's office. So many people had come and gone in the years she'd lived here. Businesses closed and businesses opened, especially saloons, which dominated the town. As such, she knew so few of the townsfolk.

She ventured a gaze in the deputy's direction. His attention remained fixed on her.

Had his ma never taught him it wasn't proper manners to stare?

Several men stumbled in and out of the Sticker Weed Saloon. Her own pa either gambled or frittered away on whiskey all the money he earned from working for Mayor Roessler.

Deputy Eliason stood on the boardwalk outside of the sheriff's office. She knew what he must think of her. He was a man of the law and she was the daughter of a no-good drunk. And not only that, but her appearance must look a fright. Instinctively, she reached up to smooth her hair, hair that she'd never had the chance to fix before Pa hastened her to town. Her dismal calico no longer held the pattern, but instead was threadbare with years of wear.

More than once, Hannah found some dingy scraps of material and sewed them onto the bottom of her dress, adding to its length. Thankfully, she never grew wider. There wasn't enough food for that. And being fairly flat on top made it easy to wear the same dress for several years.

Indeed, what must someone as upstanding and handsome as Deputy Eliason think of her?

Balancing on the edge of the wagon wheel, she climbed down and paused on the boardwalk, deciding where she should go. If she hurried, Hannah would have a few minutes to marvel at the clothing in the dress shop and maybe even explore the new items at the mercantile before each store closed. Starting toward her destination, she again met Deputy Eliason's stare. Did he have nothing better to do than to watch her?

He tipped his hat and nodded. Could that be a slight smile forming across his lips? Her cheeks flamed and Hannah pretended to be preoccupied with a pebble on the ground.

A few moments later, she pushed open the door of Nellie's Dress Shop and moseyed inside. Gorgeous gowns met her perusal, including a delicate cream-colored satin dress with numerous gathers and fancy ruffles. Lace adorned the two bottom layers. Hannah rubbed the smooth, delicate fabric between her index finger and thumb. Up close, she could see miniature designs—tiny flowers perhaps? She moved closer and inhaled. The dress even smelled new.

Unlike her own stained and tattered garment.

Hannah closed her eyes and tried to envision herself in such an elegant fashion. Maybe her hair would be curled or wound around her head in a thick plaited braid. Or maybe she'd don a fancy hat like she'd seen some of the wealthy ladies in town wear. She would purchase a pair of shoes to go with the dress and she'd walk around as if she was somebody.

Instead of a nobody.

Hannah continued to run her fingers along the material, delighting in its softness in contrast to the rough fabric of her own dress.

It was then that she noticed Claudelle Roessler and her mother standing nearby staring at her. Claudelle whispered something to her mother. Mrs. Roessler nodded and approached the owner, Nellie Quirke.

Hannah strained to hear their words, thoughts conflicting within her of both desiring to know what was being said, and yet dreading it at the same time.

"Is *she* going to purchase that dress?" Mrs. Roessler asked, tilting her head in Hannah's direction. Claudelle shuddered, likely for added effect.

Miss Quirke's eye met Hannah's. "I'm not sure."

"You know full well she's not," said Mrs. Roessler. "You should preclude her from handling the gowns and fabrics lest she soil them."

Hannah swallowed the lump that formed in her throat. Mrs. Roessler and Claudelle had never taken kindly to her.

"Miss Bane, if you don't mind..." Miss Quirke began.

"Yes, ma'am, I was just leaving."

Tears stung her eyes as Hannah rushed toward the door. She'd never treat people the way she'd been treated by the Roesslers. Never.

Hannah retreated down the boardwalk, the misting tears blinding her vision. So preoccupied with what had just happened, she wasn't paying attention and bumped into someone.

She tottered and wobbled until a hand on her elbow steadied her.

"Are you all right, miss?"

Hannah looked up at the man who was forever watching her. Only this time it wasn't from a distance. There was something in his hazel eyes that she couldn't ascertain. Compassion? Pity? Sympathy?

"I'm all right, thank you."

Deputy Eliason held his gentle grasp on her elbow for a second longer before releasing it.

What must he think of her?

He'd seen the tears in her eyes when they collided. A glance through the dress shop window and John Mark figured he knew the reason for Miss Bane's sadness. Claudelle Roessler caught his eye and fluttered her lashes at him. His sister, Charlotte, would say Miss Roessler had set her cap for him. He cringed at the thought.

Claudelle Roessler may be a comely woman, but John Mark would never be interested in a woman who mistreated others as she had Miss Bane.

John Mark heard a ruckus behind him. Frank and Hank Maloney bumbled toward him, words hurled back and forth between them. "Deputy Eliason," called Frank, his hoarse voice hinting at desperation.

"Hello, Frank and Hank. What can I do for you today?" John Mark took a deep breath and prepared for another benign quarrel between the elderly twin brothers. The two were a testament that not everything occurring in Poplar Springs was nefarious in nature. And while the men were exaggerated and, at times, absurd, it gave John Mark a reprieve from more serious matters.

"There's an argument and Hank started it."

"Did not."

"Did so."

"Gentlemen. How about we resolve this peacefully?"

The men proceeded to outstare each other.

Hank shook his bald head. "No can do, Deputy. This time Frank has really gone and done it."

"*I've* gone and done it?" Frank, twice the size and two inches shorter than his scrawny brother, stood next to Hank and jabbed a finger into his shoulder. "You're the one who decided to wear my boot."

"One at a time tell me the problem so I can help you resolve it."

Frank and Hank began to talk at once, Hank's higher-pitched voice rising above Frank's gravelly growl.

"Hank, you go first," John Mark requested.

Frank had something to say about that. "Why did you choose him first? Is it because he's older?"

It was going to be a long afternoon. John Mark nodded at passersby, suddenly wishing he could be rounding up horse thieves, catching outlaws, hauling drunks to the jail, or settling *real* disputes. "Hank, tell me what happened."

"See, I told you he was showing favortisms. Ain't fair." Frank crossed his thick arms across his chest and pouted.

Hank, on the other hand, stood taller, a smug look on his wrinkled face. "You see, Deputy, it's like this. When we woke up this morning and headed out to do the chores, I put on my boots like I always do."

"'Cept one of them boots ain't yours!"

"Is too."

"Is not."

"Gentlemen...let me see if I have this correct. Hank is wearing your boot, Frank?"

Hank's bulbous eyes bulged. "He just says I am."

"Because you are."

"Are you wearing Frank's boot, Hank?"

Hank peered down at his boots and John Mark immediately knew who would be winning this argument. While Hank's boots were both brown and somewhat worn, the boot on his right foot was larger. As such, the toe of the boot protruded farther than the toe of the boot on his left foot. "Hank..."

Guilt washed over Hank's face. "I was thinking one didn't fit near as well," he muttered. "My feet have always been somewhat cramped in my boots, but today, one didn't feel nearly as crowded."

Frank thrust his chest out and gloated. "See, told you so. And looky here, Deputy, my poor right foot is all bent and squeezed and my toes ain't comfortable one bit. Reckon my foot's asleep."

"Aww, you poor thing," chastised Hank. "My feet are both comfortable. Matter of fact, I might trade you both shoes."

Frank balled his fists at his sides. "Oh, no you won't. You ain't stealing my shoes like you stole my whirligig when we was young'uns."

John Mark was not going to go back into the past with these men and all of their perceived transgressions against each other. If he did, it would be his next birthday before this matter was settled. "All right, men, trade shoes so that both of you are wearing your own." John Mark leaned against the side of the barbershop and waited for the two not-so-identical twins to switch their boots. "There. All settled."

"Told you Deputy Eliason was a smart whippersnapper," said Hank. "He's always solving people's problems."

Frank nodded. "And I told you that you were wrong and I was right."

That started another disagreement.

"Have a good day, gentlemen." John Mark slipped away and headed toward the jail before the two could ask him to resolve another of their differences.

If you want to be among the first to hear about the next release, sign up for Penny's newsletter her website at www.pennyzellercom. You will receive book and writing updates, encouragement, notification of current giveaways, occasional freebies, and special offers. Plus, you'll receive *An Unexpected Arrival*, a Wyoming Sunrise novelette, for free.

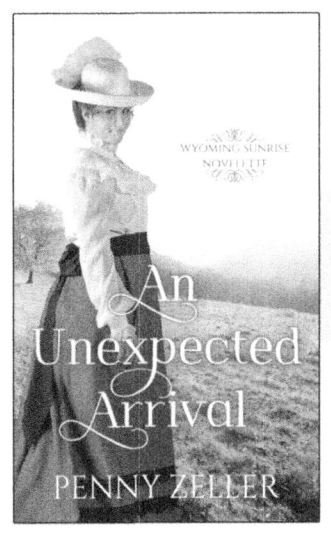

A
WYOMING
SUNRISE
NOVELETTE

If you enjoyed this glimpse into the lives of Annie and Caleb, please consider leaving a review on your social media and favorite retailer sites. Reviews are critical to authors, and those stars you give us are such an encouragement.

Author's Note

One of the exciting things about writing historical romance is delving into the past. Readers will recall that I spend a lot of time in Montana for my books; however, for *Forgotten Memories*, I was thrilled to visit Wyoming's past.

As authors, sometimes (all right, most times!) our characters and plot lines take on a life of their own. I did take some fictional liberties for the sake of the story. These include:

Altering the school schedule to fit the timeline needed for the story and making the distance between Willow Falls and the U.S. Penitentiary at Laramie City shorter in length.

In addition, I did take some additional fictional liberties regarding the prison where Cain was incarcerated. In the story, I provided a description of the U.S. Penitentiary at Laramie City, which would have been accurate in 1889, rather than 1885, when Caleb, Annie, and Reverend Solomon visited Cain. However, at the time of *Forgotten Memories*, only one cell block had been built. The middle section and a south cell block were added in 1889-1890, as was the infirmary. Because I needed Caleb and Cain to have some privacy and Cain to be somewhere his medical needs could be attended to, I allowed them to meet in the infirmary.

While Cain continued his incarceration in the prison during his illness, in later years, this was not always the case for prisoners. Taylor Hensel, Seasonal Historical Interpreter at the Wyoming Territorial Prison Historic Site, provided some interesting information on that topic. "The unconditional release process for terminally ill prisoners didn't occur until 1899, when one of the prison's last wardens, N.D. McDonald, ordered the infirmary closed in order to save on costs. Otherwise...between 1899 and 1903 when the prison shut down, sick prisoners would be released, no questions asked, with a little bit of money to pay for a train ticket and a hot meal, and whatever personal items they'd had with them upon arrival to the prison."

I can't imagine what would have happened to Cain if the book had taken place in 1899 or later, and he'd been left to his own devices while battling a terminal illness. It made me curious how real-life prisoners handled the situation if they had no nearby relatives.

There was a "no talking" silence requirement rule in place that lasted from 1873-1903, the years of the prison's operation. I took liberties of giving Cain a Bible study of sorts to tell fellow prisoners about Jesus. It is unknown if that would have been allowed in real life.

Taylor also provided some fascinating facts about the U.S. Penitentiary at Laramie City that I think you'll find fascinating. One of those items was his explanation about the "no talking" rule mentioned above. "To my knowledge, Alcatraz was the first major prison to do away with the 'no-talking' rule in the late 1920s, because prisoners began playing the 'coughing game' at meal-times, during which they would cough and talk under their breath. Eventually, the rule became too difficult to enforce, and the prison just did away with it."

I asked Taylor who, besides Butch Cassidy, was the Penitentiary's most notorious prisoner. Following is his answer: "Besides Butch Cassidy, probably our most notorious prisoner was Kinch McKinney, a cattle and horse thief active near the Nebraska border, who was probably our most rambunctious and violent inmate. He led a prison riot in January of 1893 and successfully escaped from the prison in October of 1894, but was rearrested in Grand Island, Nebraska and brought back to the prison on Christmas Day, 1894. He spent a combined 15 days in the Dark Cell (solitary confinement) for the riot and the escape, respectively. Prior to being held at the prison, he was kept over at the Laramie County Jail in Cheyenne. He escaped from there twice, the second time after having convinced his lawyer to smuggle him in a Winchester rifle and ammunition. He tried to shoot his way out of the jail, and this resulted in an all-day gunfight/siege with the Cheyenne police and local vigilantes. No one was killed or even injured, and eventually Kinch just surrendered when he realized he couldn't make it out of the prison without being shot dead. He ultimately reformed, was released from the Laramie prison in 1902, and lived out the rest of his days in Lander, Wyoming, operating a sheep ranch."

One additional note was that the U.S. Penitentiary at Laramie City became the Wyoming State Prison in 1890, the same year Wyoming achieved statehood.

I'm sure you can see why interviewing knowledgeable historians at museums is one of the best perks of being the author of historical romance!

Acknowledgments

To my family. Where do I begin? You are such treasures to me, and without you, I could not embark on this crazy writing life. To my husband, Lon, my love of a lifetime, for patiently encouraging me to continue in this, at times, unorthodox career. To my oldest daughter for shouldering the responsibility of making dinner throughout the "deadline days" without ever once complaining. To both of my daughters for being my alpha readers, offering input and suggestions, and helping me make my novels the best they can be.

To Mom. Thank you for faithfully reading my books and giving me encouragement. You are a talented writer, and I'm grateful you passed on your love of writing to me.

To Taylor Hensel, Seasonal Historical Interpreter at the Wyoming Territorial Prison Historic Site, for answering my barrage of questions and providing me with amazing insight into the lives of those who resided in the historical Wyoming prison system.

To Trent and Jodi Short for their invaluable help with the fire scene. An additional thank you to Trent for his dedication and devotion as a first responder.

To K.R., Susan, and Jan for your expertise on horses and horse injuries.

To Tracy for your assistance in answering my questions about injuries.

To my beta readers, who diligently searched for plot holes and inconsistencies. Your suggestions were invaluable. A special thank you to beta reader, Vel Zieske.

To my Penny's Peeps Street Team. Thank you for spreading the word about my books. I appreciate your support!

To my *Forgotten Memories* launch team. I appreciate you sharing space on your social media platforms with my book.

To Jenny B., for your continued encouragement.

To my readers. May God bless and guide you as you grow in your walk with Him.

And, most importantly, thank you to my Lord and Savior, Jesus Christ. It is my deepest desire to glorify You with my writing and help bring others to a knowledge of Your saving grace.

Let the words of my mouth and the meditation of my heart be acceptable in your sight, O Lord, my rock and my redeemer.
Psalm 19:14

About the Author

Penny Zeller is known for her heartfelt stories of faith and her passion to impact lives for Christ through fiction. While she has had a love for writing since childhood, she began her adult writing career penning articles for national and regional publications on a wide variety of topics. Today, Penny is the author of nearly two dozen books. She is also a homeschool mom and a fitness instructor.

When Penny is not dreaming up new characters, she enjoys spending time with her husband and two daughters, camping, hiking, canoeing, reading, running, cycling, gardening, and playing volleyball.

She is represented by Tamela Hancock Murray of the Steve Laube Agency and loves to hear from her readers at her website www.pennyzeller.com and her blog, *random thoughts from a day in the life of a wife, mom, and author*, at www.pennyzeller.wordpress.com.

Social Media Links:
https://linktr.ee/pennyzeller

WYOMING SUNRISE SERIES

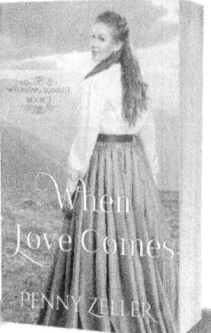

HORIZON SERIES

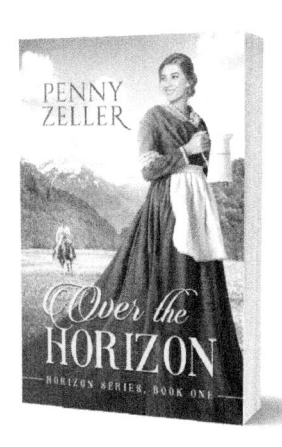

Over the Horizon — Horizon Series, Book One
by Penny Zeller

Dreams on the Horizon — Horizon Series, Book Two
by Penny Zeller

Beyond the Horizon — Horizon Series, Book Three
by Penny Zeller

HOLLOW CREEK

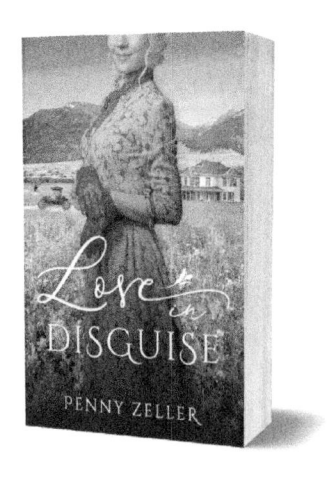

LOVE LETTERS FROM ELLIS CREEK

Love from Afar
PENNY ZELLER

Love Unforeseen
PENNY ZELLER

Love Most Certain
PENNY ZELLER

STANDALONE BOOKS

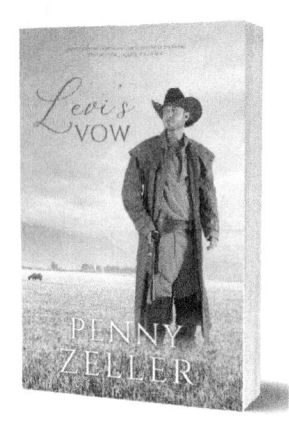

CHRISTIAN CONTEMPORARY ROMANCE

Love in the Headlines

Chokecherry Heights